Atlantis Ends

The Mars Catastrophe

Book 1

By

Paul Hillman

Sync Publishing Inc.
P O Box 5215
Aloha, OR 97006-5215
info@syncpublishing.com

www.atlantisends.com

Atlantis Ends: The Mars Catastrophe

Cover Design by Kavin King
Cover art by Julian Faylona

ISBN: 978-1-7361253-2-8

AUTHOR'S NOTE

I started writing this story in 1996, so I understand Tad Williams's comment in the foreword of *Green Angel Tower* when he called his series "The Story That Ate My Life." I feel the same way about this trilogy.

There are many people to thank for their gracious help with this trilogy. First, I would like to thank Alicia Dean, who read the first version of the story and provided excellent advice – shorten it, reduce the number of subplots, and limit the number of characters. I reduced it and eliminated several subplots, but there is nearly the same number of characters, so I included a character list at the back of the book.

Many thanks to Jason Letts at Imbue Editing, who edited the trilogy and helped create a much more readable story.

I would also like to thank two key people who inspired me to write the story. The first is my longtime business partner, David Talbott, whose work on the origin of Earth's civilizations provided the setting for Atlantis Ends. The documentary I produced, *Remembering the End of the World*, and over fifty videos on his lifetime work are available on his YouTube channel, *Symbols of an Alien Sky*, and describe a world that is indeed alien. To understand the demise of Atlantis, one needs to understand the near-extinction-level events that occurred nearly thirteen thousand years ago when Atlantis sank. David provided the key, and other researchers, listed in the references at the back of the book, supplied the details to complete the description.

Although he died before I was born, I would like to thank Edgar Cayce, the Sleeping Psychic whose books gave me a vision of a technologically advanced Atlantis. While his psychic readings explained "ships that flew through the air and water," he never described the Empire of Atlantis as I do. But his work fueled my imagination regarding a lost society with a long history of advanced technology. Those familiar with the 2,500 psychic readings he did that included lifetimes in Atlantis will recognize some elements here.

I would also like to thank my wife, Peggy Hillman, for putting up with my writing schedule. She is a model of generosity, kindness, and support. Thanks to my daughter, Cathy DeVault, and my friends Gene Knudson, Harriet Bing, Linda Erickson, author John E Stith, designer Kavin King, and many others for their gracious and generous advice and support.

In the reference section, you will find sources of information that helped me understand what was happening on Earth thirteen thousand years ago. It was the end of the ice age, the death of most large animals, and a time of recurring meteorite showers that blasted the Northern Hemisphere. The references will help you understand what life was like when Atlantis sank beneath the Atlantic Ocean.

Paul E Hillman

CHAPTER ONE

The sound of a deep, resonating conch horn awoke Acton Athu.

He jerked upright, his heart pounding and sweat drenching his body as a meteorite hit his aircraft, breaking it apart and sending it plummeting toward the mountains below, twisting and tumbling as it fell. He was falling… helplessly falling.

He stifled a scream and sucked in a ragged breath. Frantically looking around, he slowly realized he was in his apartment on SS New Hope and not falling to his death. As usual, the wall-mounted monitor beside his bed showed the Sun rising over the Orchid Garden beneath his bedroom window in the Imperial Palace at Poseidia, and its glow lit the rest of his apartment. He wiped away the sweat before it ran into his eyes and took another deep breath, exhaling slowly. Calming down, he shook his head.

The nightmares were getting worse.

Throwing the covers off, he touched the wall to turn on the lights, turned off the monitor and alarm, then walked to the bathroom. A hot shower later, dressed in his navy-blue Rescue Corp uniform and combat boots, he stopped at the mirror by the door to ensure that his dark hair was in place, his captain's badges were on both shoulders, and the tall collar was properly fastened. Since his father was a stickler for proper military attire, he didn't want anything to prompt another argument.

He looked forward to breakfast and dreaded it. Although meals with his parents always risked another fight with his father, his mother expected him to start the day with a good breakfast, and he didn't want to hurt her feelings by refusing. Since she probably had it waiting for him, he should have told her yesterday if he wanted to skip it.

Leaving his apartment, the spacious, ivory-colored hallway reminded him of the marble halls of the Imperial Palace, except it was only eight feet wide and curved slightly to follow the contour of the spaceship. The entry alcoves of the apartments he passed along the way featured plants that reflected their occupants, a rose here, a fruit tree there, a cactus on that side, and other plants, some tall, some squat, and some in need of attention. Frowning, he realized he still needed to select plants for his alcove.

When he reached an alcove with purple orchids in a small hothouse by the door, he knew he had arrived and keyed the security code to open the sliding door to his parents' spacious suite.

Crossing the foyer, then a corner of the living room, he entered the kitchen. Professor Nora Athu, an attractive woman of medium height with stylish brown hair, sat at the kitchen table reading something on her PAD, a personal accessory device. "Good morning, Mother." Acton kissed her cheek and then sat at the table beside her.

"Good morning, dear. How are you?" she said without looking up.

"Hungry." He filled a plate with eggs, sausage, and toast from a silver warmer in the center of the table. Pouring a cup of strong coffee, he glanced around. "Has Father gone to work?" he asked hopefully.

"No, he's here."

As if on cue, Commander Cana Athu stormed into the kitchen. A tall man in his fifties, he was as lean and muscular as Acton, and only a fringe of gray hair at his temples suggested his age. He looked regal in his royal purple uniform as he sat at the table. "Good morning." He helped himself to the food. "Are you on duty today?" he asked without looking at Acton.

"Yes."

"Checked your assignments yet?" Cana poured a cup of coffee.

Acton hesitated, studying his father's face. This was how their fights usually began, with some simple, innocuous question about his service in the Rescue Corp. "No."

"We're at the tail end of the Mars cycle, so the debris fall will be worse than ever." Cana didn't look up as he ate.

Since it wasn't a question, Acton pushed his empty plate away, drank the last gulp of the coffee, and didn't comment.

"I think I will reassign you to work in Control today," Cana said, focusing on his food.

"If I don't fly my missions, people will die. There are no replacements as all the rescuers are fully booked."

"I don't like you flying into dangerous areas." Cana put his coffee cup down and glared at Acton. "As a member of the royal family, you shouldn't be at risk. Let someone else rescue people and come work with me."

"We've been over this a hundred times." Acton forced himself to stay calm. "I will not do some cushy job in the safety of the spaceship while my friends risk their lives to save Atlantis. It's not right. If people need to be rescued, I'll do it because I'm good at what I do. Ask anyone."

"I can reassign you!" Finished eating, Cana stood to lean toward Acton. "You have nothing to say about that."

Nora looked at him and shook her head, but he ignored her.

Acton stood to face him. "If you do, it'll be a disaster. I may have to follow orders, but I don't have to do a good job. So, if you force me to work in some safe place, expect to have that work done as poorly as possible." He rushed from the kitchen across the foyer to the sliding door and regretted being unable to slam it as he left.

He hurried past his apartment to the lobby for the bank of lifts and punched a button to summon one. While waiting, he took several deep breaths, letting them out slowly, and willed himself to calm down. Maybe he shouldn't eat breakfast with them; that way, they couldn't fight. He entered the lift when it arrived, nodding to the other people standing in the ten-by-ten-foot elevator.

He shook his head. As the commander of the Atlantian Fleet, his father could easily reassign him. But because they had this argument several times a week, Acton was confident that he hadn't been reassigned because his mother somehow prevented it. He grinned. No one messed with his mother; as far as he knew, she never lost an argument with anyone.

The lift arrived at the central lobby one hundred forty-six floors down, and Acton hurried across it to the port lifts. One came a minute later, and he strapped himself into one of the ten cocoon-shaped seats. The seat squeezed tight as it surrounded him with a foam cushion. After nine more passengers were seated, the lift launched, gathering speed and spinning fast enough that the additional gravity pressed him farther into the cushion. Yet it didn't feel like acceleration but more like strangely spinning down. A few minutes later, the door opened to the zero-gravity spaceport lobby.

Remembering that any quick movement had an immediate and opposite effect in zero gravity, he carefully extracted himself from the seat and floated into the lobby. Grabbing a wall-mounted rail, he half walked, half floated toward New Hope's Spaceport 1, the first of five levels of spaceports and where his ship awaited him.

Approaching Spaceport 1's sliding doors, Acton noticed that the sign over them was green, indicating that the port had an atmosphere. When planes entered or departed into space, all the air was removed, and the entry was locked tight. Inside, Acton looked up at the brightly colored ropes stretching in every direction across the enormous room where dozens of shuttles and rescue ships were parked in orderly rows. The blue cable, twenty feet overhead, led to the flight desk, and he jumped to grab it. Jumping high enough was no problem in zero gravity, but he would slam into the ceiling if he missed the rope. With years of practice, he grabbed it, pulled himself to where he was above the flight desk, then used a vertical line to descend to the square workstation.

The flight officer had his paperwork ready, and a moment later, Acton headed for his aircraft, Rescue 1. It took a moment to remember that walking in zero gravity was more like guided floating, and he only occasionally toed the floor to push ahead and pressed against things to slow down or change course. After years of practice, the process was as natural as walking in gravity. From the several empty stalls along the way, he knew that other rescue ships had departed.

Rescue 1 was a bright-red, sweptwing rescue ship, like others nearby. All of them were red, but only Rescue 1 had a large "1" painted on its nose. Acton pressed against the ship to stop his forward progress, then glided along its side and under its wing. The door, at the rear and between its two large jet engines, was open, and the stairs were down and ready to use. Grabbing the stair rail, he easily pulled himself up six feet and onto the plane.

After hundreds of missions, performing his captain's duties was as natural as breathing. Acton made sure the entry lounge and passenger compartment were ready to use as he walked through them. At the refreshment center, he extracted a cup of coffee into a zero-gravity cup before entering the cockpit. He slid onto the pilot's seat on the left side and fastened his harness to keep from floating around. As usual, Cass Keltu had not arrived, and his co-pilot seat on the right was empty. He sucked the coffee, the only way to drink it in zero gravity, and studied the dashboard's gauges and dials. In the center, the pathfinder's monitor was above the avoidance system's monitor. Fuel and oxygen gauges showed they were full, and the other dials reflected that the ship was ready to depart.

"Good morning," Cass Keltu said, sounding shaky as he slid into the co-pilot seat. A tall, athletic man, he looked enough like Acton to be his brother.

"Good morning. Have a bad night?"

"No, just a late one." Cass rubbed his bloodshot eyes before studying the dashboard.

"Ready to go?"

"Sure." Cass fastened his harness and put his comm unit on.

Acton put his comm unit on his right ear, an earplug with a short flange for the mic. "Control, Rescue 1 is ready."

"Rescue 1, you are approved for positioning. Control out," New Hope's Control Center responded over their comm units and the ship's built-in speakers.

Warning alarms blared throughout the inner bay. The support crew slammed the ship's hatch closed and joined the remaining bay personnel exiting the inner port. After the alarm counted down with six short squawks, the inner port sealed all exits, and the vacuum system sucked all the oxygen out of the inner bay. A man in a spacesuit drove a tractor to the ship, attached its landing gear, and towed Rescue 1 toward the outer bay. After the huge, hundred-foot door separating the inner bay from the outer bay opened with a clang, the tractor pulled the ship into the outer bay, positioned it in front of the space portal, and then returned to the inner bay. The door closed with another loud bang.

"Control, Rescue 1 is ready to depart."

The vast outer door of the ship opened onto space, allowing a view of Earth, Mars, the debris field between them, and the periphery defense's gunners and strikers lined up in a row.

"Rescue 1, you are approved for departure. Control out."

"On it, Control. Rescue 1 out." Acton turned to Cass. "Ready, good buddy?"

"Yeah, let's do it."

Acton started the hover engine and slid the thrust forward. Rescue 1 rose and floated toward the gaping doorway. Once through the door, it hovered in space until the giant bay door closed. He switched to the jet engines, slid the thrust forward, and R1 shot toward Earth.

Acton ensured they were on the right course by checking their assignment on the pathfinder. Leaving Spaceship (SS) New Hope behind, he adjusted Rescue 1's flight path to circle around the periphery defense, a long line of small, one-person ships that defended the spaceships from any wayward space debris.

Although he saw Mars destroying Earth every day, it still overwhelmed him. It seemed unreal. He looked through his side window at Saturn, millions of miles away yet so huge that it blotted out the Sun and the rest of the solar system. Venus, the white, cloud-covered planet the same size as Earth, appeared like a large white smudge against Saturn's golden background. Assured that the rest of the collinear planetary system hadn't changed, he studied Mars.

Oscillating between Venus and Earth, since the comet disrupted the collinear system of planets, Mars was currently so close that Earth's gravity was stripping off its surface. Millions of chunks of debris, consisting of rocks, dirt, and other matter, bombarded the entire Northern Hemisphere of Earth in a rapidly moving, impenetrable stream. Occasionally, large chunks within the stream collided, and pieces shot out toward the spaceships, requiring the periphery defense to eliminate the threat.

Earth was unrecognizable. Enshrouded in a gray-black cloud with jagged, blue lightning flashes, bright red-gold spots opened briefly here and there, allowing glimpses of the all-consuming fires burning on every continent in the Northern Hemisphere.

"Looks even worse than yesterday," Acton said, studying the debris field.

"Yes, it does. Hey, I'm sorry, but I need to take a nap if that's okay with you." Cass Keltu gazed hopefully at Acton. They were nearly the same age and build with dark hair and square chins, and had been best friends since primary school.

Acton noticed his red, puffy eyes. "Sure, nothing else to do until we get there."

"Thanks. I appreciate it." Cass leaned back, closed his eyes, and was soon snoring.

* * * * *

"Hey, wake up." Acton nudged him.

Cass opened his eyes and sat upright. "Are we there already?"

"Yeah, you slept for four hours."

"Doesn't feel like it." Cass rubbed his eyes. "Thanks for letting me rest."

"Sure. What are friends for?"

"Looks like we're ready to enter the soup." Cass stared at the debris field.

Acton followed Cass's gaze and studied the debris fall (DF). From the fleet, the debris fall looked horrific, but close to Earth, it was terrifying. As far as he could see, a massive stream of various-sized chunks of DF shot past them, still distant but close enough to cause the avoidance system to occasionally override navigation and move the ship out of danger.

Below them and getting closer every moment, the clouds covering the Northern Hemisphere were denser than ever. Where he used to catch a glimpse of the fires raging below, he could not see through it.

"Where's our destination?" Cass asked.

"Africa, not far from where we were yesterday but closer to the volcano. We're rescuing three people on the river below the volcano."

"Looks like our destination is now in the DF hot zone."

"I hope not. That would be bad news. All right, here we go." Acton tensed up.

Rescue 1 entered the cloud, and the cabin instantly went dark. The dashboard lights came on, but the larger pathfinder and avoidance screens provided most of the light.

Cass checked the avoidance system. The monitor showed thousands of chunks of DF streaking down all around them. "Oh, man, it's much worse than yesterday."

"Can you see anything through your side of the windshield?" Acton asked.

"You've got to be kidding. All I see is a swirling cloud of smoke and ash. It's getting redder, so we must be close to the volcano." Cass clung to the restraining bar across the dashboard as the ship jerked and shuddered in the increased turbulence.

Suddenly, a whistling sound quickly grew loud enough to overcome the roar of the hundred-mile-an-hour winds that buffeted the ship. The avoidance system jerked R1 to the right and then tried to stop it in midair.

"Oh no! That sounds like a big one." Cass hung on and instinctively looked up toward the sound.

The screech grew louder and louder until a big chunk of DF screamed past R1's left side, barely missing the ship and close enough to suck R1 after it. The avoidance system automatically corrected the ship and then jerked it to the left as another DF screamed past R1's right.

"I hate it when I can't see!" Acton's hand hovered close to the steering stick, every instinct urging him to use it to keep from being blasted from the sky. But he had been flying rescue missions in DF zones long enough to know that steering blind was suicide. Instead, he stared helplessly at the avoidance system.

"Did you expect it to be this bad?" Cass stared straight ahead.

"How could I? We're over Africa, and that's not a hot zone."

"We're crazy to be out here at this point in the Mars cycle. If we could see what was out there, it would probably scare us to death."

Suddenly, the ship broke through the dense clouds. As far as Acton could see, hundreds of chucks of DF shot down through the thick cloud cover, leaving streamers that were instantly absorbed into gale-force winds.

As far as they could see, DF shot down, some as small as a hand, others as large as a ship. Some struck mountainsides, causing avalanches. Others plowed through the jungle, decimating the foliage, and a few hit the river, throwing water into the wind while crumbling its banks. Overhead, the cloud of smoke and ash was a grayish red-orange, more vivid in the north where Earth was a fiery inferno, but still intense this close to the volcano. The volcano's massive output of smoke, pumice, and ash made the mountain hard to see except when mile-wide lightning bolts flashed through the skies. Wherever lightning struck, everything exploded into fire. Across the terrain between R1 and the volcano, dozens of new fires raged out of control.

Acton and Cass stared at the horrific scene, stunned into silence.

CHAPTER TWO

Acton recognized his nightmare, and an icy tingle ran up his spine.

"Dear God, what *are* we doing out here?"

The avoidance system jerked Rescue 1 to the left and then back to the right as two more chunks of DF streaked past. Being suddenly thrown side to side jarred Acton from the panic sweeping over him.

"It's even worse than I imagined. We have to get out of here!" Cass's voice was an octave higher than usual, and he stared at Acton with wide, frightened eyes.

"Hey, snap out of it. It's not *that* much worse than usual." He thought he knew Cass's reactions, but fear was new. Acton glanced at him and then searched the pathfinder and the avoidance system for a less dangerous route. "What's up with you?"

Rescue 1 jerked to the right as a large DF flashed by less than three feet from its wing.

"Sumar and Metus were killed yesterday. Their frigging avoidance system moved them directly into a DF hit." Cass glared at him. "They were good pilots, good rescuers, and good friends. If they can get killed, it can happen to us." When Acton didn't respond, he returned to anxiously watching.

Acton nudged Rescue 1 to the right, suggesting an alternate course to the pathfinder and having the avoidance system analyze it. "I don't want to talk about it. Sumar was a close friend. We went from primary school through the university together and joined the Rescue Corps on the same day."

"Whether you want to talk about it or not, the same thing could happen to us. It scares me to death. I just had drinks with those guys. Now—"

"I can't think about it." Acton took a moment from finding a safer path to glance at his buddy, but Cass had returned to studying the terrain below them. "It doesn't do any good. Their deaths make nineteen of our friends who have died in the last eighteen months. Focusing on death just makes it harder to do what we have to do. That's no good." Somehow, talking or even thinking about death made them more vulnerable.

"Yeah, I know. You've said that before, but I can't stop thinking about it. I guess I'm not a hero like you. I can't focus on doing what has to be done, no matter what. I have feelings!" Cass gasped and turned toward his best friend. "Hey, I'm sorry. I didn't mean that."

Acton smiled sadly and nodded. "I know. It's all right. I had another fight with my father this morning about the same thing. He also wants me to quit." He stopped trying to find a better route and concentrated on being ready to intervene with the systems if needed.

"Well, what do you expect? You're the oldest son of the royal family. Your uncle is the emperor, and your father is the commander of the fleet. And you wonder why they want you to quit. Maybe we should retire while we still can." Cass's sadness overwhelmed him.

"Yeah, sometimes I think about quitting. But if we did, other rescuers would quit, and then who would rescue people? Some green kids right out of flight school? You know they wouldn't last a week out here." Acton gestured around them as R1 jerked to the left.

Following the river around a mountain on their right, the entire spectacle of the erupting volcano came into view ahead of them and to the right. Less than ten miles away, rivers of lava poured down its sides, and smoke and ash shot from its summit into the dark clouds as hundreds of DF bombarded it. Multiple lightning strikes danced around its peak as though igniting the eruption.

"Hey, we could get killed too. What makes you think we're any better?" Cass said.

"We have over four hundred missions on our log. What we know can't be taught in school. It requires experience."

Rescue 1 jerked back as a large chunk of DF streaked in front of them and hit the river, throwing a geyser of water into the air.

"Every time that happens, my guts clutch up." Cass slumped in front of the window and focused on finding the research station.

"Yeah, me too." Acton pushed the stick to the left, taking the ship around the water plume, and then returned R1 to its course. He rechecked the pathfinder, and the red dot of Rescue 1 was nearly on top of the blue dot of the research station. "Target is ahead at the foot of the volcano." The ship jerked to the right as DF shot past, then returned.

"There's nothing but the same old shit out there," Cass muttered.

Acton frowned. Cass was his oldest and closest friend, and they always got along well because they were constantly joking around. During their three years at the university and almost two years flying rescue missions for the fleet, their sense of humor got them through everything. But lately, it was harder to laugh. Too many lifelong friends were dead.

Acton studied Cass, clinging to the safety bar and staring through the windshield. It was almost like looking at himself. Both stood over six feet, weighed one hundred and eighty pounds, were muscular and fit, and had the same traditional square jaw and thin, tight lips. But the similarities ended there. Cass's family were prominent industrialists who had operated manufacturing facilities on three continents. Acton's father was Fleet Commander Cana Athu, leader of the military and in charge of building the spaceships needed to escape Earth's destruction. His mother was Professor Nora Athu, who created the agricultural systems essential to survival on the spaceships. His uncle, Maximus IV, Cana's older brother, was Emperor of Atlantis. None of them were pleased that he flew rescue missions.

Acton couldn't sit safely on the sidelines while his friends and classmates joined the periphery defense or shuttled people and materials from Earth to the spaceships. His family was saving Atlantis by heading into space. How could he stand aside? When he graduated from the university, he volunteered for the most dangerous work, Rescue Corps, and dozens of his friends and hoops teammates signed up with him.

"Hey! Ahead, on the right, I see...." Cass sat up straight, totally captivated by what was ahead. "I'll be damned! You don't see *that* every day." He sounded more like his old self than he had all day.

"What?" Acton slowed R1 and checked to see if he could hover.

"A naked woman is hanging onto the top of that tree." Cass pointed at the woman with blonde hair. She was buck-naked with her legs wrapped around the tallest dead tree in the area. Quite attractive, thin, yet muscular, she was frantically waving one hand and appeared to be screaming at the top of her lungs.

Acton engaged the hover engine and started to unbuckle his seat harness. "All right, take control. I'll get the scooter and—"

The volcano's summit exploded, shooting millions of pounds of rock, lava, smoke, and ash thousands of feet into the air. The volcano's nearest side collapsed and slid into the lake at the head of the river, creating a flash flood. A second later, the eruption's concussion wave hit the ship, throwing it up and away from the woman.

Rescue 1 was swept up with the wave and then slammed back down when the avoidance system automatically re-stabilized it. Strapped into their seats, Acton and Cass rode it out, then quickly checked to see if the naked woman was still there. The tree swayed violently, but she hung on with both hands.

"Take the controls." Acton released his harness. "I'll get the scooter." He dashed toward the back of the craft. "On my signal, use the laser to cut the tree off below her," he shouted back.

"Hey, why do you get to rescue her? I saw her first," Cass whined, sounding even more like his old self, but he grabbed the controls.

"Yeah, but I acted first, Nummy." Acton grinned. He had called Cass "Numbnuts" back at the university, and some people were offended, so he shortened it to "Nummy."

"But you already have a girl," Cass complained.

Acton chuckled as he pressed a button on a panel near the entry. A hatch slid into the ceiling, and the wind burst into the ship and shoved him against the wall. A compartment near him opened, revealing a strange, hybrid vehicle with jet and hover engines. It had handlebar controls in front of where the driver straddled the scooter and a passenger seat behind the driver. The small craft had a large variety of rescue devices.

Acton scooped the helmet from the seat and put it on. Hopping onto the scooter, he pressed the start button while a harness automatically wrapped around his thighs, securing him. "Testing," he said over the built-in mic that activated when he put on the helmet, and the engine started with a rumble heard over the wind howling into the ship.

"Hear you loud and clear." Cass kept Rescue 1 steady for the launch.

"Exiting ship." Acton twisted the handle, and the scooter rose and flew out of the ship. Once outside, he advanced the thrust to make better headway against the wind and was forced to close the helmet's wind guard to see where he was going. The small aircraft shot toward where she hung onto the treetop.

After the scooter launched, Cass brought R1 level with her. The sleek red craft hovered and slowly approached, only to jerk to the right to avoid DF and then return.

As he flew closer, Acton keyed a series of buttons on the handlebar and lightly closed his fingers around a handle in the center. The timing was critical.

"You ready?" he said as a chunk of DF screamed past him.

"No, I'm too busy playing with myself." Cass chuckled.

"Yeah, right. Better than nothing." Acton grinned. "On three." He kept the scooter about ten feet from the woman and began the countdown. "One… two." He squeezed the handle. A rubbery rope, so sticky it held fast to anything, shot from the scooter and wrapped around the woman and the tree. She squealed as it drew tight around her. "Three."

A bright green laser beam shot from the front of Rescue 1. It sliced through the tree inches below where the woman clung, and she shrieked as she fell toward the river. Acton pulled up on the control, taking them away from the flood.

A safe distance above the flood, Acton punched another button on the handlebar, and the rope started retracting into the scooter, pulling the woman and the tree trunk away from danger. While retracting, he brought the scooter up another hundred feet and pressed a button to enclose the front of the scooter with a padded surface that would be comfortable for her.

"You better hurry. We have a nasty cloud of ash and pumice coming straight at us." Cass brought Rescue 1 closer to the scooter.

As a wall of water and debris crashed into the trees below them, Acton looked at the ash cloud getting closer every second and pressed the button on the dashboard to retract the rope faster. As the woman and tree trunk approached the scooter, he twisted the hand control, and the scooter leaped toward R1's bay. He worried about the rope being fully recovered before they arrived. Only seconds before reaching Rescue 1, the woman was snug against the padded front of the scooter and frantically tried to cover herself with her hands. Crying too hard to say anything, she stared at Acton in wide-eyed shock.

"Hi." He smiled reassuringly, looking into her eyes. "Don't worry. We'll be on the ship in just a second."

As they got to the rescue ship, Acton pressed another button on the handlebar, and the ship's bay floor tilted down to allow the scooter to enter more easily. As the cloud of ash and pumice hit R1, the scooter entered the bay and landed on the inclined floor. As soon as it touched down, the floor rose and extended to the rear of the bay to support the scooter, and the rear hatch closed. When the ship was intact, he shut the scooter off.

"We're inside. Go," Acton said to Cass over the helmet's comm.

The rescue ship zoomed up and away from the volcano, leaving most of the hot ash and pumice behind.

Even though his leg restraints retracted when the engine died, he clung to the scooter while the ship zoomed upward. When R1 leveled out, he jumped off, returned the helmet to the seat, and peeled the sticky rope from the woman. Fortunately, it had wrapped around her waist, and he didn't have to remove it from more intimate areas. As soon as the rope was loose, it retracted into the scooter, and the treetop fell to the floor. She stood shakily, turned away, and desperately tried to cover herself. Acton deliberately looked away.

"This way." He walked into the passenger area, using the handholds for support as the ship jerked and swayed in one direction, then another. She followed him, grasping the same handholds. "You'll find a robe in the closet." He pointed at the closets lining one wall of the passenger compartment while he got a towel from a cabinet. "Are you injured?"

"No major injuries," she said between sobs, "but it feels like I'm raw and sunburned, and it's painful." She hurried to the closet and grabbed its door to keep from falling.

"We have some balm that will help until you get medical attention." He heard the closet open and assumed she was getting a robe. "Where are the other two people?" Acton asked, still looking away from her.

"The others left by boat this morning." The closet door closed with a bang. "I was supposed to take the last boat and follow, but it wasn't there."

"Are you covered?"

"Yes, thank you."

As she tied the robe closed, Acton opened a cabinet near the seats. After taking a jar from a drawer, he offered her a towel, and she tenderly blotted her face. "You should wrap the robe around your lower body so I can put some balm on your back, and then you can put it on your front and legs."

She nodded as Acton turned away. A moment later, she said, "Okay, I'm ready."

Acton sat on the seat behind her. The robe covered her from the waist down, and she sat hunched over with her hands covering her chest. Her skin was red and somewhat pitted. Scooping up some of the ointment, he gently put it on her back, starting at her neck and spreading out to cover her back and sides. "Do you want me to put some on your bottom and the back of your legs?"

Blushing, she straightened to look back at him over her shoulder. "No, thanks. I can do that. Thank you for rescuing me and the balm. I feel better already." She smiled.

"You're welcome. That's what we're here for." He put the lid on the jar and set it on the seat beside her. "There are drinks and food in the cabinet." He pointed to where they were. "Help yourself, and then use the seat belts to secure yourself to the seat. It's a bumpy ride." The ship jerked to the right as though in demonstration of his warning.

She grabbed the edge of the seat to keep from falling over, then faced him using the towel to cover her breasts.

Acton watched her for a moment to make sure she was all right. "I'm Captain Acton Athu. May I ask your name?"

"Lola Laset. Thanks again."

"You're welcome." He started to leave and then stopped. "If you don't mind me asking, how did you end up naked on a treetop?"

"Oh…" She instantly blushed while staring at the floor and then looked up at him. "I went down to leave, and the boat was gone, so I searched for it and got all muddy. After I called for help, I decided to shower and clean up. While showering, something hit the house, and it collapsed and started sliding down the bank toward the river. I jumped to a nearby tree and climbed to the one where you found me. All my clothes were in the house and went into the river." She shrugged and smiled awkwardly.

Acton smiled and shook his head. "Makes perfect sense." He returned to his seat in the cockpit and noticed that R1 was already ten miles from the volcano, heading away from the eruption and the heavy concentration of DF. He took control of the ship.

"Lucky stiff," Cass pouted as he started to get up.

"Give her a minute before you go back. She's putting some balm on her chafed skin. After hours in the ash, pumice, and wind, she's raw."

The ship's comm squawked, and Acton answered by clicking the earplug in his right ear. "Rescue 1."

"Rescue 1, this is Control. What's your status?"

"Control, Rescue 1 is ready." Acton cleared the pathfinder for new data.

"Rescue 1, approximately fifty miles southeast of your location, Research Station 217 is in the path of advancing floodwaters and in danger of a landslide. Rescue five people. Coordinates are mapped to your pathfinder."

"Control, Rescue 1 is on the way." He checked the pathfinder for the destination.

Cass slipped out of his seat and headed for the passenger area.

"Good luck, Rescue 1. Control out."

"Rescue 1 out." Acton turned toward Cass, who was halfway to the passenger area. "Hey, Nummy, we have a new mission. Make sure she's strapped in, and let's go."

"Oh shit, there's no justice," Cass said.

CHAPTER THREE

Rescue 1 flew southeast toward Research Station 217.

With Cass in the passenger lounge bantering with Lola, Acton leaned back and let the pathfinder and avoidance system fly the ship. Soon after joining Rescue Corps, he learned to relax when he could. Rescues were stressful life-or-death situations, usually followed by time to recover before the next emergency.

Thirty miles from where they rescued Lola Laset, there was less DF, and it had a wider dispersal, allowing the avoidance system to make more gradual changes instead of violently jerking the ship in one direction or another, which allowed a break.

In a way, Cass was right. They were living on borrowed time. Fleet would take two more years to build the rest of the spaceships, and then Atlantis would leave Earth to find a new home elsewhere in the universe. Two years… Would he still be doing this in two years? If the next two years were like the last two, twenty more friends would die. Did he even have twenty more friends who were rescuers? There were limits to everything.

Shaking his head, Acton tried to stop worrying as there wouldn't be anyone to save in two years. After the spaceships were built,

Atlantians would be living on them. As the fleet got closer to completion, rescue missions would have to decrease. But rescues would continue for the next year or more while the fleet gathered materials for their voyage.

Acton glanced out at the undulating hills below the ship. Blackened stumps and scorched soil extended for miles where a previous fire had destroyed everything. Wanting something more uplifting, he checked the pathfinder and found they would eventually cross the ridge to go farther south, and the avoidance monitor showed less DF in that direction. He switched off the pathfinder and took manual control of R1.

He flew over the ridge and swooped into a valley of lush trees and dense jungle. A wide, turbulent river flowed through the steep walls of a rocky ravine at the bottom. All along the river, monkeys leaped from tree to tree or swung on vines dangling from high branches; he could almost hear their chatter. Hundreds of multicolored birds took wing, probably due to the sound of his engines echoing in the ravine. They swirled in an intricate formation before flying south. It was easy to imagine abundant wildlife residing in such an unspoiled setting.

Smiling, he reset the pathfinder and enjoyed the natural beauty of the wilderness. As though to remind him of reality, DF streaked down here and there, destroying parts of the jungle.

The river flowed toward him from his right and farther south. Studying the pathfinder, he noticed that his route followed the river, which meant Station 217 was along it. The flash flood was on this river. Acton gazed at the environment outside his window as his stomach sank. Most of this valley would be destroyed in the next half-hour, and he may be the last to see its beauty.

He had seen so much destruction over the last two years that he thought nothing would bother him anymore. But it did. He was still fifteen miles from the research station, and the river disappeared around a bend a couple of miles away. The flash flood wasn't visible yet.

To the northwest, the volcano spewed lava, pumice, and smoke into the dark clouds overhead, but Rescue 1 was far enough away not to be hit by its projectiles. Lightning flashed across the clouds, blinding Acton and momentarily hiding the world in a bright white flash. He leaned back, no longer interested in what would soon be destroyed.

Occasionally, he heard Cass talking with Lola in the passenger lounge. They seemed to be getting along, but Cass was so eager for a good time that most girls soon caught on. Loud laughter came from the lounge, and Acton smiled.

The station was still twelve miles away, so he sat back and watched the steep rock walls of the valley as the ship flew past. The darkness outside was usual, even though it was late morning. Since the debris fall began, the days were twilight. Most of his missions were in the shadow of the debris fall, making every day dark. If that wasn't depressing enough, it also seemed like an eternity.

In the north, beyond the volcano, the horizon was bright red-orange, where the entire northern latitudes were on fire. Acton was amazed that there was anything left to burn. The debris fall began at the North Pole and spread south over the last three years. With the DF bombardment came the gigantic, mile-wide lightning strikes. Within months, everything was on fire. The inferno-driven gale-force windstorms spread the fire from coast to coast. Atlantians, native people, animals, and birds escaped to the south, abandoning thousands of miles of farms, towns, cities, and civilization.

To the west, dense clouds hid most of Mt. Aswanga, and he couldn't see much of it, but he knew Mya was at the Aswanga Mine.

Acton immediately envisioned Mya Moriset. She was so beautiful, tall, and slender, with long brown hair, brown eyes, and an irresistible smile. Imagining her brought a smile to his lips, followed by a frown. The last time he saw her, they had argued. He wanted her to go to New Hope, but she insisted on staying to care for her ailing father. Sitting up straighter, Acton stared at the clouds like he could see Mt. Aswanga. Was DF also bombarding the mine?

The pathfinder buzzed loudly. They were five miles from their destination, and Acton keyed his headset. "Cass." No response. "Hey, Nummy, get up here," Acton shouted, then grinned.

A few moments later, Cass flung himself into the co-pilot seat. "Classy. That was really classy, you hairball."

"If you kept your headset on, I wouldn't have to shout at you." Standard operating procedure (SOP) dictated wearing the headset when on duty.

"What do you want? Are you looking for tips on how to win lovely ladies?"

"From you? You can't be serious. No, we're five miles from the target." He didn't have to tell Cass to start searching, as that was also SOP. They searched the river below the ship for the research station.

Around a bend, the valley narrowed and ran through a forest of tall trees. Several miles ahead, a massive wall of water raced toward them, gobbling up everything in its path. The churning, tumbling mass of tree trunks and foliage plowed through the forest and jungle, ripping up trees and plants and adding them to its aftermath.

Acton keyed his headset. "Research Station 217, this is Rescue 1. Respond." With no response, he switched off the autopilot and took manual control of the ship. "Watch the right."

"On it."

Acton took the ship down to a hundred feet above the churning waters. The avoidance system took over, jerking R1 to the left to avoid a chunk of DF and returning it to his control. They followed the river around another bend and found a bare rock protrusion extending twenty feet over the river from the mountainside.

Cass pointed. "On the ledge, I count five people, two women and three men."

Acton switched to the hover engine and banked the ship toward the rocky summit where the people waited. R1 jerked wildly to the right to escape another chunk of DF and then returned to a course level with the top of it. He slowed and rotated the ship as they got near so the ship's entrance faced the people.

* * * * *

While Acton brought R1 into position, Cass dashed to the rear. He opened the door by pressing several buttons on the panel near it, and a four-foot-wide walkway extended from the ship. Cass stopped the walkway as it touched the rock and, gripping the handhold firmly, reached out to help the scientists enter. "Come on! Get in here!"

As a tall, distinctive man reached for Cass's hand, a six-inch chunk of DF hit him in the chest, knocking him off the edge. He disappeared below the ship as his handbag fell to where he had stood an instant before. Cass gasped and jerked his hand back. He looked over the side; the man was gone.

Forcing his attention back to the other people, he shouted over the hover engine's roar, "Get in here, quick!" He grabbed the next woman's hand and pulled her across.

The other four people hurried across the walkway, carrying their bags. A bald, heavyset man helped a gray-haired woman who was wailing hysterically. Another man in his forties stopped to stare at where his associate had disappeared and grabbed his bag. The younger woman crowded the older couple onboard, wiping tears from her eyes. They were coated with dirt and had multiple scratches, bruises, and scrapes.

"Jacco went right off the edge," the older man exclaimed as he gripped Cass's hand and stepped onto the ship. "He's gone." He pointed to where Jacco had disappeared.

Cass nodded as he took the old man's hand. "Yes, I'm sorry." The other people crowded in behind him. "The passenger lounge is on your left. Drop your bags in the bin with the rope mesh. There are blankets and refreshments in the cabinets across from the seats. Help yourselves, then take a seat and buckle in."

As they found seats, Cass retracted the walkway, closed the door, and keyed his comm. "Acton, we're on board. Go."

Rescue 1 soared away from the area as Cass hung onto a handhold near the door.

Cass stepped into the passenger lounge, held another handhold firmly, and smiled sadly at everyone. "Sorry for your loss." He noticed they had fastened their seat belts. "Does anyone need a bandage, painkillers, lotion, or anything?"

"No, just a few scratches and scrapes," the older woman said. The others nodded.

"Okay, stay buckled in. The ride is bumpy." Getting nods and thanks from the new passengers, Cass staggered back to the cockpit, holding onto the walls for support as the ship gained speed. He dropped into the co-pilot seat and strapped in.

* * * * *

"A tall man got hit by DF right after I opened the hatch," Cass blurted.

"Really? You saw it hit him?"

"Yeah, I reached for his hand, then wham. The DF hit him in the chest and knocked him off the edge. I don't think he even knew what hit him, and he was just gone." Cass stared wide-eyed as though reliving it.

"That's crazy."

Behind them, the wall of water and debris swept closer with every second. The thrusters kicked in, and the rescue ship rapidly gained altitude as it gained speed. They left the valley as the torrent of water overwhelmed everything.

Acton keyed his headset. "Control, this is Rescue 1."

"Rescue 1, this is Control."

"Control, Rescue 1 is headed to ASB with four new passengers. Lost one to DF."

"Acknowledged, Rescue 1. Africa Shuttle Base will be ready for you. Control out."

"Rescue 1, out."

At two thousand feet, Acton adjusted the controls to level out as Cass keyed the coordinates for the Africa Shuttle Base into the pathfinder. The ship banked to the right and came to its new heading.

A chime on Acton's headset announced a call received on his wrist comm. He keyed the watch-sized, combined comm, computer, and camera so they could receive it over their headsets.

"Hey, this is Farl." Over their headsets, her sensual voice sounded like she was seated between them.

"Hey, Farl, what's up?" Acton asked.

Acton and Cass smiled. Besides being extremely attractive and the fleet's most famous female pilot team, Farl Falco and Trice Danti had been their close friends since prep school. They were also the pilots of Rescue 2 in Acton's squad.

"Not much. Cass, are you listening too?" A humorous tone to Farl's voice made her sound like she was always having fun.

"Farl and Trice, the most glamorous pilots in rescuing," Cass chuckled.

"I'll have you know that we just rescued five of the most beautiful girls you ever saw," Trice said. While Trice was technically the co-pilot, like Acton and Cass, that didn't mean much.

"Yeah, sure, the youngest is probably seventy-two." Cass laughed again.

"Hey, we are on the air." Acton redirected the talk, although he was grinning as much as Cass. "What do you need, Farl?"

"Just wanted you to know we're also headed for ASB. Should be there in fifteen clicks."

Acton checked the pathfinder. "That's our ETA as well."

"See you soon then," Farl said sensuously.

Acton silently mouthed the word "tease," and Cass could barely keep from laughing. "Looking forward to seeing you." He turned the comm off.

"I wonder if they did rescue some beauties?" Cass pondered.

"Want to bet?"

Cass glanced at Acton like he must be nuts. "Stupid question."

Acton's wrist comm chimed again, and he glanced at the dial, then answered. "Pad?"

"Yeah, Zetu and I are also headed for ASB. Our ETA is forty minutes, though." Pad Nedin was the captain of Rescue 3 in Acton's squad, and Zetu Ordia was the co-pilot. They were friends from the university and flight school.

"We haven't seen you guys for a week, and I'm looking forward to it," Acton said.

"We are, too," Zetu said in his thick Lamatian accent.

"See you there," Acton said, then ended the call.

CHAPTER FOUR

Rescue 1 flew toward ASB – the Africa Shuttle Base.

After Cass went back to check on the passengers, particularly Lola, Acton sat back and relaxed for a minute. To the north, the debris fall rushed south even faster after hitting Africa. To the ship's right, he could see Mount Aswanga through the murky, dust-and-smoke-filled air. Seeing the ancient volcano returned his thoughts to Mya, bringing up all the feelings he tried to keep buried.

Cass returned and flopped onto his co-pilot seat. "Everybody is tucked in and content."

"We're only a few miles from Mt. Aswanga, so I'm going to see Mya for a minute." Acton toggled the engines into hyper-drive, and the ship shot forward.

Cass frowned. "Are you nuts? You're going to deviate from orders to see Mya?"

"Yeah, nobody knows we aren't scheduled for a stop except you, and you won't tell on me. Will you, good buddy?"

"Hmmm, let's see." Cass stroked his chin. "This ought to be worth something—"

"Before thinking too big, remember what you owe me already."

"What?" Cass stared at Acton, but his expression reflected his recollection of the hundreds of little incidents Acton had on him. "You wouldn't—"

"Oh, wouldn't I? You tell. I tell. No telling where it'll go," Acton said emphatically.

Cass threw his hands up in mock exasperation. "Oh, go ahead. You'll do it anyway. I might as well not be here." Cass scrunched down as though dejected but smiled.

"Thanks, old buddy." Rescue 1 swung right and swooped down toward Mt. Aswanga.

The mine sprawled across the western side of the ancient, dormant volcano rising out of the dense jungle of northern Africa. Most of the mountain had been mined for over a thousand years, leaving dozens of tunnels deep below its surface. The steep mountain towered over the mine's office and residential complex like a brooding giant. In its prime, Aswanga Mine employed thousands of workers. But lately, most of its tunnels had been mined to exhaustion, and only a few shafts were still producing sufficient uranium to stay operational. As Acton brought the rescue ship down, he saw evidence of fresh landslides across the steep, upper slopes of the mountain. "Things have gotten worse."

"It doesn't look good. Do you think DF caused the slides?"

"No, I think it's probably due to earthquakes." Rescue 1 lined up for a landing on the mine's staging field. He could easily see the widespread damage to the buildings, equipment, and countryside this close to the mountain.

"Smoke is coming from a few of the tunnels." Acton pointed to their right at the pock-marked surface of the mountain. "You think it may be active again?"

"You know as much about it as I do. I never was any good at geology."

"Thanks, you're a big help." Acton positioned the ship with the rear door facing the mine.

Switching to the hover engine, the rescue ship settled onto the ground, kicking up a cloud of dust. Some of the buildings at the farthest end of the field had collapsed.

"Looks more and more like earthquake damage." Acton leaped out of the pilot seat and hurried toward the rear door. "You stay with the ship. I'll be right back."

"Abandoned again." Cass sighed as he followed Acton into the passenger lounge.

Seeing the passengers, Acton stopped. "We will only be a few minutes, so please help yourselves to some refreshments. We will be departing soon, so do not leave the ship." They seemed puzzled but said nothing.

The rear door hissed open, and Acton jumped to the ground without waiting for the stairs to lower. He ran toward the office buildings and noticed some other buildings appeared unstable. The main office seemed in better shape than the others but still had broken windows on the top floor. Ore carts were parked haphazardly around the grounds, but the mine's ore transporters were lined up neatly in a row. Two shuttles parked near the offices were dented and damaged. Nearby, six African miners and six Gen-x AG laborers, genetically altered humans with four legs and four arms to better work in the tunnels and shafts, loaded transporters with partially milled ore.

"Does anyone know where I can find Mya?" Acton yelled as he approached them.

A thin, African miner stopped and stared at Acton. Grinning, he walked toward him. "She at office." His thick native accent made his speech barely understandable. "I saw her minutes ago. You Acton?"

Acton stopped and studied the black man. He was taller than Acton but extremely thin. He wore filthy, torn remnants of tan pants and what used to be a pullover shirt but was now no more than a rag. "Yes, I'm Acton." The miner stopped a couple of feet from him.

"I Shorty. Good friend of Mya. She tell me of you."

Acton shook his hand. "Pleased to meet you, Shorty, and thanks." He ran toward the office, leaving Shorty astonished and staring after him.

He was near the office entrance when Mya exited the building and saw him. Even in dirty, dust-covered overhauls, she was beautiful. Her shoulder-length brown hair was swept back into a ponytail. Her brown eyes sparkled with excitement as she ran toward him, and a smile lit up her face.

Acton stopped and caught her as she leaped into his arms. Swinging her around, he pulled her to him and kissed her. All the anxiety, fear, and concern he kept buried suddenly dissipated. Finally, feeling the eyes of a dozen workers watching them, they stopped and held each other as though they would never let go.

"What are you doing here?" Mya stared into his eyes and grinned.

"Seeing you." He squeezed her tight with a big smile. "Are you well?"

"Yes, but things are getting tough. Several of the tunnels have collapsed due to the earthquakes."

"I see some of the buildings have collapsed as well."

"Things are getting worse."

"Then, come with me, now, right this minute." Acton pulled her toward his ship.

"Acton, we're almost done with the last load. We will be out of here tomorrow or the next day and on our way to the fleet. I can't leave my father until he is ready to go."

"Yes, you can." Acton stopped grinning and gazed at her longingly. "Lots of workers can do the rest. Come with me. I worry about you all the time."

"I know. I'm sorry, but my father is working too hard. His health gets worse every day, and he needs me to handle all the office stuff."

"Come on, Mya. Do I have to beg?"

"No, don't beg." A tear ran down one cheek. "Just be there to welcome me when we get to New Hope."

Acton stared quizzically at her. "You're taking the last load to my father's ship? I thought it was already full."

"I don't know why, but that's where we've been ordered to go."

"Are you sure you can't leave now?" He stopped and turned back toward the offices, tugging her with him. "Perhaps if I ask your father, he'll let you leave now."

"No." Mya stopped and pulled him to her. "He is frantic with worry but will finish the job. After this load, it's all over. He doesn't know what he will do on the fleet ships, but he is adamant about getting his work done."

Acton looked into her eyes. "I love you, Mya. I don't know if I can leave you here."

As she started walking toward his ship, tugging Acton with her, Cass stepped onto R1's stairs and stared at them.

"I love you too. You know that. But I love my father too. I can't leave him here to do this on his own. He is extremely sick, and I worry about him collapsing at any moment. I have to get things done so that he will leave willingly." Her eyes pleaded with him. "Don't you see?"

Acton exhaled deeply and shook his head. His wrist comm chimed, and he punched the speaker button.

"Acton, we have to go." Cass's voice sounded frantic. "DF hit Rescue 2, and they went down. We have to rescue Farl and Trice."

"Oh no!" Acton turned the comm off and took Mya into his arms. "You take care. I will be back when you're ready to go. Just call me."

"I will. Thanks for coming to see me. I miss you so."

He kissed her. "I love you."

"I love you too. See you soon."

Acton nodded and ran toward the ship.

"Nice to see you, Mya," Cass shouted from the ship's open door.

"You too, Cass."

When Acton arrived at R1, he pushed Cass inside and glanced back at Mya. He blew her a kiss, then closed the door behind him.

A few moments later, the engines fired, and Rescue 1 took off.

* * * * *

Mya strolled toward her apartment in the office building.

She crossed the grounds, entered the offices, and climbed the stairs to her room while tears streamed steadily down her cheeks. Thankful that she didn't meet anyone along the way, she had never felt so alone. Mya sat on her bed and rested her head on her hands. Tired of holding the tears back, she let her feelings overwhelm her.

Images flooded her mind. Pictures of her mother singing with Mya as they prepared dinner in their condo. Songs of joy and peace that she learned at a retreat for One God followers during Mya's first year at the university. After walking on the ocean shore, they shared a special meal under the trees when her mother made an unexpected trip to visit her because she thought Mya might be homesick. Visiting the hospital room where her mother was dying from a fall from the second story onto the patio below. Her mother's final kiss and blessing minutes before she died.

She remembered her friends at the university and how much she enjoyed their company and the choir's beautiful music at the Temple of the One God. Acton, the most popular guy at school, paid attention to her, a nobody, a girl from a small village near Mt. Atlan. After Acton made the winning shot at the hoops tournament in their final year and was riding out of the gym on his mates' shoulders, he jumped down to lift her and kiss her exuberantly. The many late-night walks and quiet talks they had long into the night. Acton told her he loved her as the wind blew his hair into tufts and took her head tenderly into his big hands to kiss her so sweetly.

Tears fell, wetting her cheeks, hands and dusty, dirty overhauls. She wept for all the time she spent alone and for her father, who was as lost as she had been since her mother died. All her friends were in service to the fleet or on spaceships. Unlike her, they were anywhere but stuck in Africa at a dirty, miserable mine surrounded by Gen-x workers and rough, crude miners.

She wiped her eyes, took a tissue from the table near her bed, and blew her nose. She had made friends with Shorty, the other native miners, and most of the Gen-x people, but only to see that they had what they needed to survive by taking food and clothes she could steal without causing a problem. She loved them, but it wasn't the same.

"Mya, are you upstairs?" Her father's voice interrupted her thoughts from downstairs. Monty Moriset was a sick man. He could barely stand and walk on his own. His strong, muscular body had wasted away, and what was left was weak and unstable. His gray hair was thin enough to easily see his scalp through it, his skin was a splotchy red, and his eyes a dull gray.

She sniffled greatly and cleared her throat. "Yes, Father, I'm in my room."

"Are you okay? Shorty said Acton came to the mine. Is everything all right?" Monty sounded hollow and weak.

"Yes, everything is fine. Don't worry." Mya tried to sound reassuring.

"Good, I'm glad. We will be on our way to the fleet tomorrow or the next day, and things will be much better. Right?" He unsuccessfully tried to sound optimistic.

"Yes, Father, that will be great." She started to cry again.

"Are you getting lunch ready soon?"

"Yes, get some rest. I will be right down." As Mya settled on the bed and tried to stop crying, she heard Monty shuffle away from the stairs.

CHAPTER FIVE

Acton rushed into the cockpit, leaving Cass to close the hatch.

As soon as Cass joined him, Acton took off and shoved the forward thrust to its stops. Rescue 1 jumped into the sky, throwing Cass against his seatback and the passengers against their restraints.

"Easy, buddy. Remember, we have passengers." Cass jerked a thumb over his shoulder toward them.

Acton stared blankly at him for a moment. "Yeah, sorry. I forgot." He eased the thrust back a couple of notches and stared straight ahead at the murky sky. The ship jerked to the left to avoid DF and then returned to its course. "Where are we going?"

"North about five miles. It's on the pathfinder, and we're on the way now."

"What happened?"

"Apparently, DF hit a wing, and they crashed."

Acton nodded and flew automatically, reviewing his conversation with Mya in his mind. All he wanted to do was make sure she was safe. Was that wrong? He understood she felt responsible for her father, especially since he was sick. But how could he protect her if she wouldn't safeguard herself? What if something happened to her? He wouldn't even know unless he checked on her daily, and he couldn't do that because they had promised each other not to when she had proposed that before.

Rescue 1 jerked to the left and returned to its course as a chunk of DF shot past.

He took a deep breath and tried to relax. He found he was gripping the stick too tightly and released it. Gazing out the window at the jungle, he tried to find a way to handle his feelings. Somehow, he had to stop wanting to protect Mya, but even the thought made him feel like someone had gut-kicked him. Plus, he didn't understand why she didn't want what he wanted. Usually, people went along with whatever he decided was best. Why wouldn't Mya?

He hated his emotions dictating his actions, which only happened when he was around Mya. How did he lose command of the situation? Lately, things seemed to be going wrong. Was his luck changing? Was there even such a thing as luck? He had always thought he created his destiny, and circumstances had little to do with it. He remembered a particularly persuasive speech he made at halftime in a hoops game when his team was losing. He had convinced his teammates that luck was created. Luck resulted from going the extra mile and doing what their opponents wouldn't do. Luck was risking it all and being ready to lose everything to win.

Acton turned toward the side window away from Cass, who still watched him worriedly. How do you risk all when it means losing what you valued most? This wasn't a game. This was real. Mya wasn't a trophy; she was the woman he wanted to marry and share his life with. How could he risk that?

"Hey, there they are!" Cass pointed ahead and slightly to their right.

Acton stared forward like he had just awakened from a dream. They had only gone a few miles, but he could easily see more DF coming down all over the area. Rescue 2 was a pile of twisted, smoking metal. Most of one wing was on the ground fifty feet away, almost intact, while the other was crumpled under the ship. The hatch was open, and five people stood twenty feet away, two wearing Rescue Corps uniforms. Two passengers writhed on the ground as Trice helped them.

"At least Farl and Trice appear to be okay," Cass said, sighing with relief.

Acton switched to hover engines and landed a safe distance away. While he shut down, Cass ran to the hatch, grabbed a medical kit, and hurried toward the injured people.

On his way out, Acton stopped in the passenger lounge. "We need to make room for more people. I know it will be tight, especially with two injured, but do your best to make room. I'll be back in a minute."

He jumped to the ground and ran toward Farl. When he arrived, Cass was already wrapping bandages around the legs of one of the injured passengers while Trice assisted another person. Farl urged the rest of the passengers toward Rescue 1.

Acton walked with her. "What happened?"

Farl Falco's red hair was messy, and she had smudges on her cheek and forehead above her thick eyebrows. But somehow, she still looked spectacular in her trim rescue uniform, and her green eyes flashed as she faced him. "DF straddled us. The right one hit our wing and cut off a chunk. The impact flipped us, and we did a full rotation as we came down. We landed on the shortened wing and broke off the other as we landed. Fuel was all over, so we quickly got everyone out." She nodded at the two on the ground. "A cabinet broke loose on impact and fell on them. I think their legs are broken. We had to drag them out of the ship."

Acton hugged her warmly. "That's incredible! I'm so glad that you are okay. I don't know anyone else who survived a crash like that. Thank God you're all alive."

"Well, I'm not too thrilled." Farl pushed him away. "This won't look good on my review."

"You're the only one who would worry about something like that now." Acton chuckled and lightly punched her shoulder.

Suddenly, a large chunk of DF hit Rescue 2, crushing the pilot's cockpit and igniting the spilled fuel. The fire raced through the crumpled wreckage, which exploded, sending pieces in all directions. A large portion landed only feet from Rescue 1.

"Holy Atlan! We better get out of here," Acton exclaimed. "Cass, let's get the stretchers and the injured passengers onto R1. Trice, help get everyone else onboard."

Trice ran to Acton and gave him a quick hug. Her brown hair was messed up, her beautiful face was smudged, and a cut over her left eye bled into her eyebrow. "Glad to see you. These people will need some strong painkillers."

"We'll get some at ASB. Try to situate people so we can get everyone on board. It's going to be tight." Acton hurried to R1 while Farl and Trice helped the passengers to the ship.

DF struck all over the area as Acton and Cass carried the injured people to R1. They ran to the ship with the last injured person and had to put their stretcher in the aisle. Acton rushed to the cockpit as Cass closed the hatch.

The passenger lounge was full of people, leaving an aisle less than a foot wide. The original five passengers, plus the seven people from Rescue 2, made two people over the recommended maximum.

"Hang on!" Acton shouted as he started the engines. "We're taking off." He eased the thrust forward and brought the nose up. A chunk of DF shot past, barely missing the ship. He punched the pathfinder and set it for ASB as Cass joined him in the cockpit. Farl squeezed into the co-pilot seat with Cass, and Trice stood between the seats, clutching the handholds as Acton flew toward ASB.

"I'm glad it's only a few miles," Trice said.

Acton keyed the comm unit. "Control, this is Rescue 1."

"Rescue 1, go," Control said over the ship's speaker.

"Control, we have picked up Rescue 2's crew and passengers and are heading for ASB. Please advise ASB that we have passengers that need medical assistance for their broken legs."

"Rescue 1, will do. What is your ER at ASB?"

Acton glanced at Cass.

"One minute," Cass replied. "Hey, look!"

Acton leaned forward to see more clearly. He keyed the ship's camera and zoomed in on ASB.

"Control, smoke is rising from ASB. Shuttle 36 has crashed, and Shuttle 15 is parked at the refueling station. Near it, two pilots are on the ground and appear to be dead. Two unidentified shuttles are near the operations center, and rebels are loading them with material from the center."

"Do what you can, but be careful, Rescue 1. Control out."

"On it. Rescue 1, out," Acton responded automatically. He swung Rescue 1 around and landed behind a ground transport bus halfway between ASB's apartment complex and the fueling station.

By the time R1 came to rest, Trice was getting Rescue One's laser pistols, blasters, and battle goggles from the weapons lockup. They hurried to the hatch, stepping around the injured people in the aisle. Acton and Cass took the two blasters while Farl and Trice prepped the laser pistols.

Armed, Acton stepped into the passenger lounge. "ASB is under attack by rebels." They nodded with frightened faces. Turning to his team, he assessed everyone's condition. "Trice, would you take Rescue 1 a mile away and make sure no one follows you? I will call you on your wrist comm when it's safe to return."

Trice appeared to be disappointed but nodded. "Sure, I can do that. You guys take care." She handed the laser pistol to Farl and walked into the cockpit.

When he turned back to Cass and Farl, they had already put their battle goggles on. The white goggles wrapped around their heads and covered their eyes with a plastic screen as dark as sunglasses but contained a laser-sighting scope that measured the distance to objects and worked with the blasters to direct shots to selected targets.

He accepted a pair of goggles from Cass, noticed it was ready to use, and put it on. "All right, let's go kick some rebel butt." Acton opened the hatch, jumped to the ground, and was quickly followed by Cass and Farl. They closed the hatch and ran to take cover at the rear of the transport. Acton studied ASB's layout as Rescue 1 took off.

The shuttle base had ample space to park six shuttles, each forty-eight by fifty-seven feet, and still had room for six rescue ships. The jet fuel depot's tanks were buried beneath the complex. The base had a one-story operations center, a pilot's lounge, and apartments for the base personnel. On the other side of the field, far away from the fuel depot, a tall, crystal pyramid sparkled blue and gold even in the dim light. Like dozens of other crystal towers worldwide, it was a power tower that transmitted electrical energy over a wide area.

After the DF bombardment began, bases like the Africa Shuttle Base had been set up wherever evacuations were staged. All the ones north of ASB had already been destroyed, and ASB was probably only a month away from being abandoned.

"They're trying to steal Shuttle 15." Acton pointed at four rebels running toward the fuel station. "Let's stop them." He activated his goggles' infrared targeting, and the rebels lit up in his viewer with small numbers beside each, indicating the distance to them.

They waited until the four men came closer, and then Acton and Cass opened fire with their blasters, the fleet's version of blast rifles that worked with their goggles. The rebels dropped to the ground and shot back with their blast rifles.

"Cass, give your blaster to Farl, crouch down, and get to the crashed shuttle. We will hold them down, and if any try to shoot at you, we'll take them out. When you arrive, get one of its blasters and shoot anyone heading toward Shuttle 15."

"On it." Handing the blaster to Farl, Cass waited until they started shooting at the rebels, then ran a zigzag pattern toward the shuttle.

As the rebel closest to Shuttle 15 rose to sight Cass, Acton targeted him by touching a button on the blaster and shot him. The rebel flew back, landed on his back, and didn't move. A moment later, another rebel aimed at Cass. When Farl shot him, he flew sideways, landed hard, and stayed down.

A chunk of DF screamed down and hit the middle of the field, not far from the fuel pumps and about a hundred feet from the operations center. Acton followed it down and then saw another ten rebels with blast rifles spread across the field from the operations center and run to support the four rebels near Shuttle 15. Before Cass arrived at the crashed shuttle, rebels were stalking the transporter from two directions.

"Uh oh, this isn't good. Farl, take over on this side while I move to the other end of the transport." Acton hustled to the cab and shot at the approaching rebels from there.

Cass got one of the blasters from the crashed Shuttle 36 and hid behind the wreckage to shoot at the rebels near him.

The rebels moved steadily closer, alternating shooters and peppering the transport with blasts from multiple directions. Then, from above ASB, the unmistakable sound of a hover engine filled the air.

"If that's more rebels, we're cooked," Acton said, pinned behind the transport.

Numerous blaster shots suddenly struck across the field near the rebel positions. Acton leaned out and peered around the transport. Rescue 3's scooter hovered overhead, and its pilot, Pad Nedin, fired on the rebels with two blasters using his goggles. His first shots killed two rebels instantly.

"It's Pad! Let's go! Shoot! Shoot!" Acton yelled as he stepped beside the transport and shot at the rebels nearest him. Behind him, Farl did the same, and Cass rapidly fired at the rebels from the crashed shuttle.

Suddenly, the rebels broke and ran in multiple directions, trying to find cover. One second, they were pressing the attack; the next moment, they panicked and were on the run. Their shots at the scooter missed it entirely. Ones aimed at Cass went wide, and others toward Acton and Farl didn't come close. They ran toward their shuttles.

Another chunk of DF hit close to the rebels who were rushing to their ships. When the shuttles started their engines, the rest of the rebels quit fighting and ran to their ships. Pad swung the scooter around and shot at the ships as they took off with half their people still boarding and headed south with several hanging out of the hatches.

Pad pursued them until they left the base, then returned to ASB's landing field. "Make sure there are no hostiles before I land," he said over their squad comm.

"Pad, you crazy man, you sure saved the day." Acton carefully checked on the downed rebels, ready to shoot if any moved. Farl and Cass joined him, but he could see they were dead. He pushed his goggles onto his forehead. "Trice, you can return to ASB and land near the center," he said, knowing Trice was listening to the squad comm.

"On it," Trice replied.

Pad landed the scooter near the operations center while holding both blasters in one arm. Climbing off the scooter, he removed his goggles, leaned back, and yelled exuberantly while shaking the blasters over his head. "Oh man, that was fun! I've wanted to do that ever since I joined Rescue Corps." Pad looked like the country farm boy he was. He was rugged and lean, with short dark hair and a closely cropped beard on his chiseled face.

They ran to Pad as he leaned the blasters against the scooter. Surrounding him, they congratulated him. "Pad, that was the craziest stunt I ever saw. I thought you wouldn't be here for thirty minutes," Acton said.

"When we heard what was happening, we punched it to get here in time not to miss any of the fun." Pad grinned.

"You have a strange definition of fun, but you sure saved our butts. We were going down to overwhelming numbers until you arrived," Acton said.

Rescue 3 descended over ASB and landed nearby. Zetu Ordia left the ship and walked toward them. A Lamatian, he was at least six inches taller than anyone else and in better shape than most. He had bushy eyebrows, dark-brown eyes, and dark braided hair that hung down his back. "That worked," he said as they congratulated him with palm slaps and hugs.

"It sure as hell did. You guys are the heroes of the day," Acton said. As things calmed down, he took a deep breath and studied the situation. "We better get back to work."

While Farl watched for rebels, the rest went to the pilots near Shuttle 15. Colin Zefin and his co-pilot, Mak Mesen, died from blaster shots. Both were young, fresh from flight school, and no one on Acton's team knew them. They carried the pilots into Shuttle 15 and covered them with a blanket as Rescue 1 landed near the operations building. The crashed ship, Shuttle 36, was too damaged to get into the cockpit and too mangled for anyone to have survived. Acton and Cass flew Shuttle 15 closer to the operations center, landing close to Rescue 1. They deplaned, and the team quickly regrouped as more chunks of DF hit close to the transport vehicle and farther from the building.

"I don't understand why, but more and more DF is coming down all over. We better get airborne so the avoidance systems can protect the ships. Trice, you take Rescue 1. Can some of the passengers help with the injured?" Acton asked, and Trice nodded. "Pad, you take Rescue 3. Cass, you take Shuttle 15. Go south until you are out of the DF and stay in the air so the avoidance system can protect you. Zetu, can you stay near the center and watch for rebels? We don't want surprises, so fire a few warning shots if you see any." Zetu nodded.

The pilots hurried to their ships while Zetu stood guard near the building with one of R3's blasters. The ships headed south as more DF struck across the field.

Acton turned to Farl. "Let's see what's happening inside." They hurried toward the base's operations center. Besides smoke rising from somewhere in the back of the building and scattered luggage carts across the field, the operations center appeared normal.

CHAPTER SIX

As Acton and Farl got close to ASB's operation center, they heard voices calling for help.

Adjusting their goggles over their eyes, they hurried to the entrance, pushing the door open, and Acton ducked low to the right and Farl low to the left, ready for anything. The voices were louder but not urgent, so they quickly surveyed the large room with their laser pistols ready.

With the infrared on, Acton didn't see any heat signatures. To the left of the entrance, the passenger waiting area provided seats for forty people. A food service area with tables and chairs was beyond the seats, and a long counter with stools ran the length of the wall. A tall counter surrounding several desks was across from the service area, in the middle of the building, and was the communication center, management station, and passenger service desk. Next to it, a small store offered food and personal accessories.

"Back here!" a man called, and the other voices went silent.

Suspicious of a trap, they stalked closer with weapons in hand. Clothing, baggage, and other personal items were scattered across the waiting area. The store shelves were nearly empty, and food products and other goods were broken or strewn across the floor. As they got closer, they saw people lying on the floor behind the counter with their hands and feet tied. They holstered their pistols, raised their goggles, and rushed to them.

"Thank God, I thought we would be here for hours," the man said. "I'm Base Commander Surg Sideral. Seven people are my team members, and the rest are passengers for the next shuttle."

They untied Surg and the other uniformed people. When freed, each helped free the others. "Did you recognize any of the rebels?" Acton asked.

"No, they wore masks."

"Did any of them wear goggles like these?" Acton touched the one on his forehead.

"No, just face masks."

"How many were there?" Acton noticed that all the center's comm units and monitors were missing.

"Hmm, let's see… There was one who was obviously the leader. He was tall, over six feet, and had a laser and a blaster. He threatened to use the blaster if we didn't do what he said." Acton nodded for Surg to continue. "Four others came into the building, but more were outside as they forced the field crew inside. They took Shuttle 15."

"No, we stopped them at the fuel station."

"Thank God."

Farl and the base personnel helped the other people move to the seats in the waiting room while Acton and Surg spoke quietly by the counter. Someone found food and water for people while Farl and others took care of the passenger's injuries, mostly rope burns, cuts, and bruises.

"What happened to Shuttle 36?" Acton asked.

"Just after the rebels stormed the building, Shuttle 36 requested permission to land. The rebels answered the call and approved their arrival, but I think the captain suspected something was wrong. He aborted the landing and tried to contact Control, and they shot it down."

"I thought so. You better take it easy for a while." Acton helped Surg to a seat in the waiting area. "We'll make sure everyone gets to the fleet."

"Thank you."

Acton waved Farl over. "Farl, if you could get people ready to go, I will put out the fire and see if there is anything else we need to do."

"Someone found some painkillers for the injured people. Also, I learned that the rebels took all the computers, comm equipment, supplies, fuel and oxygen canisters, and ship parts they could find," Farl said.

"You found out more than I did. Good work. Finish up here, and I'll be back in a minute."

Using the goggles again, he walked toward where the smoke rose at the back of the center. When he arrived, he found the repair department's door had a large hole and hung from one hinge. "Looks like they blasted their way in and set fire to something," he muttered.

"Hey!" a deep voice shouted from his right.

Drawing his laser pistol, he turned toward the sound and found a man propped up on his elbows against the wall. He was singed and bleeding from his nose and ears.

Acton re-holstered his pistol and rushed to the man's side. "How bad are you hurt?"

"I can't hear you. I think my eardrums burst." The man's ID badge indicated his name was Mico Malin. "I was inside the door when they blasted it. Damn near brought the wall down on me and set off a barrel of liquid fuel I use to clean engine parts."

Acton checked to see if he could be moved. Besides his bloody face and minor burns, he appeared to be in no immediate danger. "Let's get you to where they patch you up."

"I think I can move. Give me a hand." Mico struggled to get up.

Acton helped Mico walk to where two people were bandaging people's wounds. Farl was waiting for him near the passengers.

"Thanks." Mico stretched across the seats.

Acton leaned close. "You're welcome." He turned from Mico and stepped closer to Farl. "Get a fire extinguisher and put the fire out. Gather any other people scattered around the building and get the base commander or one of his staff to account for everyone."

"Right." Farl started toward the fire.

"Wait, we have five people from your ship, two of whom are injured, right?"

She nodded. "Right, five people, three women and two men, all from the waterworks at Glymfi."

"So, you have five, we have five, and twelve people are at the base. We need to transport twenty-two, plus ourselves, making it twenty-six people. I think we should leave the injured people on Rescue 1 with a few people to make sure they are comfortable. Then, you should take Shuttle 15 and the rest of the passengers back to New Hope if Control approves."

"Been a while since I flew a shuttle, but it shouldn't be a problem."

"Are you up to it? I can have Cass fly it if you prefer."

"Hmm, that might be a good idea. If you're taking the injured, Trice should go with you, as she's the best one to tend to their needs. Then Cass could come with me in case I need him."

"All right, get going. I'll call Control." Acton hurried toward the entry door as Farl headed to the rear of the building. As he ran onto the field, he remembered that all the ships were airborne and south of ASB. He keyed his wrist comm. "Pad, can you pick me up so I can report to Control?"

"Be there in a minute," Pad said.

As Rescue 3 landed nearby, Acton turned to Zetu. "I'm going to report to Control. Let me know if any rebels return." Zetu nodded. When the hatch opened on R3, he climbed onto the ship and ran into the cockpit. "Take it back up. This will take a minute."

"On it," Pad said as R3 took off again.

Acton keyed the ship's comm. "Control, this is Acton Athu on Rescue 3."

"This is Control. Go, Rescue 3."

Acton explained the situation. "I think we should bring everyone to New Hope," he said, finishing his report.

"Are the base personnel too injured to continue at the base?"

"Possibly not, but there are no supplies, food, computers, or comm equipment. DF is coming down all over the place, and there's nothing they can do here. Plus, they need medical attention."

The response took a minute. "Use Rescue 1 and Shuttle 15 to transport the ASB personnel and the passengers to New Hope."

"Thank you, Control. We will depart as soon as possible." Acton nodded at Pad.

"Rescue 3, Acton, your father says he wants to see you when you get here."

He grimaced. "Please tell him I will report as soon as I arrive. Rescue 3, out."

"On it. Control out."

"Did you screw up?" Pad asked.

"No." Acton chuckled. "I don't think so anyway," he added less confidently.

"Glad it's not me reporting to the fleet commander."

"Let's get everyone on board and get out of here."

"Wait, I want to check on something." He keyed the comm. "Control, this is Rescue 3, Pad Nedin reporting."

"Rescue 3, this is Control, go."

"Control, since we are at ASB, we can help transport people to New Hope."

"Rescue 3, proceed to Island Shuttle Base 2, ISB2, to bring the regional governor and his staff to New Hope."

"As ordered. Rescue 3, out." Pad did not sound happy.

"Control out."

Acton keyed the comm. "Rescue 1 and Shuttle 15, did you copy my report to Control?"

"Rescue 3, I copied. I'm on my way back to ASB. Rescue 1 out," Trice said.

"Copy that. Shuttle 15 is enroute to ASB. Shuttle 15 out," Cass said.

Pad landed close to the operations center. Minutes later, Rescue 1 and Shuttle 15 landed nearby. He waved for Cass to follow him and motioned Trice to stay on Rescue 1.

Acton and Cass ran to Rescue 1 and entered the passenger lounge. "We will leave for New Hope as soon as we get everyone on board. I need a few volunteers to help with the injured people. The rest should move over to Shuttle 15 because there isn't enough room on this ship." One man and two women volunteered by raising their hands. "Thank you. Please make yourselves as comfortable as possible. The rest of you, please move to Shuttle 15."

He stepped into the cockpit with Trice and Cass. "Trice, since you are probably the best to provide medical assistance, would you stay with Rescue 1 while Cass moves over to Shuttle 15 to back up Farl? I think she is a little more shaken up than she thought."

"Sure, no problem, whatever works." Trice smiled.

"Me and Farl, huh? All right, I like that." Cass grinned.

"Come on, let's get going." The three pilots followed the passengers outside.

Farl joined them and stepped close to Acton. "The base commander confirmed all are accounted for and ready to make the trip."

"All right, good work," he said. "We're taking everyone to New Hope." She nodded.

Pad Nedin and Zetu Ordia joined them from the direction of Rescue 3.

"Glad it's you guys going to ISB2. I hate flying that far over the ocean. It's so boring," Acton said. ISB2 was on the other side of the Atlantic Ocean and the long peninsula at the bottom of Nolantis.

"Yeah, me too." Zetu grinned.

"Well, we better get to work." Acton nudged Cass toward the center. "You guys take care, and don't fall asleep over the deep blue."

"No problem, that's what autopilot is for," Pad said with a chuckle. "Besides, Zetu has to stay awake and keep watch. I plan to sleep the whole way."

Zetu punched Pad's shoulder as they walked toward their ship.

"What was that for?" he asked, rubbing his shoulder.

"You better not sleep all the way to ISB2."

As Pad and Zetu walked to Rescue 3, Acton and his friends entered the operations center to board the ships to SS New Hope.

CHAPTER SEVEN

Genesi Forcu hurried toward the Temple on SS New Hope.

"Oh, I can't be late," Genesi muttered quietly. She nearly swore, seeing she should be there at this moment, but didn't because church acolytes didn't curse, at least not in public. She looked up from checking the hour on her wrist comm in time to dodge a woman she was about to run into, waved her apology, and hurried down the hall.

Genesi was not herself this morning. Usually, she was early for every appointment, especially with Master Ono, head of the Church of the One God and her employer. But she had tried to do too much and now was sure she would keep the master waiting, which would be intolerable. Her silky, floor-length, light-blue acolyte robe fluttered around her legs as she hurried. Her long, brown hair, which ordinarily hung stylishly to her shoulders, was streaming back as though caught in a modest breeze. A few feet from the Temple, Genesi recognized a church member walking toward her. He frowned at her haste, but after she gave him one of her special smiles, a quirky uptick on the right side, he smiled back and waved to her.

She arrived at the double-doored main entrance to the Temple, pulled the right door open, and stepped inside. Hurrying down the wide center aisle, Genesi hardly noticed the fifty rows of fifty empty seats cascading to the stage over thirty feet below the entrance. Twenty-five hundred seats seemed like a lot, but with nearly one hundred thousand people living in New Hope, there were eighteen church services a day, seven days a week, to accommodate everyone.

Dimly lit, the empty Temple was eerie. Something about the rows of empty blue seats on a darker blue carpet seemed expectant. She preferred the Poseidia Temple with its rich wood, lofty stained-glass windows, and soaring steeple. In comparison, this Temple was sterile, all molded plastique and metal, soulless without the rich wood tones reflecting the brightly colored light streaming through the windows.

Arriving at the front, Genesi hurried up twelve steps onto the large stage that filled the front of the theater and could hold hundreds of people. She dashed across it to the door behind the gold curtains at the back, where the church offices were located to be convenient for acolytes like her to do so many services. As she entered the office, the staccato sound of her shoes on the metal floor, painted to appear like wood, still echoed throughout the cavernous amphitheater.

Inside the office, Genesi turned right and silently placed her bag and shawl on her desk only a few feet from the door. Her good friend, coworker, and long-time roommate, Marlenel Nete, sat to the left of the entrance. Similarly dressed, Marlenel was shorter and stouter than her, with dark hair and brown eyes. Leaning close to Marlenel, she whispered. "Is he in?"

Looking up from her monitor, Marlenel nodded as she nervously glanced at Mara.

As the gatekeeper for Master Ono, Mara's desk was at the back of the room, the last obstacle before his door. Older than either acolyte, she ran the office with a firm hand, including the Temple's personnel, but Mara was focused on her monitor and hadn't noticed them.

Genesi nodded her thanks. Brushing her robe free of tangles, she smoothed her hair into place, took a deep breath, and walked to

Mara's desk at a stately pace. "Good morning, Mara," she said from across her desk. "I have an appointment with Master Ono."

Mara, a reservoir of serenity, glanced up from her monitor and smiled. Her dark-brown eyes seemed like openings into another dimension. "Good morning. Yes, he's expecting you," she said in a hushed tone, then returned to her monitor.

Genesi nodded her thanks and stepped around Mara's desk to the master's door. She knocked softly and opened the door to listen.

"Come in." Master Ono's voice was a deep, baritone sigh.

Genesi slipped through the door and closed it softly. His office was as tranquil as if on another plane of existence. The large room was dark and comfortably furnished with sofas, cushioned chairs, and small wooden tables. She carefully walked between the furniture toward the only bright light in the room.

Master Ono sat at his desk, working on something on his monitor. The bald space in the middle of his white hair reflected the overhead light and his long white beard seemed to glow. His white robes, designating his position as the head of the Church of the One God and Master of the Way, were iridescent, nearly sparkling. As Genesi approached his large mahogany desk, he looked up. His piercing blue eyes seemed lit from within as he smiled warmly.

"Hello, Genesi. What can I do for you?" He motioned for her to sit on one of the white cushioned chairs in front of his desk.

"Thank you for seeing me, Master." She sat on a chair close to him.

"Always a pleasure to see one of my favorite coworkers."

"I am worried, Master. I haven't seen Pal in three days, and it's not like him to disappear. I've been meditating on where he may be but without enlightenment," she said, referring to Pal Athu, the youngest son of Fleet Commander Cana Athu. She lowered her head to hide the tears suddenly brimming in her eyes.

"Hmm, that's a long time. Have you checked with his family?"

"No, I didn't want to bother them. They do so much already."

"Yes, I understand." Master Ono leaned back in his chair, making a steeple of his fingers as he stared into space. "I think you are right to be concerned, and I suggest you notify the L.E.T. of Pal's disappearance and tell them I would like them to look into it." On the spaceships, the Law Enforcement Team was the police.

"Yes, Master, I will. May I have some time off today to do so and to meet with some of Pal's friends from the university to see if they have seen him?"

"Yes, of course. Arrange with Mara for someone to do your services and take whatever time you need."

"Thank you, Master. I appreciate it."

"You're welcome. Go with God." Master Ono smiled as he delivered the usual blessing sincerely but automatically and returned to his monitor.

Genesi quietly left his office. After arranging for a replacement to lead her church services near the lunch hour, she called the L.E.T. and made an appointment to see Captain Nortin Ketsu after lunch. With everything organized, she got ready for her day's first service. She entered a secluded nook next to the office, sat on one of the cushioned chairs, and quietly chanted. A few minutes later, she entered meditation, and her anxiety slipped away. By the time of her first service in the Temple, she was serene and ready.

Each service, a spiritual exercise, lasted from thirty minutes to an hour. The attendees determined how long a contemplation they wanted to experience. Genesi's three services took less than an hour each, and she was ready for lunch by the end of the third.

Before work, she reserved a large booth in the Social Club, a restaurant one floor below the Command Center. Genesi took a lift to the club and stopped at the reception desk.

The host arrived a moment later. "May I help you?"

"Yes, my name is Genesi Forcu, and I reserved a booth for six."

"Yes, I remember. Several people have already arrived. Follow me." The club had well over a hundred tables, yet it had a quiet, hushed quality. The subdued lighting and rich colors created an ambiance that made the club feel more intimate than its large size typically would. He led her to the booths along the left side of the restaurant.

Genesi recognized one of the people sitting in the booth as she arrived. She thanked the host, then sat next to one of Pal's closest friends. "Linga, how are you?"

"I'm good. How are you? You sounded so worried when you called that I became worried." Linga Forst was about her height with short dark hair and brown eyes and wore loose-fitting clothes like most university students.

"I am very concerned." She turned to a tall man sitting next to Linga. "Are you Jonna?"

"Yes." Jonna Kerol was taller and thinner than Linga, had blond hair and blue eyes, and wore a sports top and loose-fitting pants. "Nice to meet you." He was on Pal's hoops team.

"You must be Sula Kens, right?" Genesi smiled at a short, deeply tanned woman with long dark hair and brown eyes.

"Yes, I am. Nice to meet you, finally. Pal has spoken of you so often that I feel like I already know you." Sula wore a brightly colored slip-over dress.

"Have you known Pal for a long time?" Genesi asked.

"Yes, we grew up together. My family has the farm next to the Athu Farms."

"I've looked forward to meeting you. Thanks for coming."

A waiter arrived at the table and brought their drinks. Placing plates of tiny sandwiches and fresh vegetables in the center of the table, he took Genesi's order of iced tea.

"I ordered some lunch items. Please help yourselves." She passed the plates around, and everyone took a few sandwiches and veggies.

Suddenly, a scrawny little man with dark hair and large ears arrived at the table, wearing rumpled gray pants and a loose pullover shirt. "Hello," he said.

"Hi, Denna." Jonna leaned forward to shake his hand.

"Are you Denna Garric?" Genesi asked, and he nodded. "Please have some lunch."

Denna sat next to Sula and took several small sandwiches.

"Well, that's almost everyone, so let's begin. I am terribly worried about Pal. No one has seen him in three days. I just wanted to ask you if you have seen him recently." Genesi took a sandwich.

"I haven't seen Pal since I started driving a tractor in the port after the term break." Denna quickly ate a sandwich.

"It's been a couple of weeks since I saw him." Sula leaned forward to get her drink.

"Not since school." Jonna took more veggies.

"Me too," Linga said.

"Does anyone have an idea where he might be? Do you remember him saying he was going away or doing anything unusual? You know, something he hadn't mentioned before." Genesi hopefully studied each of the others.

"No, I'm afraid not." Linga leaned back against the seat.

"Last time I saw him, he wondered if that guy would be back at school this term. You know, the one who's always competing with him, Harcu Simoon," Denna said.

"Hmm, I invited him here today." Genesi studied their reactions.

"I'm not surprised he didn't come. We don't really know him," Sula added.

"I've never met him. Have any of you?" Genesi sipped her tea.

Jonna took the last sandwich. "Harcu has been around the school and in the same classes, so he must be on a similar course of study. But I don't think he has ever been close to any of Pal's friends. At least, not that I know of."

"Yeah, I think Harcu is anxious to get better grades than Pal. Hard to do, you know?" Denna took the last of the veggies.

"Hmm, thanks," Genesi muttered. "Can anyone remember anything about Pal that was different or out of the ordinary? You know, strange?"

One by one, they all glanced at each other and shook their heads.

"Hey, I've got to get back to work," Linga exclaimed, looking at his wrist comm.

"Yeah, me too." Denna stood.

"Thanks. I appreciate your meeting with me. If you hear anything regarding Pal, please let me know. You can reach me at the Temple." Genesi stood to let Jonna and Linga out of the booth. After Denna stood, Sula scooted toward the end of the seat. "Sula, do you have a few more minutes?"

"Yes, sure."

Genesi and Sula waved at the others as they hurried to the exit and sat in the booth.

"You've known Pal longer than most people. Is it like him to just disappear?"

"No, never. Pal is one of the most considerate people I know."

"I'm so worried. Pal hasn't been seen in such a long time." Genesi glanced at the table, then wiped away the tears brimming in her eyes.

Sula scooted around the booth to be closer to her. "Oh, you really are upset, aren't you? Do you think something is wrong?"

Genesi gazed into her eyes. "Are you a member of the church?"

"Yes, of course."

"All right, I had several premonitions in my contemplations that something is wrong, but I don't know exactly what." Genesi had to wipe her eyes again. "I miss him so much."

"You and Pal are in love, aren't you?" Sula held her hand as Genesi nodded. "I thought so, but he never said so."

"Yes, for a couple of years now." Genesi smiled sadly.

"How did you meet Pal?"

"Oh, it was one of those chance things." She smiled at the memory. "Two years ago, my roommate, Marlenel, didn't want to sit around the apartment, so she dragged me out to a hoops game at the university. I knew nothing about hoops, so she explained the game and how the points were scored. And one player was in the middle of every play, Acton Athu. So, I asked Marlenel about him. She didn't hear me, but the guy sitting beside me did. It was Pal, and of course, Acton was his brother. We started dating then, and it didn't take long to fall in love with him. He was so lonely. His family had a full agenda, and Acton was the most popular guy at the university. Whatever Pal was doing never seemed important enough to get their attention. And, since I have felt that way since my parents died three years ago, we just seemed to fit together."

"Oh, I'm so sorry to hear it. That's terrible. I wouldn't know what to do if my parents died." Sula held her hand more firmly.

She took a deep breath and sighed. "Anyway, Pal has been the center of my life since then. And now, with him gone, I'm so worried." Genesi wiped her eyes.

"I can imagine. We'll have to find him. Have you contacted the L.E.T.?" Sula stroked Genesi's shoulder.

"Yes." She sniffled, then glanced at her wrist comm. "In fact, I have an appointment with them in a few minutes."

"Oh, I better go so you can meet with them." Sula scooted toward the edge of the seat, and Genesi stood to let her stand.

She gave Sula a warm hug. "Thanks for listening."

"Hey, anytime. Let's get together again soon."

"Yes, let's do that."

Sula waved as she left the restaurant, and Genesi returned to the booth.

CHAPTER EIGHT

Genesi waited for Captain Ketsu in the Social Club.

Even though it was after the lunch hour, the club was still crowded. She didn't see anyone else wearing an acolyte's robe, and some diners stared at her like it was strange for her to be there. Apparently, few acolytes patronized the Social Club.

A man with short dark hair and a mustache, wearing the sky-blue uniform of the L.E.T. with a captain's braid on each shoulder, entered the club and stopped at the entrance to look around. She stood and waved, and he hurried to the booth.

"Captain Ketsu?"

"Yes, are you Genesi Forcu?" He bowed slightly and motioned to return to the booth.

"Yes, I hope I am not interrupting anything important by asking you to meet with me." She returned to her seat, and Captain Ketsu sat across from her.

"Not at all. May I call you Genesi?" He smiled.

"Of course, Captain, please do."

"You may call me Nortin. It's not quite so formal. What can I do for you, Genesi?" He removed a PAD from his pocket and laid it on the table to record the conversation instead of making notes.

A waitress stopped at the table, and they ordered iced tea.

"Captain… Nortin, I am very concerned. Pal Athu has disappeared."

"Disappeared may be a bit premature, don't you think? He simply hasn't been home for a few days. Isn't that correct?"

"No one has seen him for over three days. His apartment hasn't been used in that period, and it appears none of his clothes have been touched either," Genesi said, warming up to the urgency she felt.

"You've been inside his apartment?"

"Yes." She hesitated because she didn't know if she had broken any laws. "Pal and I are very close, and he gave me access to his apartment several months ago."

"I see. Does Commander Athu know you have access to his apartment?"

"I don't know." Genesi blushed and looked away from Nortin. "I can't think of any reason why *he* would know."

"Do you mind if I mention what you know and how you know it to the commander?" Nortin gazed at her expectantly.

Confused, she asked, "What do I know?"

"His apartment has not been used, and his clothes have not been disturbed."

"Oh, that. Yes, I have no problem with you mentioning it."

The waitress appeared with their iced teas, put them on the table, and departed.

"I think the commander would want to know that there may be a problem."

"Yes, I can understand that." Genesi took a much-needed sip of her tea, surprised that she was so nervous.

"You mentioned you were meeting with Pal's friends. Have you?"

"Yes, today at lunch. I spoke with four friends, but none have seen Pal in a week. They said they didn't know where he was and that he hadn't mentioned going away."

"May I know who you spoke with?"

"Of course, I called each of them to ask them to come to lunch today. Jonna Kerol is a student on Pal's hoops team. Linga Forst is a longtime friend of Pal's and is in the same classes at the university. Sula Kens is a lifelong friend of Pal's, as her family has the farm next to Athu Farms. And Denna Garric is another classmate, but not a very close friend."

"Why do you say Denna is not a close friend?"

"I never heard Pal mention him. When I asked others who else to invite, someone said to invite him," Genesi explained.

"Was that everyone you invited?" Nortin calmly sipped his tea.

"No. One person didn't show up, Harcu Simoon. And that's weird." Genesi leaned forward, warming up to the interview.

"Why is it weird?"

"It's a little bit complicated. Harcu is another classmate of Pal's and has always been very competitive. Whenever there's a test or competition, Harcu has always tried to do better than Pal. Even if neither of them was at the top of the event, it's like Harcu has made it his life goal to always be better than Pal. It's weird."

"Hmm, that's interesting. And you say Harcu did not show up today?"

"Yes, correct."

"Let's drink up. I want to go see Pal's apartment for myself. Do you still have access?"

"Yes, of course." Genesi took a drink of her tea. "I'm ready when you are."

Nortin took a big gulp of his tea. "Excellent, let's go."

After paying the club, they quickly walked to the lobby and summoned a lift. One arrived almost immediately, and Genesi and

Nortin took it to the floor where the Athu family apartments were located. They walked down the hall toward Pal's apartment.

"Have you always been in the military?" She quickened her steps.

"Yes, why?"

"You tend to march rather than walk." Genesi smiled and took another skip-step to keep up with him.

Nortin laughed. "Yes, I do, and you seem to glide. I can't hear your footsteps at all."

She chuckled. "Hardly gliding. I'm just smaller than you, you know?"

"Yes, there is that."

"Here we are." Genesi stopped in front of an apartment with a rose bush in the alcove. She entered the code in the entry panel, the door slid open, and the lights came on as they stepped inside.

"Wait here and let me look around," Nortin instructed firmly without a trace of humor.

"Of course, Captain." Genesi noticed the window-sized monitor on the wall changed from showing the Imperial Palace and its beautifully manicured lawns, shrubs, and trees to the colonnade that connected it to Poseidia University in the capital city of Atlantis.

The door closed, and she stood beside it as Nortin searched the apartment. He walked around the living room and into the kitchen. She heard cabinets, the refrigerator door, and other doors opening and closing, and it sounded louder than usual. He left the kitchen and went into the bedroom. There were more sounds of doors and drawers being opened and closed and items moving around. Finally, the captain returned to the living area.

"How do you know his clothes haven't been used?"

"There are no new clothes in the hamper, and the closet is the same as a few days ago when I looked." She stared innocently back at him without batting an eyelash.

"You'd make a good detective, Miss Forcu."

"Thank you, Captain. I love Pal, and that gives me a strong interest in his welfare."

"Yes, it usually does. I will definitely check into this. I'm glad you brought it to my attention, and I'll be in touch. If you hear anything else, please let me know."

"Are you going to ask Harcu Simoon what he knows?" Genesi turned as the captain walked toward the door.

"Yes, I will check on Harcu Simoon. I'll let you know what I find." Captain Ketsu pressed the open button, and the door opened. "Have a good day, Genesi."

"Thank you, Nortin. Good day."

When the door closed, she was alone in Pal's apartment and noticed his absence so deeply she nearly cried. Genesi couldn't return to church services on the verge of tears, so she touched the wall, then ran her hand down it to lower the lighting to a more comfortable level. She walked to the sofa, kicked off her shoes, and sat cross-legged with her feet tucked under her. Closing her eyes, she chanted her favorite contemplation, but it took longer than usual for a sense of peace, love, and tranquility to infuse her.

Nortin entered his office and sat at his desk.

In his gut, he knew Pal Athu was probably in trouble. He punched his computer, opened a search engine for personnel on New Hope, and typed the name Harcu Simoon. A few moments later, a picture of a young man in his twenties, with bright red hair, big ears, and a comical facial expression, appeared on the screen. He was tall, played hoops, was doing well in school, and wanted to be a spaceship captain someday. Nortin transferred the information to his PAD, signed off the computer, and left the office.

Harcu Simoon shared an apartment one floor above New Hope University with Duc Fenmenk, whose name seemed familiar, but

Nortin couldn't place where he had heard it. It must have been an inexpensive apartment because it was about as far from the lift as possible. Ordinarily happy to walk, Nortin rode the people-mover, a flat escalator portion of the hallway, to get there twice as fast as walking and was still tired of checking the apartment numbers when he got to Harcu's. He stepped off the mover, compared the door's number to the one on his PAD, and knocked.

"Yeah, what do you want?" someone shouted through the closed door.

"Harcu Simoon?" Nortin shouted back.

"Yeah, wait a minute. I'll be right there."

Nortin knew there wasn't a back door, and windows were nonexistent on a spaceship, so he waited. A minute later, the door opened.

Harcu Simoon wore a red shirt with yellow bananas painted on it and baggy brown pants. His hair was in spikes all over his head and still dripping water, and his feet were bare. His ears were big, and the comical expression on his photo seemed to be permanently on his face.

Nortin had a hard time keeping a straight face. "Are you Harcu Simoon?"

"Yeah, are you with L.E.T.?" Harcu stood a little straighter and forced a smile.

"Yes, I am Captain Nortin Ketsu. I'm making inquiries about a student named Pal Athu. Do you know him?" He carefully watched Harcu's face when he said Pal's name and was happy there didn't seem to be any response other than that the crooked smile got more crooked.

"Yeah, sure, I know him. We are in some classes together at New Hope University. Why? What's Pal gotten himself into?"

"Nothing, we're trying to locate him. When did you see him last?"

"Hmm, must have been in a class before the term break, and I haven't seen him since."

"Do you know a girl named Genesi Forcu?" Nortin noticed there was no reaction.

"Yeah, I heard the name. I think she's Pal's girlfriend, right?"

"Yes, that's right. Any reason you didn't go to lunch today per her invitation?"

Harcu's eyes widened.

"What invitation? I never got an invitation. Just a sec." Harcu walked into the living room, picked up his comm unit, and studied it as he returned to the door. "Nope, didn't get an invitation, sir."

"She didn't call you and ask you to come to lunch today?"

"No, I never heard from her. I'm sure I would remember." His smile got even more crooked, and his eyes sparkled.

"Okay, if you see Pal or hear from him, please call the L.E.T. and let me know. The name is Captain Nortin Ketsu. All right?" He handed Harcu his card.

"Sure, no problem, be glad to." He put the card in his pocket as he stepped back inside the apartment. "Hang in there." Harcu shut the door.

Nortin walked back to the lift with a smile on his face. He didn't know if Harcu would ever become a spaceship captain, but he was pretty sure he could get a job as a comedian, even if he didn't say anything funny.

CHAPTER NINE

Someone knocked on Pal's door, interrupting Genesi's meditation.

Straightening her robe as she stood, Genesi slipped on her shoes and smoothed her hair on the way to the door. Presentable again, she turned the lights back up. "Door open." The door opened to the strangest person she had ever seen. He wore a red shirt with pictures of yellow bananas all over it, baggy pants, and sandals. His red hair was disheveled but organized as if it were intended to look unkempt, and he had a big smile.

"May I help you?"

"You're Genesi, right?" He seemed genuinely excited to meet her.

"Yes." She cautiously stepped back.

"I'm…" He paused for emphasis. "Harcu…Simoon," he announced with arms held wide, presenting himself like the next act in a stage performance.

"Oh, hi, nice to meet you." She offered her hand, and he took it.

Still holding her hand, he peered around her. "All right if I come in?" he asked with raised eyebrows.

"Yes, please do." Genesi stepped aside and tugged her hand free of his grip.

He swept into the apartment as though royalty and headed for the sofa. "I had a visit from Captain Ketsu a few minutes ago asking about Pal." He waited for her to sit before he sat. "I thought I should come by, on the off chance you might still be here, and introduce myself. I also thought you would like an update on what I told the L.E.T. officer."

"Well, how very kind of you. Why didn't you just come to lunch today with the others?"

"I didn't come today because I had no idea I had been invited. I never got your invitation," Harcu said with a sad face.

"You didn't? Didn't I call you earlier today?"

Harcu shook his head and pouted.

"Oh, I wonder who I spoke with then?" Genesi blushed.

"No idea. What number did you call?" He stopped pouting and gazed at her curiously.

"I don't have it anymore. I called the number I was given for you."

"Who gave you the number?"

"Oh dear." Genesi looked away and blushed even more. "I don't remember. You see, I was calling people who knew Pal, and one of them suggested I also call you."

"Which one?" Harcu asked, more to have fun embarrassing her than a need to know.

"I don't remember. I'm sorry," she said sincerely.

"No problem at all. What's the news on Pal? Any word yet?"

"No, nothing, but it's only been an hour."

"Well, that's not cool. What are they waiting for?" Harcu declared and then laughed. "Sorry, I know it's a serious matter, but I just don't have a serious bone in my whole body, so I have to have fun with everything."

"I wish I could do that."

"Stick around me, and maybe it will rub off." He laughed.

Genesi couldn't help herself; she laughed. "Hey, it's working. That's the first laugh I've had in days, and I'm usually a pretty up person, too."

"I don't know about being up..." He paused for emphasis again. "...but you certainly are pretty."

"Oh, stop. You're embarrassing me."

"Sorry," he said, obviously not sorry at all. They sat there for a minute, not saying anything. "Did I mention how pretty you are?" he asked seriously, and when she frowned, he leaned back, loudly laughing.

"You're incorrigible."

"Yep, and proud of it." Harcu suddenly sat upright. "Hey, I bet I know who you called." He keyed his wrist comm and punched a number.

A man's voice answered over its speaker. "Yes?"

"Hey, Duc? Did you get a call for me to go to lunch today?"

"Oh, man! Yes, I did, and I forgot to tell you. I'm sorry," Duc Fenmenk said with a thick Lamatian accent.

"I found out through the L.E.T. They came to our apartment because I didn't go to lunch. I could have been arrested or something."

"That's too much. It was a sweet girl's voice, Jenny, or something like that, not the L.E.T." Duc's voice trailed away.

"Duc, you moron, you can't get anything right." Harcu laughed. "But since I met her today anyway, I forgive you."

"Thanks, man, sorry about it. I'll do better next time."

"Next time? There won't be a next time. Bye, you moron."

"Bye," Duc said as the call ended.

"At least that answers one question." Genesi leaned closer.

"Yeah, but don't tell Captain Ketsu. I don't want him to think I'm going behind his back, so let me tell the L.E.T." Harcu laughed.

Genesi smiled and nodded. "So, who is Duc?"

"Oh, sorry, Duc Fenmenk is my roommate. The big jerk is so scatterbrained that I'm surprised he can remember where our apartment is located, let alone anything else."

"He's not alone in that department. Does he know Pal?"

"I don't think so. I don't know, but I don't think so. Duc is into the arts, and none of my classes with Pal were art classes." Harcu thought for a moment. "Why do you ask?"

"When I called, whomever I spoke with knew Pal and who he was. If it was Duc, I think he must know who Pal is." Genesi frowned.

Harcu keyed his comm again. "Hey, Duc, do you know Pal Athu?"

"Yeah, I know him. I mean, I know who he is, but I don't know him like as in he knows me too. We're not close or anything."

Harcu laughed. "Yeah, I know. Have you ever met him?"

"No, but I saw him the other day though."

"What?" Genesi exclaimed, although she wasn't on the phone.

"What?" Harcu exclaimed a moment after her.

"What, what?" Duc asked.

"When did you see Pal?" Harcu asked seriously.

"When? Hmm, let's see. It was before I went to see Mory, and that was the day before yesterday. I was talking to someone when I saw him–"

"Try to remember, Duc. It's important," Harcu said.

"Oh, all right. Was it Teta? No, that was yesterday. Was it… Zat? Hmm, yes, I was talking with Zat when I saw Pal, and he was with a bunch of people."

"Where was this, Duc?" Harcu asked.

"Hmm, you know my memory ain't that good."

"Try, Duc. Even the L.E.T. wants to know where Pal is." Harcu stared at Genesi as he spoke with Duc, seeing she hung on every word.

"I think it was at the university. Yeah, I was going to play hoops with Zat, and Pal was talking with a bunch of guys on the other side of the court. It looked like maybe they had played a game."

"All right, that's good. When was this?" Harcu asked.

"Oh, I don't know exactly. It was about four days ago, I think. Does that help?"

"Yes, very much."

"Ask if he recognized any of the people," Genesi softly pleaded.

"Oh, good idea. Duc, did you recognize any of the other people?"

"Hmm, I don't think so. There was something funny about the others, though. They all wore dark gym clothes."

"Good work! Thanks, Duc, that's good stuff. You could be a hero!"

"Ah, yeah, for sure. Ain't I always?" Duc laughed.

"Anything else?" Harcu asked Genesi.

"Dark clothes? What does that mean?" she asked.

"Almost everyone wears brightly colored clothes for a game, so I think it means they were from another ship," Harcu said to Genesi, then returned to the comm unit. "Thanks, Duc. I'll be home in a while. See you then."

"All right, bye." Duc signed off.

"That's something anyway," Harcu said.

"Yes, it is. That's outstanding work, and I so appreciate it. Let's go find Captain Ketsu and tell him what we found." Genesi jumped up and hurried to the door.

"Yes, let's do it." Harcu followed her.

Genesi and Harcu found Captain Ketsu in his L.E.T. office.

After hearing their story, Nortin had Harcu call Duc and ask him to join them. A few minutes later, Duc Fenmenk arrived wearing baggy black pants and a pull-over blue shirt covered in various-sized white dots. He had a dark Lamatian complexion, was skinny enough to be wiry, and wore his hair short.

"Duc, this is Genesi Forcu." Harcu stood to introduce them, and the others also stood.

"Hi, sorry about forgetting your invitation." Duc seemed genuinely embarrassed.

"It's all right. Nice to meet you," Genesi said.

"And this is Captain Nortin Ketsu of the L.E.T."

"Captain," Duc said as he shook the officer's hand.

"Duc, thanks for coming. Please, have a seat, everyone." Nortin placed his PAD on the desk while waiting for people to sit. "As you know, we are trying to find Pal Athu. Genesi and Harcu told me you remembered seeing Pal with some people at the hoops court about four days ago. Is that right?"

"Yeah, that's right. I was there to play hoops with Zat–"

"Zat, who?" Nortin asked.

"Hmm, dang, I don't know. He's in my painting class."

"All right, go ahead."

"Like I said, I was there to play hoops with Zat, and we were waiting for a court. I saw Pal with a bunch of other guys–"

"How many others?" Nortin asked.

"Maybe five or six." Nortin nodded for Duc to continue. "They were on the other side of the court."

"What were they doing?"

"Looked like they might have played a game."

"But what were they doing when you saw them?"

"Oh, just standing there. They were all in a circle, talking."

"Was Pal part of the circle or inside it? Were they all around him?"

"No, he was just one person in a circle of five or six people, and they were talking." Duc looked around, noticing that everyone was giving him their full attention.

"Did you recognize any of the other people?" Nortin asked Duc.

"No, not really."

"Would you recognize them if you saw them again?"

"Maybe…I'm not sure," Duc said nervously.

"If I showed you pictures of people who play hoops at the university, could you spot one or more of them?" Nortin asked.

"I can try, I guess. Don't know until I try."

"Good. Come with me, and let's look at some pictures."

Everyone followed Nortin into another room where a computer was available, and a large screen hung on the wall. He sat at the computer and started typing on the keyboard. "Have a seat. I'll show you pictures of hoops players. Stop me if you see someone you recognize, okay?"

"Sure." Duc sat on the left, Genesi sat in the middle, and Harcu sat on the right seat of a three-seat row.

"Okay, here we go."

The pictures started appearing on the screen. One after another, the screen showed guys wearing gym clothes.

"Stop," Duc said after ten pictures went by.

"You know this guy?" Nortin asked, checking the name on the slide.

"Yeah, I know him, but he's not one of the ones who was talking with Pal."

"Okay, let's try it again." Nortin began showing pictures again. A minute later, he stopped the show. "Hey, you said the other guys wore dark gym clothes, right?"

"Yeah, right." Duc turned around to look at the captain.

"That's significant. Hold on." Captain Ketsu stepped out of the room.

"What's significant about it?" Duc asked.

"I think it means they were from another ship," Harcu explained as Nortin returned.

"Yes, I thought so too. I checked on team rosters for all the ships, and the only teams with dark-colored outfits were teams from Belial ships."

"What? Belial? Why would Pal be talking to people from a Belial ship? Let alone playing hoops with them?" Genesi asked.

"Excellent questions." Nortin sat at the computer. "We will want to pursue that further, but for now, let's view the players from other ships. This is getting more and more disturbing." He loaded a different database, and they viewed players from Belial ships next. One by one, pictures of young men and women appeared on the screen.

"Hey, that guy could be one." Duc pointed. "I'm not sure, but he is familiar."

"Okay, let's keep trying." Nortin selected the picture and started a new file for prospects. Then he returned to the database, and a few seconds later, another image appeared.

Over the next fifteen minutes, Duc recognized six people he thought might be part of the group talking with Pal.

"I'll check and see if these people have anything in common. I'll be right back." Nortin left the room again.

"All right, Captain." Genesi turned to Duc. "I can't tell you how much I appreciate your help finding Pal. I think we are finally onto something."

"Oh, I'm happy to help." Duc grinned at her.

"Genesi, what are you doing when we get done here?" Harcu asked.

"Oh." She quickly checked her wrist comm. "I've got to get back to the Temple. I should have been there a half-hour ago."

Captain Ketsu returned. "All six are part of nine students who came to New Hope to learn more about how to repair hydroponic systems and get better irrigation through them. They came from SS Qusar Kalif. There's no record of any of them returning to their ship, and the addresses on the computer are phony."

"Now that's what I call a lead," Harcu said.

"What does it mean, Captain?" Genesi asked.

"I'm not sure yet, and I don't like to jump to conclusions, but either there is a massive mistake here, or this could be quite serious. You have been very helpful, and I appreciate you narrowing down who we are looking for. I have no idea whether any of this is pertinent to Pal's disappearance, but it definitely makes the situation more urgent. I will be in touch as we proceed. If you see any of these guys, let me know immediately." Captain Ketsu shook hands and handed everyone a card with his contact information.

"For sure." Harcu stepped aside for Genesi to stand.

"I will, Captain. Thank you." She stepped toward the door.

"Yeah, if I can help, give me a call." Duc followed her.

"We will be in touch." Nortin sat at his desk.

Genesi, Harcu, and Duc walked back to the lobby, caught the next lift, and exited on the Temple's floor.

"Thanks again, Harcu. And you too, Duc. I really appreciate it." Genesi hurried toward the Temple's entrance, and the others followed.

"Glad to help." Duc's grin was nearly as big as Harcu's.

"My pleasure," Harcu said. "Are you conducting services for the rest of the day?"

"Yes, my last one is at five. I've got to go. See you later." She entered the Temple.

"Bye, see you later," Harcu called after her. With Duc, he walked back to the lift.

CHAPTER TEN

The Control Center was a hive of frenzied activity.

Located in the hub of the Atlantian Fleet, the Command Center on the top inhabitable floor of SS New Hope, all activities of the military, rescue, and fleet operations on Earth and in space were reported to it. One thousand feet in diameter, Command employed hundreds of people of every ethnic origin or genetic construct. Their work supported the hundred people working in the Control Center.

The Control Center, more commonly referred to as Control, served as the brain of the fleet's operations. Its management occupied a semi-circular theater with eight tiers of cubicles that encircled a fifty-foot wall of screens reporting the status of every aspect of the Atlantian Empire on Earth, in space, or on any ship. The top level of the theater was reserved for the officers in charge of operations, and each had an office made of clear plastique.

Fleet Commander Cana Athu, a man with steel-blue eyes and dark hair graying at the temples, stood in front of his Control office. As always, he was resplendent in his royal purple uniform – only a member of the royal family could wear purple.

More than any other person, Cana was responsible for the Atlantian Fleet, from its conception through its current operations. His office was in the middle of Control, on the top tier overlooking the wall of screens. From it, he had immediate access to all the people in Control and Command. He was nearly as fit today as the day he reported for duty thirty-two years ago.

Cana studied the screens showing the status of the fleet, from the operational statistics of New Hope to the deployment of the gunners, strikers, shuttles, spaceship construction platforms, and the other eighteen inhabited spaceships. But the largest screen covering forty percent of the wall showed Mars so close that Earth was sucking the surface off the smaller planet.

Although the sight sickened him, Cana stared at what he knew would eventually be the end of Earth. His family had ruled Atlantis for the last ten thousand years, and everything they had accomplished was being destroyed. He couldn't do anything about it, and his helplessness threatened to consume him. He racked his brain daily, but he was doing everything possible. He clenched his fists and stood there day after day, month after month, making critical decisions to avert life-threatening catastrophes. Ever since the comet, his life had been a never-ending stream of decisions that made the difference between life and death, and the weight of making the decisions was evident in his bloodshot eyes. Yet, he stood ramrod straight, unflinching, and commanded what had to be done, even while it ripped his guts out.

"Excuse me, sir?" Captain Thegan came to attention near Cana. A short, middle-aged officer in a blue uniform, he was the communications officer for Control. His sector employed over one hundred and fifty comm operators twenty-four hours a day.

Cana pulled his attention away from the screens. "Yes, Captain?"

"Atlantis Pride requests redeployment to sector sixteen for repairs due to DF damage."

"How extensive?"

"Minor, sir. A small bit of DF deflected off a striker kill."

"All right, have the other ships in its triad cover for it while in repairs."

"Yes, sir." The captain walked back toward the comm desk.

Another officer approached. "Sir?"

"Yes?"

"A large chunk of DF has destroyed a transport ship carrying iron beams."

"What the hell?" He pressed the button on his comm, an earpiece clipped over his right ear. "Halo," he said through gritted teeth, and the unit buzzed.

A moment later, Halo Hajac, the construction manager in charge of building the Atlantian Fleet, answered, "Yes, sir."

"Damn it, Halo, I've told you a million times that the freighters have to pull back when Mars is this close. Now, I hear one has taken a direct hit."

"Yes, sir. I just learned of it."

"What do I have to do to get you people to–"

"Cana, I don't know why they were so close. I'm checking into it. Let me call you back with the facts." Halo was one of few people who could address Cana by his first name as he was one of Cana's closest friends. They were classmates from primary school through graduation from Poseidia University and had worked on many projects over the last thirty years.

"Make it quick." Cana ended the call.

Cana's personal assistant, Salia Vericus, a petite woman with auburn hair and green eyes, stopped a few feet away. She had worked with him so long that he considered her the daughter he never had.

"Yes, Salia," Cana muttered, trying to calm down.

"It's time for your emergency meeting with the emperor. You need to leave now."

"Oh, damn." Cana checked his wrist comm for the time. "Right, thank you." He rushed toward the lifts. Leaving Control, Cana fumed as he hurried down the central aisle through Command, and people quickly stepped out of his way.

He didn't even see people as he continued to analyze his problems. Everything seemed to be going wrong; DF struck ships, gunners were destroyed, rescuers were killed, and the list kept growing. He had studied the stats for hours to find out why the things that had worked well for three years weren't working anymore, but he wasn't any closer to knowing why.

As Cana arrived, a lift's double doors opened, and he quickly entered. A student in an orange shirt sprang out of the lift carrying a tray of trinkets. Concentrating on the small figurines, he crashed into Cana in the middle of the lift's open doors. The young man fell, and Cana was thrown out of the lift, struggling to stay on his feet. The tray hit the floor, and the figurines scattered across the lift lobby, many breaking on impact.

As soon as Cana regained his balance, he shouted, "What the... Why don't you look where you're going?" Cana stopped as he glanced down at the student scurrying around the floor.

"I'm so sorry." The student rose to his knees and only then realized he had collided with the Fleet Commander. "Oh, sir, I am so sorry." He hurriedly gathered the figurines, putting them on the tray. "Are you okay? Should I call someone?" The student watched Cana so intently that he could barely find the trinkets to gather them.

The lift doors automatically closed, and the officers and other Command employees anxiously watched them, waiting for the inevitable angry explosion the Commander was notorious for.

Cana laughed. "Calm down." Cana chuckled again, and then, noticing the spectators' stares, he glared sternly at the student scurrying about the lobby floor. "What are those things anyway?"

"They're replicas of the university's hoops mascot, Terrible Tiger."

"You're selling them?"

"Ah, yes, sir. They're a fundraiser for the team." The student focused on picking up the pieces of the figurines.

"How much are you asking for them?"

"Ten credits, sir." The student tentatively smiled.

"How many broke?"

"Hmm, let's see…." He quickly counted. "Twelve, sir."

Cana checked his wrist comm; he was late. "Okay, go to Control and see Salia. Tell her I will buy the broken ones."

The student grinned as he looked up at the Commander. "Yes, sir. Thank you!"

"Next time, watch where you're going." He successfully stifled a grin. After all, he had a reputation to maintain. Another lift arrived, and Cana entered with three other people.

"Conference level," Cana instructed. He keyed his comm unit and advised Salia to pay the student. Then, he redirected his future calls to Control's receptionist.

The lift arrived, and Cana hurried to the conference center near the lift lobby. He pushed through the double doors and stopped to allow his eyes to adjust to the dimmer light. A white, oval conference table dominated the darkened room, and the overhead spotlights, the only lights in the room, lit the table with near-blinding white light. The room was dark enough that its gray walls seemed nonexistent, and darkness surrounded the meeting space. At the back of the room, the table joined a raised pyramid of desks, one on each side of an elevated center position.

Emperor Maximus IV peered over the conference table from the highest desk as he stroked his lapdog, a small animal with long hair and pointed ears.

"Commander." Emperor Maximus nodded, acknowledging Cana. Max was Cana's older brother, and as usual, he was regal in his royal purple robes of state. The gold woven into its borders glittered under the spotlights. Max looked a lot like Cana, except he made sure his hair was black with no gray. While he seemed bored, his dark blue eyes noticed everything.

Cana bowed slightly. "Emperor." Walking around the right side of the conference table toward his elevated desk at the emperor's left, he checked to see who else was in attendance.

On the other side of the emperor, seated on the opposite raised section, was Master Ono the Fourth, head of the Church of the One God, the official state religion. He was a cousin, Cana's father's sister's son. His iridescent white robe seemed to radiate light as proof of his holiness. He sat at the desk, making a steeple of his fingers. Cana smiled and nodded to him, receiving a smile and nod in return.

On the other side of the table, away from it and against the wall, were three elevated rows of luxurious seats for the nine Imperial Council members. They were occupied by nine elderly people who had served the empire faithfully for many years and now served as advisors to the emperor. As old as they were, the youngest was seventy-seven, their gray, wrinkled faces were sunk in the folds of their gray, woolen robes. Only their bright eyes were noticeable when they peeked out. Several appeared to be asleep, and the rest were bored.

Next to Ono, on the other side of the table from Cana, twelve scientists were only partially visible behind the mounds of paper they had brought to the meeting. Seven men of varying ages and five women, who may have been related to the men, sat quietly conversing as they occasionally pawed through the documents. The university insignias on their light gray uniforms and the braids of distinction on their shoulders easily identified them as professors.

Cana sat at the raised desk next to Emperor Maximus and turned to the men on his side of the table. Closest to him was Captain Marnin Clovus, Captain of SS New Hope, and his aide, a young man with short blonde hair. Next to him was Captain Steril Magneson, another battle-tested and trusted aide, and his assistant, a short man with a beard and mustache. The officers sat straight and alert as if they were in a crisis. Cana smiled and nodded to his staff members. Both captains had been with him through dozens of campaigns, including the suppression of the Lamatian rebellion twenty years ago and the negotiation of peace with Zu a few years afterward. Their alertness made him proud.

Once seated, he noticed an empty seat at the end of the table closest to the doors, usually reserved for whoever presented something. Cana turned to Max. "Who are we waiting for?" Max seemed preoccupied.

Captain Clovus leaned forward and cleared his throat. "Professor Norvis Scintillian, sir. He called this meeting."

"Where is he?"

No one answered. Max, Cana, and the officers looked to the scientists who were associates of the university's professor of physics and astronomy. They shrugged, turned to each other, or stared back.

"Send someone to find him," Cana ordered Captain Clovus as he leaned back.

"Yes, sir." Clovus nodded to his assistant.

The junior officer hurried toward the door, but the double doors burst inward as he arrived. A short, old man with thinning white hair and his arms full of papers collided with him as the doors banged shut behind him. The old man wore a light gray uniform with an extra layer of insignias on his shoulders, indicating he was a department head at the university.

"Excuse me." The old man juggled the papers but didn't drop any.

"My apologies, Professor. I was going to find you."

"Thank you. I am here." The professor smiled at the young aide.

The officer returned to his seat as Professor Norvis Scintillian dropped his papers on the table, cleared his throat, and glanced around the room. "Emperor Maximus, Master Ono, Council Members, Commander Athu, fleet officers, and fellow scientists," the professor nodded to each as he addressed them, "please forgive my tardiness. I was detained with last-minute information."

"Quite all right, Norvis. Please proceed as soon as you are ready." Emperor Max chuckled quietly and continued to stroke his dog.

Cana stifled a smirk as he watched the old man. He had first met Norvis thirty years ago when he was the newly appointed professor of physics at the university. His hands had always trembled, whether he was nervous or had an affliction. Whatever the reason, it had only worsened over the last thirty years.

"Thank you, sir." Norvis sat and raised the top edge of the table to reveal a series of controls contained within a hidden compartment. He flipped a switch, and a monitor rose from the table along with a keyboard. He entered commands.

The room grew darker, and a holographic screen appeared over the oval table. The screen was a gray ethereal box, the length of the table and four feet high, which floated three feet above the table. The screen grew darker, and the grayness switched to a view of the solar system with stars twinkling in the background as it rotated to where its width faced the emperor. After all the planets appeared and gradually attained their true colors, the picture focused on the ones in the collinear configuration: Jupiter, Saturn, Venus, Mars, and Earth, in that order.

Orbiting around the Sun as a group, the five planets rotated around Saturn as the center of the collinear configuration, keeping Jupiter constantly facing the Sun. Situated next in line, Saturn blocked Jupiter and the Sun from the smaller planets, and all the hundred-plus moons in the system orbited Jupiter and Saturn. Venus, Mars, and Earth were always in the shadow of Saturn, except for a crescent of sunlight peeking around Saturn.

From Earth's view, at the end of the configuration, the planets formed what the heathens called the "Eye of God." Saturn was a huge gold-orange disc filling forty degrees of the sky directly above the North Pole. In the center of Saturn, Venus was the white iris of the "Eye." In the center of Venus, Mars was the red pupil. The bright halo of sunlight moved around Saturn, making the eye appear to rotate in the sky continually.

Cana had seen presentations on the holographic screen many times. Still, the clarity of the solar system was so sharp that the planets seemed to be inside the meeting room. To see every detail so close and lifelike was breathtaking.

Gradually, the view of the system changed to show the distance between each planet. Then, a comet swept toward the collinear configuration from outer space beyond Saturn. The comet's white tail stretched for over a million miles, and its fiery red surface was like a massive sparkler, shooting projectiles in every direction.

Professor Norvis Scintillian stood and cleared his throat. "As you know, seven years ago, a comet nearly the size of Earth swept through the collinear configuration, nearly striking Mars." His deep voice was automatically amplified so everyone could hear him. In the screen, the comet curved into the collinear system, passing between Mars and Earth. "The Mars Space Command estimated that the comet passed within fifty thousand miles of Mars. As a result, Mars was pulled out of alignment with the other planets and, following the comet, closer to Earth."

Instantly, Cana remembered that fateful day. He was Commander of the Mars Space Command, and images of it flooded his mind's eye. He had exited the Control Tower and stood on the plaza far away from its buildings to see better. Around him, hundreds of men and women ran to save lives and protect property. With a mighty roar, the likes of which he had never experienced even in battle, the comet flew overhead, filling the sky from horizon to horizon. Everything shook like a plaything in the hands of a giant, and buildings collapsed, including the tower he had exited. He screamed and fell. The ground rose toward the comet like a child reaching for its mother, and Cana was more helpless than ever.

After the comet moved away, thick clouds of smoke and fumes from the comet's tail engulfed Mars like the world was on fire. The entire planet quivered and lurched forward, following the comet. Below the plateau where the Space Command was located, the ocean pulled up, revealing its bottom. It piled high into the sky, smoke and water combining, and then fell on the plateau's cliffs, sending spray across the complex and out into the fields beyond. Cana climbed to his feet and ordered the evacuation of Mars before the air even cleared.

Norvis's voice broke through his memories, and Cana quivered like a child.

"Mars became so unstable that we removed our personnel and fleet resources within a month after the comet's near-miss. All surface buildings and settlements were destroyed by quakes and gigantic ocean waves shortly after evacuation. Since then, Mars has not returned to its usual position in the system.

"The collinear configuration is a delicate balance, and the displacement of Mars affected all the other planets. Venus slipped its position and was swept into Saturn's gravitational field, traveling hundreds of thousands of miles along Saturn's rotation. And Earth was pulled toward the comet and, therefore, toward Mars. The combined gravity of Earth and the comet pulled Mars even farther from its historical orbit. We estimate that Mars traveled nearly five hundred thousand miles closer to Earth before the comet escaped the gravitational force of the collinear system." The computer graphic showed Mars following the comet's path, away from the alignment of the five planets. Mars moved closer to Earth, getting closer and closer until the comet broke free and traveled out into space.

Cana groaned. The sound was lost in Norvis's discourse.

Max leaned closer to Cana and whispered, "Should we interrupt this history lesson?"

"No," Cana whispered, "if we do, he will just start over again. Better to let him finish on his own." Cana quickly looked back to Norvis and saw that the old man had not noticed their conversation.

Norvis continued. "As you can see, during the twelve months after the comet's near-miss, Earth returned close to its original position in the collinear configuration. Venus never returned to the central axis and continues to follow Saturn's rotation, farther weakening the axis."

As Mars moved away from Earth, it appeared smaller. Beyond Mars, Venus streaked across the face of Saturn, leaving massive white vapor trails in its wake.

"Released by the comet, Mars swept back toward its historical position in the system. However, it did not stop there. Due to the speed of its return, Mars continued toward Venus and Saturn. Too small to exert much influence on its own orbit, Mars traveled nearly five hundred thousand miles closer to Saturn. Since then, Mars has oscillated between Saturn and Earth.

"At first, we thought Mars would eventually return to its neutral spot along the axis, and the collinear configuration would return to normal. It took nearly eighteen months after the comet to determine that Mars came closer to Earth with each oscillation.

"During that time, the university and government observatories focused on Mars to determine if it would return to normal. Finally, all the scientists agreed with the proposed Mars Equation. With each oscillation, Mars got closer to Earth, and they would eventually collide. At that point, we knew that life on Earth would never be the same, and the final decision was made to escape Earth by building a fleet of spaceships.

"That was nearly five years ago, and the equation has been proven accurate. Since then, Mars has lost all rotational stability and continues to erratically switch poles, causing catastrophic damage. Mountains have thrust up over five miles, continents have collided with other continents, causing volcanoes to erupt, and other mountains have collapsed.

"Beginning three years ago, when Mars came close enough, Earth's gravity stripped Mars of its atmosphere. Life on Mars ended that day. During the last two years, Earth's gravity started stripping Mars of its oceans and surface."

The presentation switched to show Mars so close to Earth that its oceans were pulled from the planet. The planet's water streamed from Mars to Earth, closely followed by a reddish-black mass of rocks, dirt, and debris. The surface matter struck Earth at the North Pole like water poured from an enormous pitcher. The deluge washed across the frozen pole, melting the ice and sweeping away all surface features toward the continents south of the pole. Then, the rocks, boulders, dirt, and debris struck the northernmost latitudes. Massive lightning bolts flashed between the planets, scaring Mars's surface with deep, jagged trenches and blasting Earth's frozen tundra and ice.

"The debris fell across the northernmost latitudes of Earth, causing enormous damage to the polar region and releasing millions of gallons of water that raised the oceans over two hundred feet. Poseidia and our coastal cities were severely damaged, forcing the populace to relocate to higher ground. As a result, we expected that the return of Mars on this year's oscillation would bring widespread damage to latitudes much farther south than last year."

The holographic screen shifted from computer animation to live video of Mars and Earth, as seen from the Atlantian Fleet of spaceships. The two planets appeared very close together.

"This is a live broadcast of Earth and Mars. We had no idea the destruction would be as bad as this. All the way to the equator, the entire northern latitudes are heavily bombarded by debris. Lightning bolts between Mars and Earth are causing widespread fires around the world. A dense black cloud of smoke, dust, and ash covers Earth from the North Pole to nearly the equator, and a thinner cloud covers the rest of the planet. The bombardment is causing severe earthquakes, and many volcanoes have erupted."

Mars filled the screen, and the debris stream was like a bridge between the planets moving in one direction toward Earth. Fires burned so fiercely that they were occasionally visible through the smoke and ash. Lightning bolts flashed through the space between the planets like massive laser shots. Some of the large rocks caught in the debris field struck others and were thrown from the debris fall toward the fleet of spaceships orbiting Earth over Atlantis. Gunners and strikers, small ships shaped like arrowheads, were fully occupied, destroying the errant chunks of DF before they could endanger the fleet.

"The violence and destruction of this year's Mars oscillation caused us to reevaluate our calculations. Measurements made from fleet ships show that Mars is closer to Earth than predicted. Instead of receding toward Saturn, Mars has continued toward Earth. This explains why the debris fall and destruction have been much greater than expected." The lights came on as Dr. Scintillian ended the holographic presentation and faced the emperor.

"Emperor Maximus, I am sorry to tell you that we believe Mars will not recede but will continue toward Earth." Except for the scientists, everyone in the room gasped. "Instead of colliding with Earth in two years, as we previously forecasted, we believe the planets will collide within the next twenty-four to forty-eight hours." As though exhausted, Professor Scintillian collapsed onto his chair.

Cana, Emperor Maximus, and the others were stunned.

CHAPTER ELEVEN

The three gunner ships in Squad 902 of the periphery defense departed SS New Home.

Vin Neblu, Captain of Gunner 902 and squad leader for the two other gunners in his sector, made sure his squad stopped at the designated staging area, an otherwise empty spot in space two miles from New Hope. In their bright yellow gunners, designed to shoot DF before it could hit the spaceships, they awaited the other gunners and strikers in this shift rotation.

Like most people, he rarely had an opportunity to see the fleet close-up. Alone in his single-pilot ship, he leaned back in his comfortable leather chair and looked through the front windows. Vin was of average height and thin, like most young gunners, but with the blonde hair of a southern islander rather than dark hair like most Atlantians. After graduating from the flight academy a year ago, he quickly became the lead gunner in his sector.

Facing the debris field created by Mars and Earth, Saturn was to his left and close enough to block the Sun, Jupiter, and most of their moons. Vin could see Venus's white vapor trail against the backdrop of Saturn, but so far away that he only recognized it because he knew what it was. Saturn's moons looked like balloons against the face of the gas giant, even though the smallest ones were thousands of miles in diameter.

Gazing through his left side window, Vin could easily see the bright white command ship, SS New Hope. But he could only see a portion of the other two ships in its triad, the green agricultural ship Grand Poseidia and the gray manufacturing ship New Venture, as New Hope blocked them. The triad was closest to Earth and nearest to the debris field. Leaning forward to look back through his left side window, he could see some of the other triads, but the closest was fifty miles away.

All nineteen spaceships were deploying gunners and strikers for the current rotation of the periphery defense. Each spaceship had twelve gunners and four strikers per shift, enough for four sectors of three gunners and one striker per sector. The gunners and strikers staging near the other spaceships were so far away they looked like pinpricks. Besides the other two gunners in his squad stationed to his left, he knew the rest of New Hope's gunners and strikers were behind him but blocked from his view by his own ship.

While the ships got into position, he studied SS New Hope. The first spaceship to be built, all the others were modeled after it. The ship looked like an elongated and streamlined egg mounted at the front of a square structure. Inside the egg, positioned like its yolk, a huge sphere with three hundred floors and a diameter of three thousand feet spun fast enough to create gravity comparable to Earth's, although slightly more gravity near the outer edge and a little less near its core.

On the exterior, the egg-shaped portion and the massive structure housing the ports, engines, fuel, and munition depots were covered with pyramid-shaped crystal towers. They captured energy from the universe, broadcasted power like radio waves, and linked the fleet's communications. The crystal towers lit up occasionally, making the ship twinkle like a star.

He was proud that Squad 902 was closest to the debris field and was the anchor position for the entire array of gunners and strikers. And he was equally proud that his position was the nearest point to the debris field.

"Periphery defense," the comm announced, "this is Control. Deploy to your assigned positions. Control out."

"All right, guys, let's go," Vin instructed his team on their squad-level commlink. He pressed the thrust, and his bright yellow gunner with the number 902 stenciled on top and bottom quickly reached cruising speed. All gunners were yellow triangular ships with dozens of blasters, cannons, and laser weapons along the front and top surfaces.

"On it," Yassa Afari answered over the comm. Yassa flew Gunner 903, the middle gunner in Squad 902, and was the first to follow Vin toward their spot in the formation.

"On it." Edo Tasari flew Gunner 906, the far-left spot in Squad 902's formation. He pulled in behind Yassa.

"You guys look real pretty this morning," Lado Strifa said over their shared commlink. He flew Striker 113, which was assigned to Squad 902. Strikers were longer, sleeker ships than gunners, and their engines were much larger. Even though strikers had fewer guns, their weaponry was much more powerful than gunners. Like all strikers, Striker 113 was bright white, with its number stenciled on top and bottom.

"We are so happy you think so. How are you?" Vin searched for Lado's striker.

"Couldn't get much better." Lado flew above and a little behind the squad.

They flew toward the debris field. Mars appeared to be closer to Earth than ever before, and its massive debris field covered the space between the planets. Millions of chunks of rock, soil, and other matter tumbled and bounced off each other in their mad dash to Earth. Some debris was as small as a fist, and others were larger than a spaceship.

Lightning lit the debris field every few minutes as it shot between Mars and Earth. As a perfect background for the lightning show, Earth was covered by a dark, black cloud across the entire northern hemisphere.

As they got close, Vin could see that the squad they were relieving, Squad 602, was fully engaged in shooting chunks of DF that had ricocheted toward the spaceships.

Vin pressed a large green button on his dashboard, combining Squad 902's communications, automated target acquisition, and auto-firing systems with the ships they were replacing. "Squad 602, Squad 902 is ready to relieve you on your command," he announced over their combined commlink. Squad 902 slowed and hovered a hundred feet from their corresponding Squad 602 ships.

"902, commence relief." The squad leader of 602 had a familiar, feminine voice.

"Sala, are you in 602?" He grinned, thinking of the cute squad leader.

"Hello, Vin. I thought that sounded like you." Sala sounded happy to hear from him.

"Looks like you're pretty busy."

"Yes, I can't remember a busier shift."

Gunner 602 flew up and away from its other two gunners, still firing on targets as it moved. Vin flew under Squad 602 and into its place in the formation. Arriving in position, his guns automatically took over, firing on the same targets that 602's had been engaged with, and Gunner 602's weapons stopped shooting.

"Just what I need." Vin reviewed all his gauges, monitors, and dials as he settled in.

One by one, the other 902 gunners replaced Squad 602's ships, and then Lado replaced 602's striker.

"Happy hunting, guys." Sala led her squad toward New Hope.

"Thanks. Take care, Sala." Vin switched his comm back to only Squad 902. "Hey guys, Sala says there is a lot of DF today."

"Looks like it." Lado scanned the sector for possible problems. "Stay alert."

Hours later, the squad's guns were still automatically firing on more and more DF. Like all gunner pilots, Vin kept his hand on the manual gun control, ready to shoot anything the detection system might miss. Watching the computer select and fire on DF got old, making it easy to get careless. Staying alert was exhausting.

Vin could have watched the debris field through the windows above the dashboard and across the front of the ship like he had done when he first started. Back then, he trusted his eyes more than a computer program, but he soon discovered that a chunk of rock moving at a hundred miles a minute and coming straight at you was like a pinprick of light that got steadily brighter but not noticeably brighter until it hit you.

He realized if you used your eyesight to spot DF, you better have excellent reflexes. Vin also learned that the wave scanner could detect DF faster and more accurately than the human eye one hundred percent of the time, and spotting DF was only half the battle. The other half was shooting the DF before it hit your ship and killed you, or more importantly before it hit a spaceship and killed thousands of people.

Using the wave scanner, the gunner ship automatically shot ninety-five percent of all the detected DF. Which left only five percent of the DF that the ship's automatic guns didn't shoot or couldn't shoot because it had selected a more urgent target, and Vin had to destroy the remainder. That was why he was there; otherwise, a drone ship could do his job.

At the leading edge of the curved array of periphery defense gunners, Vin could not see the other gunners in his unit. He knew they were there and on the job as debris to his left would suddenly explode from a cannon blast or a streak of laser fire from their ships. To his left, a large chunk of debris was blasted into pieces. Immediately afterward, the most substantial chunks were systematically shot into tiny fragments except for one big chunk that soared up away from the rest. Vin leaned forward as it sped overhead. He knew what would happen next and eagerly awaited it. He rarely got to see a striker shoot an object.

Lado's Striker 113 arrived and blasted it. In the periphery defense, strikers were the last resort to ensuring the fleet was safe. If an object made it through the arc of gunners and was on a path approaching the fleet, strikers pursued it and destroyed it. Vin wanted to be captain of a striker. The radar-guided systems of the gunner ship only rarely allowed him to shoot anything. Most of the time, an errant object, like the one he was watching, traveled out of his sector so quickly that he would have to leave his station to shoot it. Gunners never departed until replacements arrived, while strikers could travel across the full line of the periphery defense surrounding the ships.

"Hey, Lado, nice shot," Vin called, and the voice-activated microphone on his headset broadcasted his voice to the rest of his squad. As he spoke, Lado shot another chunk, blasting it into dust.

"Thanks. How are things?" Lado responded.

"All right, a little bored. Maybe I should shut off the radar and try target practice for a while." Vin chuckled.

"Yeah, right. You do, and you'll be swamping toilets in lower Tandia before you can explain why you did it."

"Yeah, I know. I was just joking." The striker zoomed out from Vin's sight. "Are you retiring any time soon?"

Lado laughed; his voice was deep and vibrant. "I'm only a year older than you, knucklehead."

"I know. Recommend me if you get the chance, all right?"

"Sure, why not? Got to go." Lado sped away.

Vin returned to his monitors as his cannons continued to fire.

"Hey, Vin, keep trying to get promoted," Yassa Afari said in his distinctive Lamatian voice. "I want your job." Yassa was Vin's closest friend and a graduate of the same academy class.

"You can have it as soon as I'm a striker."

"Would you guys keep it down? I'm trying to sleep over here." Edo Tasari's voice overrode Vin's and Yassa's. Everyone laughed.

"Yeah, you probably are," Vin replied.

Suddenly, all the radar sensors in 902 flashed red, and warning sirens blared. Within seconds, the sensors in all the periphery defense ships went red. In the debris field, a massive chunk of rock struck another big piece, and thousands of large chunks of DF were created and thrown out toward the ships.

Vin pressed a button on his console to alert all the ships on duty. "Multiple break-out! Multiple break-out! Sector 902, all ships needed immediately." He pressed a large blue button on the console, and the radar and computers for all the ships in nearby sectors linked one by one, coordinating the selection of targets and shots.

All the ship's cannons opened fire simultaneously as the wave scanners picked up hundreds of targets moving toward the spaceships. One by one, the other gunners and strikers opened fire across the area where the fleet ships were orbiting, and more spaceships were being constructed.

Vin kept his hand on the cannon trigger, watching anxiously for any DF the radar did not pick up. To his right, a big chunk of DF burst when one of his cannons shot it, but instead of pulverizing it, the DF broke into dozens of new targets. Vin swept his gun to the right and targeted them, firing as quickly as his computer sighted them.

From above him, more cannon fire hit the DF he was targeting as Lado's striker joined him. Lado shot one large chunk, creating pieces the size of a land vehicle, and one came directly at Vin's position.

Vin's computer switched from distant debris to the immediate threat as several smaller pieces nearly struck him. As the avoidance system moved the ship to the left to avoid getting hit, he kept manually shooting DF as new cannon fire joined from his left.

"You guys looked like you could use some help." Kale Katalasou's said over the headset. He was the striker for Sector 52.

"Thanks," Vin answered, "just keep them from hitting me, and I will be forever grateful."

Their cannons started acquiring targets farther out toward the debris fall again as the last of the immediate threat was eliminated.

"Oh shit!" Edo's voice came in loud and clear over their headsets.

Immediately, Lado and Kale sped up and flew toward his far-left position in the sector, where hundreds of additional targets came into the area.

"It would be good," Lado said on air, hesitating as he fired on targets, "if you would be…a little more specific…than just saying, oh shit."

"Oh shit!" Edo repeated louder. As Kale and the striker in the next sector, Nolan Hasarius fired on the new threats in Edo's targets.

"Hey, guys?" Yassa's voice came over the headsets. "I need some help too."

Immediately, Kale swung up and over the heavy cannon fire and headed for Yassa's area. As he arrived and shot at hundreds of projectiles, Vin fired from his position on the right.

As Vin shot at fewer targets, he noticed something different within the debris field. Buried deep within the debris fall, a massive dark shape moved toward Earth. An enormous lightning bolt lit the debris field, and he saw that the vast DF was at least a hundred miles in diameter. Moving quickly toward Earth, the massive object collided with and destroyed other debris as it passed through.

Across the front, the gunners and strikers' shots decreased. The break-out ended as quickly as it had begun, and space was relatively free of threats again. It was the largest break-out they had endured since working the periphery defense.

"Man, that was something." Vin relaxed and checked the radar consoles one more time to be certain, then disengaged the combined coordination of radar and weapons.

"Oh yeah, that woke me up," Edo said.

"You guys did really good." Lado sounded relieved.

"All sectors, gunners, and strikers," the deep, baritone voice of the Control announcer came over their headsets, "excellent work. The fleet is well protected by its periphery defenses. We recorded over three thousand shots and targets destroyed. You have our thanks."

"Even got Control's attention on that one," Yassa said.

"I think we got everybody's attention on that one," Vin added. "Hey, Lado, did you see a huge object in the debris field?"

"What huge object?"

"Toward the end of the break-out, I saw something huge, maybe a hundred miles in diameter, moving toward Earth."

"Nah, I didn't see anything. You better report it to Control."

"On it." He switched to the fleet comm channel. "Control, this is Vin Neblu, Gunner 902."

"902, this is Control."

"Control, during the break-out, I saw a huge object in the debris field quickly moving toward Earth. It must have been a hundred miles in diameter."

"902, we will verify and notify all concerned. Thanks for the report. Control out."

"902 out." Vin sat back, still staring at where he saw the object.

"Way to go, Vin." The sound of Yassa's applause could be heard over the comm.

"Yeah, way to go, Vin," Edo said. "Now, let me get back to sleep."

They all laughed and continued to unwind as the guns routinely found new targets and fired.

CHAPTER TWELVE

Slowly, the silence in New Hope's conference room was replaced by moaning and weeping.

As if all the air had been sucked out of the room, everyone was frozen, trapped in a nightmare. Even Emperor Maximus and Master Ono stared at Professor Norvis Scintillian as though unable to comprehend what they had heard – the world was ending.

"Exactly how long do we have?" Fleet Commander Cana Athu's strong baritone voice asked quietly but firmly. He had been in situations like this before – the shock and dismay of disaster. In battles, war, and fierce competition, people froze when their minds could not see a solution, and their emotions paralyzed them. Then, as now, he knew someone had to take control and bring everyone back to sanity.

His calm voice and unshakeable presence cut through the despair. While everyone else visualized the utter destruction of everything they loved, Cana saw through the panic and recognized the need to take decisive action. With one question, the people's attitude changed from despair to desperation, not much better, but more hopeful.

Emperor Max glanced around the room as though looking at people who, like him, were confronted with their own doubt and dismay and were finding a way back. During the moaning and crying, the panic and frenzied fear, a beacon of hope heralded the awareness that what was real was what you believe was real. They were either utterly defeated or called upon to do something extraordinary. He gazed at Cana and Norvis with renewed expectation.

Everyone turned to Professor Norvis Scintillian.

Usually a fiery, cantankerous man, Norvis Scintillian appeared physically shaken by the events. He stood and grasped the table as though his only support to deal with the problem. "Commander, it is nearly impossible to forecast exactly how long we have. This has never happened before, and we have no data to form an answer."

"Make your best guess then." Some of the strength returned to Cana's voice. He sat up straighter and glared at the old man.

Norvis wiped his eyes and stared at the table as though the answer might be written there. He blinked several times, made meaningless gestures with his hands as though calculating something, and muttered to himself in incoherent sounds. He glanced hopefully at the other scientists at the table as each of them bowed their heads one by one. Norvis stood straighter and turned to face the commander again, somehow withstanding the force of Cana's glare. "*If* Mars continues at its current pace, the collision will happen in three days."

The silence in the room was overwhelming. Every head turned toward Cana.

"*However,*" Norvis continued, "it is doubtful that Mars will continue at its current pace. As Mars gets closer," he looked around the room into anxious faces, "Earth's gravity will have a greater impact, causing Mars to speed up. If it speeds up, Mars could collide with Earth within twenty-four to forty-eight hours, as I said earlier." The statement appeared to take all his strength, and he collapsed again onto his chair.

Cana bowed his head and closed his eyes. As murmuring filled the room, he sat absolutely still with his head down and his hands pressed to the table in front of him. After a minute, he sat upright, straightened his shoulders, and looked at Emperor Maximus as though silently seeking permission to proceed. Max nodded, and Cana turned toward Norvis and the other scientists.

"What will happen when they collide?" Cana asked in a firm voice, once again in control.

Norvis and the other scientists huddled together, whispering among themselves. Then, from the group, Norvis rose to his feet again. "We are not sure of how direct the collision will be. If Mars strikes Earth with a glancing blow and is deflected, Earth might be able to withstand the collision. However, numerous things could happen as a result – earthquakes, ocean waves a thousand feet high, every volcano erupting, and continents violently set adrift. Earth may even be thrown out of the planetary system. Even with this best-case scenario, millions would die, and Earth may not be able to support life again."

Norvis wiped the sweat from his face and continued. "*However,* most of us believe the collision will be more direct. Mars currently moves along the axis between the planets. If Mars maintains that path, it will collide directly with Earth at the North Pole. Mars is seventy percent of the density of Earth. Moving at an accelerated pace, both planets would be utterly destroyed." Norvis collapsed onto his chair once again.

Everyone in the room was numb. This was the end of the world they had feared for the last five years. Cana slowly paced the room, staring at the floor with his hands clasped behind him. After a complete circuit around the table, he stopped near his seat.

"What is a safe distance to move the fleet?" Cana asked.

Norvis revived himself and scooted nearer the other scientists. They whispered among themselves for several minutes while Cana continued to pace. Then Norvis stood. "We should move the fleet as far from Earth as possible. We are not sure what will happen, but the collision will probably result in Mars and Earth exploding. If that happens, millions of pieces will shoot in every direction. If we are nearby, the Fleet could be destroyed.

"Even if the collision is less direct, both planets could be knocked out of the collinear system. If so, the collinear configuration could come apart. Without Mars, Venus, and Earth to counter-balance Saturn and hold Jupiter in the system, Saturn and Jupiter could slip into different orbits. We do not know how fast they would move into a new orbit, but it may be so fast that the fleet could not escape their massive size." Norvis hesitated, expecting an additional question. When the commander resumed pacing, Norvis sat, shaking like he had a nervous affliction, and waited silently.

Commander Athu returned to his seat at the table and stopped close to the desk. "One more question. Do the other scientists and spaceship captains know any of this?"

Still seated, Norvis answered. "No, sir, we thought that the emperor, council, and you, as commander of the fleet, should know before sharing the news with any others."

Cana stood rigid, silently gathering his thoughts. Then he turned to face Max. "Emperor Maximus, Imperial Council, and Master Ono, I may be overstepping my authority, but there does not seem to be time for meetings and discussion. With your permission and blessing, we must act quickly and decisively to save our people." He paused for comments.

Max looked at Master Ono and the Imperial Council members and got a nod from most. Emperor Maximus leaned forward to make eye contact with Cana, "Commander Athu, I speak for all of us. You are *not* out of line, and I concur that time is critical. We must act. You were selected fleet commander to act on behalf of all Atlantians for precisely this purpose. Please proceed."

"Thank you." Cana bowed to the emperor and then faced the others. "I will hold an emergency teleconference with all fleet captains and their staff officers in an hour. While that is in preparation…" Cana turned to his two fellow officers, "…I need you to get all available data on the condition of the ships, our provisions, fuel, and relative positions. Go now and start gathering the information. Enlist as many people as you need, *but* do not tell anyone why. Tell them only that I ordered it."

"Yes, sir." The two officers hurriedly left the room, accompanied by their aides.

"Emperor Maximus and Imperial Council, I would appreciate your attendance at the teleconference in this room in an hour."

Max looked at the council members, and they nodded. "We will be here, Commander."

"Thank you." Cana turned toward Master Ono.

"Commander Athu," Master Ono said, "I will excuse myself and seek God's counsel in this terrible situation. If you like, I will return for the teleconference."

"Thank you, Master Ono. I would appreciate your guidance."

"Very well. I will return within the hour." Ono rose and walked from the room.

Cana turned to Norvis and the scientists. "Ladies and gentlemen, I need all the information you can get before the meeting. But more importantly, if we are to leave immediately, I will need ongoing information regarding the collinear system and the catastrophic events that will soon overwhelm us. Please prepare a summary explanation of what has happened and what you expect so we can send it to each science officer in the fleet *after* the meeting. We will enlist all scientists to gather and interpret the facts. For the foreseeable future, all scientists will be pressed into service for their maximum effort to keep us advised of conditions and the actions we must take to survive."

"We will do our best, Commander," Norvis said. The other scientists nodded.

"Thank you. Let's get ready for the teleconference."

As the emperor, council members, and scientists rose from their seats, Fleet Commander Cana Athu walked briskly from the meeting room.

CHAPTER THIRTEEN

After rushing to Control, Cana stopped for his messages.

The receptionist, Alsa Gen-Aga, a shapely, genetically altered woman with four arms and two legs, handed him a stack of messages with her top right hand. "Also, sir, Captain Nortin Ketsu with the L.E.T. needs to see you." She pointed at Nortin with her top left hand.

"Thank you." Cana walked to the waiting area, a cozy corner of the entrance separated by plants and flowers, and stopped in front of Ketsu. "You need to see me, Captain?"

Captain Ketsu came to attention. "Yes, sir. I have an urgent matter concerning your son."

"Acton? What's happened?" His messages forgotten, he stared anxiously at Ketsu.

"No, sir, concerning Pal."

"Pal?" Surprise and confusion registered on Cana's face. Before he could respond, Captain Thegan breathlessly rushed up to him and stopped at his side. He turned toward him, leaving Nortin standing at attention.

"Sorry, Commander, but this is urgent," Thegan said. "We must act immediately."

Cana nodded and glanced back at Nortin. "Wait in my office, please." He pointed the way and returned to Thegan.

"Yes, sir." Nortin immediately walked toward it.

"What's happening, Captain?"

"Sir, a gunner reported a large object in the DF stream. We have verified a one-hundred-twenty-mile-wide chunk of Mars is headed for the North Atlantic." He pointed to the big monitor's computer graphic of the object landing on a narrow land bridge at the edge of the Arctic Circle. The illustration showed that the tsunami created by the impact would be a thousand feet high and stretch across the Atlantic Ocean.

"When will it hit?" Cana asked breathlessly, staring wide-eyed at the display.

"Less than an hour–"

"Something that size will wipe out everything in the Atlantic...." As Cana studied the screen, he realized what he was seeing. "Good God, Atlantis!"

"Yes, sir–"

"Issue immediate orders to clear the entire area. Sound the tsunami alarms and order the evacuation of Atlantis. Order all bases and settlements within ten miles of the ocean to move to high ground. Order all ocean-going ships to land." Before Captain Thegan turned away, Cana realized one more thing, "Nora!"

"Yes, sir! Immediately, sir!" Thegan rushed back to his desk.

Cana burst through his office door, dashed to his desk, and then saw Nortin waiting at the meeting table. "Oh, Captain, I already forgot you were here. What is it? Be quick. I have an urgent call to make."

Nortin stood to address the Commander. "Yes, sir. Your son, Pal, is missing. No one has seen him in three days, and his apartment shows no sign of use. He was last seen with a group of hoops players who wore all black clothes."

Cana glared at Nortin. "What the hell does that mean?"

"The only players who wear black clothes are Belial teams."

"Belial teams?" Cana asked, his blank face reflecting his confusion.

"I need to ask you a few questions, and then I will dig further into the matter."

"Yes! Yes! What?" Cana asked angrily.

"When did you last see Pal?"

Cana keyed the monitor on his office comm as he answered. "Weeks ago."

"Do you know if he was planning on going anywhere?"

"He's at the university. I don't see him much. Too busy... Oh, do what you need to do. I don't have time for this now." He punched a button on the screen. "Nora," he said, then turned to Nortin, "You're dismissed. Close the door on your way out."

"Yes, sir, sorry to bother you, sir." Captain Ketsu quickly exited, closing the door behind him as he hurried toward the lift lobby.

"Nora?" Cana asked as her image appeared on the screen. He recognized the window behind her as the one in her office on Athu Farms near Poseidia.

"Hello, how are you?" Nora smiled warmly. An attractive forty-nine-year-old, she appeared more like she was in her late thirties with dark brown hair and brown eyes.

"Nora, listen! There's no time." Cana said frantically. "A huge chunk of DF is headed for the North Atlantic and will cause a tsunami that will destroy Atlantis. You must leave now!"

"Oh, my God!" Nora jumped up, knocking her chair over. "How long do we have?"

"I don't know...less than an hour. Are the shuttles there?"

"Yes, we have been loading all morning." Outside, the tsunami sirens wailed.

"Good, get on board and leave. Now!" Cana ordered.

"All right. Yes, I will."

The screen went blank as the call ended, and he collapsed onto his executive chair.

* * * * *

Ending the call, Nora looked through the window at empty wheat fields stretching to the horizon as the tsunami sirens wailed their urgent cry. Confused, the Gen-x Ag workers stopped working and gathered near the shuttles. Thirty-eight Gen-x AG workers, nearly all the workers on the farm, were loading the Athu family's possessions. The thousand-hectare farm was being abandoned as they moved to SS New Hope.

Nora ran from her office, past bookcases overflowing with books, scrolls, papers, magazines, and other reports interspersed with pictures of the Athu family going back a thousand years. As she raced past partially filled boxes containing the mementos of generations, tears streamed down her cheeks at the thought of abandoning everything.

The hallway to the living room was lined with pictures, paintings, and souvenirs of Atlantian campaigns on every continent on Earth. Artifacts from Mu, vases and urns from Lemuria, African headdresses, spears, and weapons of every era on Earth lined the way. Nora was crying so hard by the time she reached the living room that she could barely see where she was going.

The large living room had busts of Atlantian rulers from the Athu family during the last ten thousand years, including emperors, kings, and ministers who served during every significant achievement of the oldest and greatest empire. Under these rulers, Atlantis became the largest empire on Earth. But now, blinded by tears, Nora could only rush past them to the door. She pushed the door open and ran across the yard toward the blue shuttles. The lower level of the shuttles, designed for luggage, was partially filled with various-sized boxes.

Due to the wailing sirens, many workers noticed Nora running toward them and gathered to meet her. She ran up to Cesa Gen-Athu, the farm manager, a genetically altered human with four arms and four legs. He was over fifty years old and, with his family, had worked on the Athu farms for his whole life. His wife, children, siblings, and their families formed a large part of the thirty-eight Gen-x Ag people loading the shuttles. Cesa appeared to be one of the legendary centaurs of mythology who were part man and part horse. Atlantians had genetically manipulated humans for over fifty thousand years. Atlantian scientists designed genetically modified people to work as farmers, miners, and other workers to increase productivity.

"Cesa, forget the rest of the stuff," Nora ordered as she stopped before him, slightly out of breath. "A tsunami is coming! Get everyone onto the shuttles. Now!"

"Everyone? You know we cannot go to New Hope. It is forbidden."

"Do what I say, now!"

"Yes, of course," Cesa said, but Nora had already hurried toward the pilots. He shouted loud enough to be heard by everyone. "Put the rest of the boxes into the ships, then board the shuttles." They stared at him in confusion. "Hurry!" He turned to his son. "Herme, run to our house and bring everyone to the shuttles. Make them come immediately. We leave our homes forever. Hurry!" He watched Herme leave, then went back to work.

Nora rushed to the six pilots of the three shuttles. "A tsunami is coming, and we're taking the workers with us."

"What?" Captain Suga said. The pilots and co-pilots exchanged glances with each other. "You know we cannot do that. It's against regulations."

"I just spoke with Fleet Commander Cana Athu, my husband. Do you want to argue with him about it?" Nora held her comm unit out, daring them to do so.

The three captains looked at each other again, then back to her. "Ah, no. I don't want to do that, Professor," Captain Suga said.

"Well, then, get everyone aboard." Nora ran toward the house. She had to save some of her family pictures, papers, and valuables but would have to hurry.

"Yes, Professor, I will," Captain Suga called after her. They started getting the Gen-x people on board.

"Cesa, you and Amado, come help me. I must save some of our heritage." They quickly followed Nora into the house.

*　*　*　*　*

Cana tried to calm down. His heart was pounding, and he couldn't breathe, but his mind worked feverishly. A thousand things needed to be done, most of them urgent. His eyes grew large as he remembered that he had to schedule the meeting.

He called Captain Thegan and had him issue immediate orders to all fleet captains, and scientists to attend a teleconference with the emperor, council, Master Ono, the scientists, and himself within an hour from the conference room.

That out of the way, he focused on what would require the most time as that should be started immediately. The fleet was the primary concern; without the spaceships, no one would survive, and there would be no future. The spaceships… Yes, that was first. He keyed his desk comm and said, "Halo." The comm buzzed, and he lifted the handheld receiver to hear better.

"Cana," Halo Hajac answered, "I'm sorry I didn't get back to you about the transport that got hit by DF. It just slipped my mind."

"Don't worry, I know why it happened. I have something more important to discuss, but you need to keep this confidential for the next hour until a major announcement makes it public. But before I make the announcement, I need something, and you're the expert."

"Of course. How can I help?"

"I was just informed that Mars will collide with Earth within twenty-four to forty-eight hours, and–"

"My God! Truly?" Halo gasped.

"Yes, my friend, I'm afraid the scientists are certain. We must move the fleet to safety and abandon anyone still on Earth. We do not have time to do anything else."

"Oh no! My family is still on Earth."

"Where are they?"

"At the marine station near ISB2."

"Hold on." Cana put him on hold and called Thegan on his wrist comm to ask about missions to ISB2. "Halo, have them get to ISB2 immediately. A rescue ship is headed there now, and they can return with it. I told operations to allow them passage."

"Thank you! Thank you. I will have them go there immediately."

"Good. We have a lot of work to do before the fleet leaves. That's what I want to talk to you about. We will need the Space Construction Center (SCC) in the future. It is the nature of mankind to propagate, and I do not want to tell future generations that they cannot have children. So, we will need to be able to build additional ships in the future. If we do not take SCC, we will have to build another one. What do we need to do to take it with us?"

"It was not intended to be a part of the fleet. SCC has no gravity or living quarters and only positional engines, not the big space drives needed to keep up with the fleet. We don't have time to get it ready to go."

"Do you have any space drives that have not been installed yet?" Cana asked.

"Let me check my PAD." There was a long pause while he looked at it. "There are space drives on SCC ready to be installed."

"So, they could be installed on SCC?"

There was a long pause. "I don't know. SCC does not have the structure to attach the engines. It's just a big construction platform floating in space. There's no infrastructure in place to support the thrust of the engines. We would first have to build a whole new framework to support the engines and anchor them for thrust so that the tension doesn't tear the ship apart. Because of the time needed to create the parts and install them, it could take months. Do we have that much time?"

"No, I'm afraid not. But I thought we could tow the SCC behind one of the spaceships. Once we are free of danger, we could station the construction crews with one spaceship and finish outfitting SCC for use. Once we are out of danger, I do not think a few extra months would matter, and we could use the time to make sure all the other spaceships are functioning as intended. What do you think?"

"Cana, I think that's a marvelous idea, but I do not have the information to determine whether we can do it. We would need to make sure we have ample materials to complete the transformation from a working platform into a Fleet cruiser. Let me gather information and evaluate the possibilities. I will call you when I know. Fair enough?"

"Yes and no. Make your study, but remember that time is running out. I need to know if we can tow it before the announcement in less than an hour."

"Yes, sir, then plan on it. I will find a way to tow SCC behind a spaceship. Do you know which ship it will be?"

"I think Grand Poseidia would be best. I will let Verl Madre know that he will need to tow it. Get ahold of him and have him get his engineers working with you to make it happen. Thanks, Halo, that puts my mind a little more at ease anyway."

"You're welcome, old friend. Oh, remember, when it's time to leave, I have ten thousand people who need to be shuttled to the spaceships, and that takes a while."

"Thanks, I had forgotten. In that case, you better start sending them to the spaceships now." Cana closed the commlink and concentrated on what he needed to do at the meeting.

CHAPTER FOURTEEN

The New Hope conference room had been rearranged for the meeting.

When Emperor Max and Commander Athu entered the room, it looked completely different than an hour earlier. The rear wall had been removed to reveal eighteen monitors, each showing a conference room on one of the spaceships. Professor Norvis Scintillian and his fellow scientists sat on the right side of the oval table, and Master Ono, the nine council members, and New Hope's captain and crew sat on the left. The pyramid of seats had been removed, and cameras were situated near the monitors to broadcast the event to the other ships. Max sat on the right, and Cana sat on the left of a new head table near the entry doors.

Emperor Maximus pulled the mic stand closer. "Thank you for attending on such short notice. This could be one of the most important meetings in the history of Atlantis." He paused and studied the nervous faces in the room and the anxious faces of the people on the monitors. "I want to thank all of you. You have constructed nineteen spaceships and relocated nearly two million people to their new homes. We have a new crisis, and Commander Athu will explain the situation."

Cana stood and extended the microphone stand to his level. "Thank you, Emperor Maximus. Ladies and gentlemen, we do not have time to go into the history of what brought us to this moment. You are only too aware of the proximity of Mars and the tremendous destruction happening at this moment across the entire Northern Hemisphere of Earth.

"This morning, we were made aware of a significant change in the disaster we have been fighting for the last five years. We have anticipated that Mars would continue to oscillate between Venus and Earth for another two years, allowing us time to finish the construction of the fleet and evacuate the rest of our people. Our diligent scientists, headed by Professor Norvis Scintillian..." Norvis nodded for the cameras. "...have discovered that Mars is not behaving as expected. Instead of retreating toward Venus, it has come closer to Earth than ever. Mars has broken away from the gravitational pull of Venus and Saturn and has advanced too far to retreat."

Cana paused to clear his throat and let the news sink in. The monitors showed that everyone was stunned by the news.

"Ladies and gentlemen," Cana said firmly, "Mars will collide with Earth on this rotation within twenty-four to forty-eight hours."

The officers on the other spaceships gasped and stared at each other in disbelief. As they realized the end of the world was at hand, people's shock and alarm resulted in several minutes of tears, denial, and anger as Cana and the people on New Hope waited sympathetically.

"Captains!" Cana said firmly. "Please settle your people. We have much to do and no time to lose."

One by one, the captains quieted people and got them back on task.

"Thank you. I apologize for not giving you advance warning of this information. There was no time. We only learned of the situation an hour ago ourselves. We must act quickly to safeguard the advancements we have already achieved. Because the impact of Mars and Earth will be catastrophic, whether a glancing blow or destruction of both planets, the fleet is much too close to Earth to be safe. We must relocate to a safe distance from the catastrophe as quickly as possible.

"We have a lot of issues to deal with. I know that we have shuttles and rescue craft on missions. I am also mindful that supplies, materials, and equipment are deployed at the Space Construction Center and in stockpiles on Earth awaiting transport. The materials we have on hand are not evenly distributed between ships, causing shortages on some and too much to store on others. All of this will have to be sorted out *after* we relocate. Waiting to do so could mean the end of the fleet and our civilization. Now, as painful as it is, we must focus on the survival of our people who are on the spaceships.

"Because New Hope has more shuttles, rescue craft, and periphery defense personnel, I am ordering the relocation of the other spaceships as far from Earth as possible. We have up to two days before the collision, and we should be able to secure things well enough to allow the fleet to travel millions of miles at cruise speed. If we had more time, we could batten down and use our space drives to get farther away. Utilizing the space drives without being prepared would destroy much of the plant life, livestock, and materials we have on board. We never considered that we would have to move this quickly, so we must do the best we can.

"New Hope will remain on-site for as long as we can, up to twenty-four hours, to pick up the returning shuttles, rescuers, and others. No other spaceships will wait for their small crafts, and we can sort everything out after we are safely away."

"Pardon me, Commander Athu," Captain Verl Madre, captain of Grand Poseidia, interrupted. "I apologize for the intrusion, but I suggest that one of the other spaceships await the returning ships. With the Emperor, Master Ono, the Council of Nine, and most of the royal bloodline on New Hope, it should be the first ship to depart, not the last."

"I agree," Captain Ofre of Atlantis Pride said. "Emperor, I hope you will consider this suggestion for your safety."

Emperor Maximus looked at Cana. "They may have a point."

"As you wish, Emperor, I have always had a philosophy of never asking someone to do something I wouldn't do myself. Perhaps I have assumed more than I should have."

"Brave fellow," Max said with a smile.

"Grand Poseidia will volunteer to wait for the remaining ships and then follow the fleet with all possible speed," Captain Madre said.

"Well said, Captain Madre. I accept your request for the mission with my compliments." Cana studied the monitors for a moment. "I want all the other ships underway in twelve hours, no excuses or delays. Spend the hours between now and then to secure quarters.

"I will make a public announcement immediately after this meeting and advise all who can evacuate from Earth to do so within the next few hours. We will use the rest of the time to ensure our preparedness to depart. Expect shuttles and other craft to be rapidly incoming and alert your flight controllers to maintain safety.

"Now for the hardest part of the orders. There will *not* be any additional rescue missions or shuttle missions to Earth." The noise level from the other ships was almost painful. "Quiet!" Cana shouted. "Captains, maintain quiet in your meeting rooms." The noise gradually reduced. "I do not like this order, but there is no more time. Shuttles or rescue ships leaving now would require nine to twelve hours for the round trip, and the fleet needs to be underway before that time. Those on Earth who have shuttles will have time to get to the fleet. And the present missions headed to the spaceships will have time to arrive within six hours, allowing us time to secure the ships before the fleet departs.

"Correct me if I am wrong, Professor Scintillian, but I believe we are not certain what to expect as Mars gets closer to Earth. I believe you mentioned earlier that there is some possibility of the collinear system becoming unstable. Is that correct?"

Norvis stood. "Yes, Commander, that is correct. All our research is available through Command. Each ship's science officers should study that information and be prepared to help monitor the planets, moons, and spaceships over the next two days. It is impossible to estimate what will happen, and we need your help. Thank you." Norvis sat once again.

"Thank you, Professor. Captains, meet with your science officers and become familiar with the facts, which should help prepare us for what we may face as the end approaches."

Cana turned to Master Ono. "Would you like to add anything?"

Ono smiled and stood. "Yes, Commander, thank you." He hurried to their table. "Emperor, Commander, Council, and Officers, I have been in touch with Atlan, the Spirit of God. Although our home is lost, take heart, for God is with us. He has given us what we need to take our faith to new worlds, and we will be blessed. May we safely travel in peace and find paradise in our new home. Go with God."

"Go with God." Nearly everyone repeated, except those who followed the Belial faith.

"Thank you, Master Ono. Captains, please keep Control advised of any actions you take. We will work closely with you to get all the ships to safety. Emperor..."

"My people, go with my blessings," Emperor Maximus added.

One by one, the monitors winked out. As people departed, Cana, Max, and Ono sat at the head table. Max sat in the center, and the others were on either side of him. Most of the monitors went dark, and a moment later, three monitors showed the communications center and people getting ready for the global telecast.

"Are we ready?" Cana asked.

"Ready in one minute," a camera operator said as the countdown started on a monitor.

When it reached zero, Emperor Max began. "My people, I have grave news. Please put aside what you can and pay attention, as this announcement will affect everyone. We begin by turning the broadcast over to Fleet Commander Cana Athu."

Cana leaned forward and took the mic. "Thank you, Your Majesty. For five years, we have anticipated that Mars and Earth would collide. Each year, Mars comes closer and closer to Earth. Most of you have had to relocate to the fleet spaceships or move farther south, away from the lightning, fire, and destruction of the debris fall. For the last three years, Mars has retreated toward Venus, giving us a respite from the intense bombardment and allowing us to work more efficiently on constructing the fleet. At this moment, we *should* see Mars retreating toward Venus, but that is not happening, and the debris fall is worse than ever.

"Earlier today, Professor Norvis Scintillian and many of his colleagues at the university called an emergency meeting on New Hope with the council and the three of us here with you now. The news was devastating, and it pains me to share it with you.

"Mars is not retreating but is continuing toward Earth, getting closer and closer every minute. Mars has passed the point where it could return toward Venus and has slipped away from the gravity of Venus and Saturn. Friends, neighbors, and family, our time has run out. Mars will impact Earth within twenty-four to forty-eight hours."

Cana paused to let that news sink in. He looked at Max and Ono and then continued.

"I have ordered the fleet to move to a safe distance, and it will depart within nine hours, allowing enough time for shuttles, rescue craft, fighters, construction teams, and defense teams to get to their fleet spaceship and prepare for departure.

"I know that there are millions still on Earth. There is no time to send more shuttles to find you and bring you to the fleet. If we did get you to the fleet, the spaceships would be overcrowded. That would endanger the purpose of the fleet – to *safely* evacuate as many people as possible. Because each spaceship is designed and equipped to house one hundred thousand people, more people would use up resources faster than new ones could be created or grown. The entire fleet would be endangered. Therefore, there will be no additional shuttle or rescue missions. There is simply no time.

"Those who have a shuttle or can catch one on its last flight to the fleet do so. But each ship will be instructed to allow only its maximum number of passengers and no more. They will repel anyone attempting to force themselves onto a fully occupied craft.

"Most of you on Earth are south of the equator, the only safe place left. There is a possibility that Mars will strike a glancing blow. While this would still be devastating, it should not be the end of the world. Move as far south as possible. Stay away from the ocean, mountains, volcanoes, and large bodies of water for the next two or three days. That should provide you with the best chance of survival.

"My heart goes out to each of you. May God be with you."

Ono pulled the microphone closer. "My people, Atlantians, God's children. I have spoken with God. In this crisis, know that God is with you. I had no indication from Him that this was the end of Atlantis. God gave me no instructions for the end. Instead, He said, 'Go with God.' So, I say to you, go with God. Get yourselves to a place of safety, then put your mind on God and meditate. God will be with you." Ono sat back.

The emperor pulled the microphone back in front of him. "My people, thank you for your faith and hard work. Thank you for all the people who will journey afar to try and find a new home for Atlantis. We worked long and hard for a chance to survive, and now only some of us will have that chance. How I wish it could be *all* of us. Oh, how I wish it could be all." Close-ups of the emperor on screens worldwide showed tears flowing down his cheeks. "But we must do what the people decided and follow the best possible options for surviving as a people. I believe Cana, Ono, and God have that best interest in mind. It isn't easy, but it is what is possible. Be safe and go with God."

The three leaders covered their faces to hide the tears streaming down their cheeks as the broadcast ended.

CHAPTER FIFTEEN

In the jungles of Solantis, across the Atlantic Ocean from Africa, Cat Lipo watched the bandit camp.

She was perched on a large limb about fifty feet up a kapok tree and concealed in its dense canopy. Spending so much of her recent life spying on targets from tall trees, she was as comfortable in them as her namesake. Cat used the remote to move the camera a little to the left and watched her portable monitor to make sure it focused on the closest hut. The camera was attached to the same limb twenty feet nearer the camp. In the dense foliage, the half-inch lens was invisible from ground level.

At eighteen years old, she stood five foot six inches with short blonde hair and intense green eyes. She was athletic and strong after nearly three years of what her father, Magnus Lipo, called vermin extermination. Her custom-made vest, open to mid-breast, had a backpack with a place for a jetpack, although she wasn't wearing it now. Cat wore tight, water-resistant stretch pants tucked into knee-high boots that contained her throwing knives, blow-darts, and pepper spray. She wore fingerless gloves extending to her elbows and providing a wide variety of readily available weapons from its secret compartments.

Cat saw one of the thirty-two bandits emerge from the crude hut closest to her, pulling his pants up as he tucked his shirt in and grinning at a few of his buddies. There were no longer any screams. Yesterday afternoon, the two girls in the shack, the oldest possibly thirteen and the youngest ten or less, had stopped screaming when their captors raped them. The heavy-set brute had a scar down his right cheek, a two-week stubble of a beard, and a wide, bulbous nose. Cat memorized his image. A few minutes later, another bandit, this one short, skinny, and swarthy, emerged carrying his pants. He stopped before the hut and put them on as other bandits poked fun at him. They all laughed. She marked his image as well since both men visited the shack frequently. Excited voices carried from the far side of the camp, and most of the bandits rushed toward the sound, leaving the fat one and skinny one to keep the girls from escaping.

Cat refocused the lens to her right, stopping when she could see most of the men gathered around their leader, a tall, well-dressed man wearing a tan hat who energetically addressed them. Whatever he said, the men were excited, and she knew the only thing that motivated bandits was going on a raid.

She keyed her wrist comm and spoke softly into a tiny microphone near her mouth. "They may be going on a raid."

"Now?" Mag's voice was loud in her earplug.

"Not sure, but they're jumping up and down excitedly."

"When they leave, get a count. We need to know how many are in the camp."

"Right, I know. Hold it. They're leaving now. I'll call you back."

She adjusted the lens to watch as they gathered weapons and hurried toward the field where their three shuttles were parked. She preferred to be on the ground so she could follow and know what was happening, but she forced herself to be calm and watch the screen.

Three minutes later, the unmistakable sound of shuttle engines filled the jungle. The shuttles took off one by one, and the sound trailed them as they headed south. Cat kept her eyes on the monitor, waiting to see who had returned. After another minute, three men shuffled onto the aisle in the middle of the camp. Two stopped at the crude food hut a hundred feet away, and one joined the two bandits at the shack below the tree.

"Dad, five bandits are in the camp, three near the fuck shack and two near the food shack. A new one just went into the fuck shack."

"I wish you wouldn't talk like that."

"I'll take the three at the fuck shack. You take the other two."

"Give us a few minutes to get there before you do anything."

"Better hurry then. It's payback time," Cat said without a hint of humor. "Call me when you arrive."

Cat loaded the camera and its lead, clamp, and cable into her backpack. She got her crossbow and two bolts, each a foot long with a blunt half-inch tip, and pressed a button on the crossbow's stock to cock it. Pulling the pack onto her back, she carefully loaded one of the bolts in the groove on top of the crossbow, removed the covers from its telescopic sighting lens, and took aim at the fat bandit.

"We're in place," Mag said over her comm.

"Go." Cat pulled the trigger.

The bolt silently flew fifty feet and struck the fat man in the middle of his back. The blunt tip punched a hole in his back an inch wide and blew the entire contents of his chest out the front of his shirt so fast he never made a sound and dropped where he stood like a sack of shit.

By the time the fat man fell, Cat had the other bolt in place and sighted on the skinny man. He stood three feet from the fat man and watched him fall. Turning toward where she was hidden, he was hit in the upper left chest, and the bolt exited his lower right side with most of his internal organs. He also dropped like a wet sack.

Cat knew one man was still in the shack, probably raping one of the girls or getting ready to. She had prepared to move quickly. In the middle of last night, she had installed a wire cable from her tree to a spot ten feet north of the shack. She slung the crossbow over her shoulder, grabbed the cable, and slid silently to the ground.

She left her pack and bow in the jungle, and as she got close to the shack, she heard the man inside grunting like a pig. Cat crept to the doorway and peeked inside. The bandit was four feet inside the door with his pants down around his ankles, and his bare ass was pumping up and down as he raped the older of the two girls. She grabbed his feet and hauled him off the girl toward the door.

"What the…" the man cried as his privates were dragged across the dirt rubble. When he was released, he scrambled, trying to get up.

From behind him, Cat put her wrist next to his neck and quickly cocked back her wrist. An inch-long needle, dripping with the deadliest poison, emerged from its small compartment in her glove and entered his neck. A second later, he flopped to the ground dead.

In shock, the girls huddled at the back of the hut, whimpering and crying, as Cat dragged the dead men out of sight and then went back into the shack. The naked girls had multiple cuts and bruises on their faces, arms, and hands, and the older girl had a swollen, black eye. Their wadded-up clothes were against the back wall and had evidently been ripped from them. They cried and hugged Cat as she helped them get their clothes on, even though the big holes in their crude wraps exposed a large part of their young bodies.

"For you, Mom," Cat whispered. She was numb, no pain, no sorrow, no remorse. She had done this too many times to feel anything except perhaps the satisfaction that these five bandits wouldn't rape and murder anybody else.

A minute later, the loud sound of a shuttle landing in the camp panicked the girls, and they tried to escape into the jungle. Cat held them tight. "It's all right. It's my papa. We're going to take you to your mama and papa." They may not have understood, but they calmed down.

"Everything all right in there?" Magnus asked from outside the shack. He was tall with dark hair, steel-blue eyes, and a short beard. He wore green pants, a sleeveless tan shirt, and sunglasses, and his weapon belt held two laser pistols, a long knife, and a short knife.

"Yeah, give us a second." Cat calmed the girls. "Did you take care of the others?"

"Yes, I got one, and Opin got the other. They had some fuel cans stored at the food shack, and we grabbed eight cans of fuel and took all the weapons and ammo to give to the girls' tribe."

Opin was a thirteen-year-old native boy whom Mag and Cat had adopted eighteen months ago. Most of his fierce tribe had been systematically slaughtered by bandits and enemy tribes, and they rescued him from a battle site where his entire family had been killed. He was short, like most of his tribe, tattooed from his waist to his neck, and had designs carved into his chest and back during manhood rituals at ten years old that were meant to scare enemies. Since he had been with them, he had learned to fight with modern weapons, fly the shuttle, and do most other chores. He was family now.

"I need a couple of wraps. Their clothes don't cover them."

"Okay, be right back." The sound of Mag's footsteps faded as he walked to the shuttle.

A minute later, two simple cloth wraps appeared in the doorway of the crude shack, along with her backpack containing the crossbow. Cat slipped the pack on. Taking the wraps, she helped the girls get dressed. "Opin should wait in the shuttle. These girls are panicky."

"I go." Opin hurried to the shuttle.

"Sorry," Cat called to him as he walked away.

They left the shack, and the two girls cried pitifully as they walked with their heads down. Cat held the girls close as Mag led them to the shuttle and helped them get on board.

"Why don't you stay with them while Opin and I fly?" Mag walked through the passenger compartment to the pilot's cockpit, where Opin waited for him.

"Yeah, that sounds like a good idea." Cat took the girls to a row of seats halfway to the cockpit, putting her backpack on a rack by the door as they passed by.

The shuttle had been modified to be more of a home and operations center than a plane. Instead of eight rows of seats, two on each side of the center aisle, only four remained and were modified to be a place to sleep. The rest of the passenger compartment had been made into a home. A small kitchen with a stove, vegetable cooler, and storage cabinets was at the rear of the cabin. Nearby lockers housed their extensive selection of weapons, ammunition, and survival gear. Wire mesh bins full of clothing, boots, and everything else that didn't have a place in the cabinets were near the lockers. The baggage compartment under the cabin served as a place to store fuel containers, food supplies, tents, canvas, and other equipment that was too big or too toxic for the passenger area.

The girls huddled together, crying and edgy. Cat got a cup of water for each of them, which they eagerly gulped down. So, she got them more water, sat across the aisle, and smiled at them as she drank a cup. Saba, a ten-year-old native girl they rescued from slave traders a year ago, left the pilot's cockpit and brought the girls some bananas. Wearing a simple cloth wrap and sandals, Saba snuggled with Cat and offered her a banana. The rescued girls eagerly peeled and ate their bananas, finally relaxing.

As the shuttle flew north over the jungle toward where the girl's tribe had created their new home, Mag glanced at the picture of his wife, Marna, taped to the dashboard. She had been taken by bandits three years ago, and since then, dozens of similar rescues hadn't eased his pain. He wished someone was bringing her home.

CHAPTER SIXTEEN

Zeth Mercu saw smoke ahead, enough to be trouble.

He slowed down, forcing the five trucks following him to do the same. The road was little more than a rhino path through the savannah grass, so tall he couldn't see anything else through the side windows of the Eby all-terrain vehicle. The grass covered the plain between the distant jungle to his right and the nearer jungle to his left. As the road curved right then left, he saw thick black smoke rising into the sky near their path. He checked the rearview mirror to look beyond his towed six-wheel trailer to the truck twenty feet behind them. "We have to stop," Zeth said to his wife, Zuzu, as he slowed down. Glancing at his wrist comm, he saw it was mid-morning Atlantian time.

"We won't be able to get out here." Zuzu Mercu pointed at the grass. "Are we stopping because of the smoke?"

"Yes." He stopped the Eby, shut it off, and stepped out of the left side. It had bigger tires than the trucks following him and was at least a foot higher. The roof over the front seat had been removed, while the top over the back seat shaded his children. The shoulder-high grass allowed barely enough room to stand without being swallowed whole. Over six feet tall with short dark hair and intense blue eyes, Zeth wore his farm work clothes with the sleeves rolled up on his muscular arms.

Zeth smiled at Zuzu, beautiful even in her work clothes, and at his three children: Feri, his ten-year-old son; Marta, his eight-year-old daughter; and little Olly, his four-year-old son. The two dogs, large brown mastiffs, sensing they could get out, tried to climb over the back of the seat. "Better stay in the Eby. Feri, hang onto the dogs and keep them in the back." He closed the car door and walked toward the vehicles behind him.

"The smoke?" X'to Zylata, an African from Vandia with short black hair and dark eyes, was standing on the left side of his truck when Zeth arrived. In his two-seat, short-bed truck, his wife, Saba, sat in the front seat, and his daughters, Ki and Jea, sat in the back.

"Yeah, let's wait for the others."

A few minutes later, the other four men joined them. Perta Cermius was a tall, muscular man with a long dark beard. Dimitri Durias was nearly as tall as Perta but, although fit, was no match for Perta's strength. Kona Torinus was much shorter with a neat beard, and Volf Bezania was a short, stout man. All the men had been in the same squad in the Atlantian air corps and had decided to farm in Africa shortly after they left the service five years ago.

"There's a lot of smoke ahead." Zeth studied his friends after they formed a circle around him. "We should be prepared for anything."

"Good idea." Perta finished putting his laser pistol on his belt.

"When we arrive, let's stop as close to the jungle as possible while we see what's going on. Arm yourselves and be ready for action." Zeth made sure they all understood. "Let's go."

They returned to their vehicles. Zeth's Eby towed an extended trailer full of household items, food, tents, water, and everything they could take with them in the short time they had before leaving the African farms that had been their homes for more than four years. Sudden DF bombardment had killed their cow, Mazzie, flattened one barn and destroyed a tractor on the first day. They headed south, away from the DF, the same day before someone got killed.

In a broad clearing less than a mile farther along the trail, a farmhouse was burning, sending a boiling cloud of smoke into the hazy sky. But the barn, behind and to the side of the house, was not on fire. Zeth stopped, allowing enough room for the other vehicles to stop nearby. The field before them was strewn with trash and household items, and the house had laser burns and blast holes. No people or animals were within sight.

Zeth gathered his team near the Eby. "Perta, you and X'to, come with me. Everybody else, stay close to your truck and be ready to leave." He strapped his laser pistol to his belt, got his blast rifle from behind the driver's seat, and ensured the other men carried blasters.

They cautiously approached the burning farmhouse. The fields were barren of crops, and the neatly plowed rows showed recent signs of vehicles and people. As the group got closer, they saw everything on the ground was either broken or worthless. The fire was too fierce to get close to the house, and the barn was empty except for hay on the floor, suggesting animals had recently been inside. They hurriedly made a circuit around the buildings and returned to their vehicles.

"Anybody there?" Volf asked as they arrived at the Eby.

"Nothing here. No bodies, no animals, no equipment." Zeth put his blaster away.

"I heard that bandits are raiding more often now. You think they did this?" Kona asked.

"Yeah, I think so." Zeth put his weapons back into the Eby.

"The bandits must have attacked the farm and taken everything of value." Perta squatted, holding his rifle between his knees.

Suddenly, they heard native drumming.

"Danger drums," X'to said, "to the south and east."

"Far away." Zeth opened the Eby's door. "Let's go. There's nothing we can do here."

"Yeah, but keep an eye out, though." Perta pointed at the farmhouse. "This happened less than two hours ago."

The chest-high grass south of the farm was as dense as farther north. Zeth led the way along the narrow path, and the rest of their caravan followed. Volf was last and followed Kona's truck and trailer loaded with their small herd of goats, pigs, and chickens in cages.

Hours later, they drove out of the tall grass and entered the dense jungle. The road was wider but still not large enough for traffic in both directions. The jungle was strangely silent. No bird calls, no animal sounds. The drums were now loud enough to be heard over their engines. They broke through the last of the jungle and entered the open, choppy prairie. A half-mile to their left, a forest of tall trees stretched to the horizon, and a mile to their right, the terrain rose steadily toward the distant hills.

"Let's stop and eat." Zuzu turned to look into the back seat. "The children are hungry and need to play for a while."

Seeing Zuzu's happy expression, Zeth had to smile himself. He had never been able to refuse her anything. She was so beautiful with her long blonde hair and blue eyes that her smile made his heart skip a beat even after twelve years of marriage. "All right, dear." He stopped the Eby.

The other vehicles stopped nearby one by one, forming a semi-circle around the Eby and its trailer. The children jumped out, followed by the dogs, and joined the children from the other vehicles. A moment later, a ball was in play as they chased each other around the vehicles.

"Stay close," Zeth called to them as he stretched.

Zuzu sorted items in the trailer, getting food and kitchenware for a meal. She was slightly taller than the other women but only came to Zeth's shoulder. Her trim figure had added a little more substance after three children, but she was probably the most beautiful woman in Africa. Like most farm women, she wore work pants, a long-sleeved shirt, and boots.

Hearing the crunch of footsteps behind him, Zeth turned to find X'to approaching.

X'to was from Vandia, and like most Vandians, he was a foot shorter than Zeth. Black people were a minority in Atlantis, but he was Atlantian, first, last, and always. Vandia had been a district of Atlantis for over three hundred years. After meeting X'to in the military academy, they entered the service together and became good friends. When Zeth decided to relocate to Africa and go into farming to provide for his family, X'to and his family joined them. Neither had ever regretted the decision.

"I'm going to take Volf and see if we can find some water. If I remember correctly, there's a river east of us. I think some of us..." X'to nodded at his wife near their vehicle. "...would like to wash up tonight after we camp."

"Good thinking. There are some empty bottles in the trailer, too." Noticing how much dirt clung to X'to, Zeth glanced at his work clothes, realizing he should also take a bath and change clothes.

"I'll take them." X'to got the containers, called Volf to help, and headed east toward the trees and the river with laser pistols on their belts. No one went anywhere in Africa without a weapon.

Zeth unloaded food baskets and containers from the trailer. As Zuzu made lunch, he helped Saba get the food from their vehicle.

Suddenly, two low-flying shuttles soared overhead. Their large engines blasted the area with a deafening roar, and everyone stopped to cover their ears.

"What the..." Zeth cringed. "They're way too low."

The children stopped playing, and the youngest ones started crying. By the time parents calmed them and got them playing again, the sound of the shuttles had trailed off to the south.

Perta and Kona joined him to watch the children while the women prepared lunch.

"What about those shuttles?" Perta was a big man, Zeth's height, but much more muscular and bulkier. He was easily the strongest man in their farming village. His dark beard and long hair gave him a slightly wild look, but he was also the children's favorite person to play with, as he always let them win.

"I think they were rebels." In contrast to Perta, Kona seemed even smaller than he actually was. No taller than Zeth's shoulder, he almost appeared to be a child from a distance, except he was also muscular and wore a beard. His lighter hair made his beard almost invisible. Kona was great with animals and managed their small herd of goats and pigs.

"Yeah, I think so, too." Zeth studied the sky like the shuttles were still visible. "There's no other reason they would be flying so low."

"Do you think we should report it to Control?" Perta asked.

"No communications out here in the bush. We will have to wait until we get to Vandia. But it does give us a good reason to contact them, and perhaps we can still join the fleet."

"Yeah, I'm not going to mention it until it's confirmed." Kona glanced back at his wife to make sure she wasn't listening. "Shea would be after me every minute if I did."

Perta chuckled. "Yeah, me too."

"Let's put it on hold until we can contact them," Zeth added.

"Hey, guys, the food's ready," Zuzu called.

As they finished eating, Zeth saw X'to and Volf running toward them, carrying only one water bottle each instead of the two they took with them. He jumped to his feet and raced toward them. "What's the matter?" he shouted.

They were so out of breath that X'to had to stop to shout back. "River's raising… Over banks… Flood coming… Must leave."

Zeth turned back and shouted, "Get in the trucks! We have to leave at once!" He was reminded how much he missed their wrist comms after they stopped working when the mid-Africa tower went down.

X'to and Volf reached him, out of breath and panting. "Flash flood…" X'to struggled to catch his breath, and Volf was gasping.

"Trees and stuff are blocking the water in the woods." He took another deep breath. "Will breakthrough soon."

"Okay, get them moving," Zeth shouted.

Parents immediately got their children into their vehicles. Everyone helped toss the supplies, kitchen utensils, and food into the trailer. They followed the Eby as he sped up. Zeth couldn't go as fast as he would like, but they went as quickly as possible without crippling the animals and tossing their supplies all over the trail.

Zuzu sat in the middle of the back seat and held the children on both sides of her with the dogs at their feet. Zeth smiled to reassure them, but the children were scared.

Zeth was unsure whether the road curved back toward the river before heading south. If it did, and the river had left its banks, they were in trouble. He sped up. Better to break a few dishes than get stuck in the middle of a flood. He glanced back at the other vehicles. "Oh shit."

"What?" Zuzu asked, immediately concerned.

"We have to slow down. Kona cannot keep up without crippling the herd, and I don't want to leave anybody behind."

The road swung left toward the river. From ahead in the distance came loud cracking sounds and the thuds of heavy objects as trees broke off and fell. The canopy of leaves swayed toward them and back again.

Zeth checked where the others were located. Perta, Dimitri, and X'to were close behind him. Kona trailed a hundred feet behind, and Volf faithfully remained behind Kona to help if he could. They were too spread out and too slow. He stopped and motioned for Perta and X'to to stop next to the Edy. When X'to pulled alongside, Zeth shouted to him. "You take the trailer." He turned to Perta as he pulled up to the other side of the Edy. "Perta, take Zuzu and the children with you. Get past the flood, find high ground, and wait for the rest of us."

"Are you sure?" Zuzu asked.

"Yes, I have to help Kona get the animals through the water, or he and Volf could get washed away." Zeth nodded toward the jungle ahead.

The jungle seemed to sink as water rushed through the trees carrying logs, limbs, and other foliage. Water already covered everything halfway to the road.

Zeth got the trailer unhitched while Zuzu, the children, and their dogs moved to Perta's vehicle. Once the trailer was on its stand, he jumped back into the Edy and pulled it around in a semi-circle facing Kona. X'to immediately drove to where the Edy had been, and they got the trailer hitched to X'to's truck.

"Go!" Zeth called as he jumped back into the Edy and drove toward Kona.

* * * * *

X'to, Perta, and Dimitri reached cruising speed as the water broke through the trees along the roadway. The largest trees caught the logs and debris, creating a dam as the raging current tried to go over, under, and around it. The water already covered the road, and the vehicles drove into it. The spray from the big tires shot up from both sides of X'to's vehicle like giant wings. The children squealed with delight, pointing at the water flying into the air.

Perta followed twenty feet behind X'to, keeping an eye on the much lighter and more buoyant trailer. "Geta, hand me the rope behind my seat," he said to his wife.

Geta leaned around her children in the middle of the front seat and reached for the rope. Zuzu, her three children, and their two dogs were scrunched into the back seat of Perta's truck. Zuzu reached around her children, past the dogs, and grabbed the rope from the floor. Untying the slip knot that had kept it in a tight loop, she handed the rope to Geta, who gave it to Perta.

"Grab the wheel and keep us behind the trailer," he shouted.

Geta leaned closer and took the wheel while Perta created a lasso with the rope.

Standing in the roofless truck, he lassoed the corner post of the trailer and pulled the rope snug over the windshield. Getting back behind the wheel, he took the rope in one hand and steered with the other. He sped up to give the line a little slack. "Thanks." As the water rushed around the trailer, the rope slid to the side, and Perta pulled it tighter to keep the trailer squarely behind the X'to's vehicle.

* * * * *

As Zeth reached Kona, the water surrounded the last two vehicles. "Stop, let's get the animals down so they don't break their legs," he shouted to Kona.

"Is the water high enough to drown them?" Kona asked anxiously.

"I don't know, but they will surely break their legs when we have to go faster."

Kona nodded as he stopped, and Volf pulled up behind him. The three men climbed into the trailer, got the animals onto their sides, and tied them. The water was up to the vehicle's axles by the time they finished.

"Go as quickly as possible." Zeth jumped into the Edy. He pulled in front of Kona, trying to redirect water away from the trailer if possible. All the vehicles created a large spray as they sped up. Zeth could see the other trucks as they drove through deeper water. Seeing how Perta kept the trailer on the course, he pulled out of the way and fell back to where he could shout to Volf. "Get a rope on the trailer and keep it lined up with the truck." Zeth pointed at the other trailer. Volf quickly got a rope on the animal trailer as Zeth drove back to the lead position.

* * * * *

X'to kept an anxious eye on the trees as the floodwaters got deeper and more debris threatened to break through and overwhelm them. The closest trees leaned more toward them each minute. He glanced behind and saw the others were underway but too far behind to be safe. With nothing else he could do, he pressed on.

Ahead and to his left, X'to saw a space between the trees that may be big enough to allow the vehicles through. But did it lead back to the road or into a denser jungle, forming a trap? Also, with water a foot deep, he couldn't tell if the ground was level or hid dips and shallow areas. Without knowing if it was safe, he drove on what he thought was the current road with a prayer for everyone to get through before the dam gave way. Thirty feet later, he sensed the roadway turned left. He couldn't tell for sure with the water over a foot deep, but he turned right and drove up a slight rise. The tires slipped, and the truck bogged down before getting enough traction to go up the incline.

The sound of shattering trees grew louder and more frequent as X'to, Perta, and Dimitri followed the roadway to the right, slower due to slipping but away from the dam. Behind them, Zeth led the other three vehicles into ever-deepening water.

✲ ✲ ✲ ✲ ✲

The leakage through the congested dam was rapidly becoming a river. Zeth kept an anxious eye on the other trucks so he could stay close enough to help if needed. He wished all the trucks were Edy all-terrain vehicles, bigger, heavier, and sturdier than the others, but they had to accept what they had.

A five-foot, broken tree trunk slammed into the Edy. It bounced off, got caught in the rushing water, and hit the front of Kona's vehicle, shattering a headlight and jamming under the bumper. Kona came to an abrupt halt.

Zeth stopped the Edy. Removing the roof over the back seat and putting it on the seat, he climbed into the vehicle's bed. Behind him,

Kona tried to back up, but the current kept the tree trunk under his truck's bumper.

Zeth grabbed a tent pole from the side of the Edy. "Kona, wait until I can push the tree trunk into the current." He shoved the tent pole against the tree trunk, but after Kona backed up, he was too far away. Jamming the tent pole back into place to prevent it from being washed away by the current, he climbed back to the driver's seat, backed up a few feet, and stopped again. The water was about to flow over the side of the Edy as Zeth took the pole and tried to dislodge the tree trunk. The stump was caught on its tires and refused to budge.

"Kona," Zeth shouted, "when I push on the trunk, back up so it can come free." Kona nodded. As he got in place for another try, Zeth noticed Volf had pulled alongside Kona's truck. Volf fashioned a lasso and tried to rope the tree trunk as Zeth positioned the pole again. "Okay, now!" Zeth shoved against the pole with all his might.

Kona backed up as quickly as he could, and the tree bobbed up against the bumper as Volf's lasso caught the stub of a broken limb. As Volf pulled and Zeth pushed, the tree trunk swung around in the current, slammed into the side of Kona's vehicle, and was swept away in the water. Volf was nearly yanked out of his window as the tree trunk swept by, but he held the rope tight against the door frame long enough to whip his ever-present knife out of its sheath and cut the line. The tree trunk disappeared in the raging current.

Zeth jammed the pole back into its spot, climbed into the driver's seat, and drove forward again. Kona quickly followed him, and Volf waited for Kona to pass him so he could again be in the rear. The current was so fast now that the vehicles made little headway.

Studying the forest where the logjam held the water back, Zeth noticed only a few trees continued to resist the pressure of the raging current. Soon, the entire dam would burst, and he doubted the vehicles could escape so many tree trunks. He searched for Perta and the others and found them on an incline across from the jammed dam.

He waved at them and noticed X'to frantically pointing at something between them, but Zeth couldn't see what.

The three vehicles slowly moved forward. The water was deep enough that the trailer full of animals was now a floating barge held in place by the hitch and Volf's rope.

Fifty feet closer to the dam, Zeth saw what X'to was pointing to. A gap in the trees was big enough for the vehicles to drive up the incline and join the others. More explosive popping sounds came from the dam, and massive tree trunks, limbs, and brush tumbled past the Edy. Zeth leaned on his horn and motioned to detour to the right. In his rearview mirror, he saw them follow as he turned into the gap.

The water was even deeper in the gap. Zeth sped up to keep the Edy moving. He looked back and saw Kona had difficulty following, and the trailer floated away from the truck. Hopelessness threatened, but nothing else was possible now. They were committed.

Slowly, foot by foot, the Edy moved forward, slipping and sliding but refusing to stop. Kona was not as fortunate and moved as much to the right with the raging water as he went ahead. Volf had an even bigger problem trying to keep the trailer in tow and drive simultaneously. They were only moments away from disaster, powerless to prevent it.

Suddenly, with an explosive sound like a hundred cannons firing, the front trees holding back the flood snapped and flew out into the raging water. A massive surge of water, six feet deep, rushed directly into the area where the three vehicles struggled to escape. The water shoved them to the right and started to wash over them.

As the Edy jerked to the right, its tires made solid contact with the ground, and it came free of the raging current to drive onto the incline.

The water shoved Kona's vehicle to the right, climbed up the driver's side, and flowed into it. Shea and her daughter Zala, who had been clutching their seats and enduring the wild ride, suddenly screamed. They grabbed whatever they could to keep from being swept into the water. Behind Kona, the trailer lifted faster than the truck and pulled the vehicle with it. Suddenly, Kona's right tires made solid contact with the ground, and the truck jerked forward, bringing the trailer back into line and moving up the incline.

The rope edged across the windshield and threatened to slip out of Volf's control. Kayl and her son Quina fought the rising water's efforts to suck them out of the vehicle. But as the water threatened to capsize them, their tires hit the ground solidly enough for the truck to surge forward and follow Kona up the incline.

As catastrophe had seemed inevitable, they drove onto higher ground and stopped next to X'to, Perta, and Dimitri. Below them, the raging floodwaters carried the remains of the jungle forest downstream.

Zeth and the others slumped onto their seats, exhausted but happy to be alive.

CHAPTER SEVENTEEN

The emperor's image faded from the monitor in Rescue 1.

His last words still echoed throughout the ship, "Be safe and go with God."

"Damn." Acton softly muttered as though coming out of a trance. As he stared through the front window toward where SS New Hope was still a speck in the distance, the news wouldn't register in his brain. Shaking his head in disbelief, he saw the same shock on Cass's face. The nightmare was real; the end was here. "Damn!"

He turned on the rear camera and watched Earth receding behind them on the pathfinder's screen. Earth's black-shrouded atmosphere was only partially visible through the debris field and then only recognizable by scattered smudges of fiery red and massive lightning bolts shooting erratically through the clouds.

"I can't believe it." Cass shook himself out of his stupor.

To their right, Acton could hardly see Mars. The debris field blocked most of its view as it seemed to burrow into Earth, throwing off DF in every direction. Massive lightning bolts shot between Mars and Earth, one after another, as though one ignited another, and it set off yet others in an endless jagged burst of blue fire.

The passengers' anxious voices reminded Acton that he wasn't alone. The broadcast had been piped throughout the ship, and the passengers' moans could be heard in the cockpit. He brought the pathfinder back up and checked their route. They were scheduled to arrive at New Hope in an hour.

"I have to go get her," Acton mumbled, more to himself than Cass.

"Say what?" Cass asked.

"Mya is still down there. I must go get her." Acton studied the dashboard gauges to see they had a quarter tank of fuel and less than half of a tank of oxygen.

"We can't go back now." Cass looked at his friend's anxious face, swallowed hard, and nodded. "Do you think your father will give you a ship?"

"He has to! I can't leave her on Earth!" Acton exclaimed, becoming more emphatic by the moment. He checked their speed; Rescue 1 was going as fast as possible.

"I'll go with you," Cass stated.

Acton looked at his lifelong friend and smiled. "Thanks, Cass. I appreciate that."

"No problem, I have to safeguard my winnings."

"Your winnings? What winnings?"

"You still owe me twenty credits from the last hoops game."

"Like hell I do."

"Just before the end of the game, I bet you Stondu would score and ensure the win. He did. You owe me." Cass leaned smugly back in his seat and grinned.

"I didn't bet on that, you moron. He shot before I could respond."

"You were going to, though, so you owe me."

"Fat chance of collecting on that." Acton's wrist comm chimed, and he automatically punched the speaker button.

"Acton, do you copy?" Farl's voice was loud and clear.

"Yes, Farl, go ahead." He glanced to his left through the side window and saw Shuttle 15 flying parallel with Rescue 1.

"Do you think your father will let us have a ship to rescue Mya and her father?"

"What are you, a mind-reader? We were just discussing that." Acton stared at Cass and saw he was also surprised.

"I don't have to read minds to know you would go after Mya, and knowing Mya, she wouldn't go without her father."

"I think he will. We have plenty of time, and he said he wasn't sending any additional rescue missions, so no problem."

"Yeah, but what you want *is* another mission," Trice interrupted. "Do you think he will allow it?"

"He will. He has to." As Acton stared toward New Hope, he suddenly got a pain in the pit of his stomach.

"Trice and I will go with you. Just in case you need us," Farl announced.

"Hey, thanks. I appreciate that. Cass said he was going, too. That's above and beyond, as always. Let's get together on New Hope, and we'll go get her."

"Right." Farl ended the call.

"Starting to get a little crowded. Better get a big enough shuttle for everyone." Cass grinned at Acton.

"What are you grinning about? Any shuttle will do."

"Right." Cass agreed as though he knew something Acton didn't.

Acton keyed the ship's comm unit through his headset. "Mya Moriset." It buzzed.

"Did you hear the announcement?" Mya answered.

He could hear the panic in her voice. "Yes, listen, I'm coming to get you."

"We have a shuttle –"

"Don't use it. The ones I saw at the mine are damaged and won't make it back to New Hope."

"Father said –"

"They'll never get out of Earth's gravity. They're too beat up and will leak air. I will get a shuttle and come get you. Understand?"

"Yes. Oh, Acton, I can't believe this is happening. So many people are still here –"

"I know, sweetheart, you must be brave and wait for me. You know me. When I say I'll do something, I always do, right?"

"Yes, but –

"No time now, Mya. I'll see you in a few hours. Wait for me. Promise you'll wait."

"Of course, I'll wait." Mya started crying.

"I love you. I'll be there as soon as I can."

"I love you too." Mya sobbed.

Acton ended the call.

"That's ballsy, isn't it? What if the commander won't let you have a ship?" Cass sounded worried.

"He has to." Deep in thought, Acton stared straight ahead and flew toward New Hope.

* * * * *

Genesi and her roommate, Marlenel, listened to the announcement in their apartment.

The video of the emperor ended, and the wall monitor returned to a picture of the Temple in Poseidia. Sitting on their sofa, Genesi used a handkerchief to wipe tears from her eyes and cheeks. "I can't believe the world is ending." Genesi sobbed.

"I always thought we'd return to Poseidia one day," Marlenel said through her tears.

Genesi took a deep breath and sat upright. "We're so fortunate to be here. When I think of all the millions still on Earth–"

"Oh, my cousin and his family." Marlenel bolted upright. "They're still in Salincia." She stared at Genesi, wide-eyed and quivering. "That's pretty far south. Maybe they'll be all right." She took a deep breath and shuddered as she tried to calm herself.

Genesi scooted closer and hugged her friend. "I hope so." Her wrist comm chimed, and the ID showed Master Ono was calling. She quickly answered, "Yes, Master?"

"Genesi, I need you and Marlenel to come to the Temple as soon as possible."

"Yes, right away."

"Thank you. Hurry, please." Ono ended the call.

Genesi stood and turned to Marlenel. "Come on. The Master needs us in the Temple. We can help." She pulled Marlenel up and opened the door as Marlenel dried her tears. They rushed to the Temple.

* * * * *

The announcement still echoed across Aswanga Mine's staging field.

The mine workers, including Monty and Mya, gathered to hear the announcement over the large speakers scattered around the field. When the broadcast ended, Monty stepped onto the porch of the office building and turned to face the miners.

"Hear me, now! You heard the commander. We have shuttles and will use them to go to the fleet. Gather your families and personal belongings and meet at the shuttles. The transport pilots will take their transporters. We will leave in two hours, so hurry." He sagged as he finished speaking. If Mya hadn't steadied him, he would have fallen.

"Oh, father…" Tears brimmed in Mya's eyes.

"Come on. Let's get our stuff. You will be with Acton soon." With Mya's support, he hobbled toward the door.

"Father, Acton called while you were addressing the workers. He said our shuttles will never make it to the fleet and made me promise to wait for him to come to get us on shuttles that are in better shape than ours."

"If he gets here before we leave, we can go in his shuttles. If not, we'll go on ours. They will make it to the fleet."

"But I promised him that we would wait for him."

"We'll see."

As they arrived at the office door, Shorty ran up to them. "Monty, my people?"

Monty turned to see the African and Gen-x AG workers gathered around the porch. "Everyone who works at the mine can come with us, including their wives and children, but that's all. No others. I cannot leave you here to die, but I cannot take too many. Zelk, Neez, and all the Gen-x people join Shorty and the other Africans and meet me at the shuttles in two hours."

"Thank you, Monty." Shorty ran toward his shanty as the other Africans and Gen-x workers ran to theirs.

Monty leaned heavily on Mya as they entered the office. "Thank you, Father. I appreciate you taking them with us even though we'll have trouble when we get to New Hope."

"One problem at a time." Monty collapsed on the sofa.

Mya sat next to her father and wiped the sweat from his face with her tissue.

* * * * *

Spaceship construction stopped as the announcement began.

Beyond where the fleet spaceships orbited, three spaceships were in various stages of completion. Ten thousand workers in spacesuits welded frames together, moved supplies where needed, or wrestled equipment into place.

Everyone stopped as the emperor's announcement was received on each spacesuit's monitor. Across the construction site, the workers looked at where Earth and Mars were locked in a death hold as they listened. When the announcement ended, they moved toward SCC. Those close to SCC used their jet packs, and the ones working on more distant spaceships went to the ship's freight port to await the shuttles that would take them there.

"All construction workers, this is Halo Hajac. Immediately return to SCC. Shuttles will arrive shortly to take you to your ship. Make sure you sign off on the SCC terminals so we can account for everyone. Check with dispatch at the SCC terminal because some of you will report to Grand Poseidia instead of where you were stationed. We have an important job to do before the fleet leaves. I will be in touch after we arrive on the spaceships. Hajac out."

* * * * *

After the emperor's announcement, Vin Neblu was stunned.

"I knew things were bad, but not that bad," he whispered in the isolation of his ship. Looking around, he was alone and wanted someone to console him. But he was the squad leader and couldn't say anything that sounded weak.

He also didn't know what he was supposed to do. Should he head for New Hope or wait until they were ready to depart? A moment later, he knew. He should follow orders. The DF and the lightning were worse than ever, and he was needed.

Massive, mile-wide lightning bolts exploded between Earth and Mars, racing between the planets like giant laser gun blasts. Each bolt quickly zig-zagged through the debris field, hitting and exploding debris into hundreds of smaller chunks large enough to destroy his gunner or put a massive hole in one of the spaceships.

Another lightning bolt tore through the debris field, displaying everything in the debris field. In the brightness, he saw thousands of big chunks of DF shooting toward the fleet ships. He switched to the control comm.

"Control, this is Gunner 902, multiple breakouts! All ships needed now." He slapped the blue button to link all the ships' radars and weapons. Working in unison, each ship's guns selected targets and fired.

"All gunners and strikers, multiple breakouts, respond immediately," Control announced a second after Vin's message.

The other gunners and strikers responded within seconds, and laser and blaster fire erupted across all the sectors. The strikers held back and watched for any DF that wasn't destroyed. Soon, the strikers were fully engaged as well.

"Control, this is Striker 113. All ships are fully engaged, and more targets are being formed. Need reserves as soon as possible." Lado Strifa fired on dozens of chunks of DF.

"Striker 113, all reserves have been assigned. Expect them soon. Control out."

"Well, I guess that answers that question," Vin said loudly enough to be heard over the squad comm.

"What question?" Lado asked.

"Whether we should return to the fleet and prepare to leave." Vin shot any DF not destroyed by the automatic system.

"Fat chance of that," Edo Tasari responded from his position in Vin's group.

"Shut up, guys! Can't you see how busy I am?" Yassa Afari continued shooting at debris.

"Dang, didn't your instructors teach you to maintain radio silence during a breakout?" Kale Katalasou, another striker, asked.

"Silence? If you miss any of the incoming DF, you'll have all the silence you could handle," Nolan Hesarius said. He stopped talking while his guns continued to fire repeatedly.

Suddenly, twice as many shots erupted across the entire sector.

"Wahoo! The reserves are here," Vin cried.

"Dang, Vin, keep it down. You nearly broke my eardrums," Yassa said.

"Sorry, Yassa, but don't those guys shoot good?"

Lightning continued to erupt between Mars and Earth and lit the entire debris field.

"Hey, look at that," Lado shouted. "The lightning is ripping up thousands of miles on the surface of Mars." Four times the usual amount of rock and debris was suddenly thrown into the debris field.

"It's carving a huge canyon on Mars," Vin said. "It must be thousands of miles long and hundreds of miles wide."

"How do we stop all of that stuff?" Edo asked.

After Edo said what everyone thought, the giant guns on SS New Hope fired. Firepower, a hundred times the strength of the gunners and strikers' guns, destroyed the more massive DF created by the excavation on Mars.

The comm suddenly came alive with orders. "All ships, this is Commander Athu. Except for New Venture and Grand Poseidia, fleet spaceships will depart now. Immediately pull back to staging area one, as shown on your pathfinder. New Venture, assist the gunners and strikers in protecting the Space Construction Center and the last returning shuttles. Grand Poseidia, reposition to the SCC and defend it until it can be towed to safety. As soon as ready, take SCC in tow and fall back with the rest of the fleet.

"All gunners and strikers will immediately report to duty. All gunners and strikers will be stationed on SS New Venture until the fleet has departed. You will fall back to a safe distance as soon as the fleet ships are safe. Control out."

"Dang, so it begins," Vin said.

* * * * *

Zeth Mercu was at the Tandia Shuttle Base in central Africa.

He entered the store to get food and supplies and encountered anxious people crowding the service desk. The announcement was on the monitors, and everyone stared at the screens in shock as Commander Athu and Emperor Maximus spoke.

As the people around him grabbed food from the shelves, Zeth moved closer to the exit. The broadcast ended, and the people rushed to the counter to demand a shuttle from its three attendants. He stepped outside and hurried across the empty shuttle lot to where his family and friends waited.

Arriving at the Eby, Zeth saw that meal preparation had stopped, and everyone stood around the back of the Eby. The food chest was out, but Zuzu sat on it, holding Marta and Olli close to her. "Hey, guys, gather around. There was an announcement –"

"We heard it," Perta interrupted. "Kona had his comm unit on."

Zeth saw their anxiety. "The people in the base shop are panicking, and we have the only vehicles in the area. We better get out of here before anyone gets any ideas."

"Makes sense," Perta agreed.

"We have to go through town to go south," X'to said. A small village had formed around the shuttle base, mostly lean-tos and tents, where a hundred people waited for a shuttle.

"Yeah, that's the way, but it's a problem, too many people." Zeth glanced at the building to ensure nobody had followed him. A dozen people pointed at the vehicles as they talked.

"Maybe we can loop around the town, through the fields," Dimitri offered.

"That would be slow," Kona said. "Maybe we can drive through Vandia as fast as possible and brandish our weapons if challenged."

"I don't think we have time to plan anything better." Zeth looked at Zuzu and his young children. The two youngest were ready to cry. "If we're going through town, we better do it now. We don't want to give them time to plan."

"Right," Perta said, "let's go."

Everyone returned the food to their vehicles, rounded up their children, and got them in their trucks. Zeth grabbed the food chest and put it back in the trailer. "Feri, get the dogs in the Eby," he instructed his oldest son. Feri whistled for the dogs, and they responded immediately and were back in the Eby in less than a minute.

Zeth checked the line of vehicles to make sure everyone was ready to go, then got into the Eby as Zuzu got the children to tighten their seat harnesses.

"Were you able to get any supplies?" Zuzu asked.

"No, people were panicking, and I didn't want to fight for it." Zuzu nodded.

Zeth started the Eby, and the caravan pulled forward and onto the road through town. People were on the roadway as they approached the base store, and Zeth leaned on the air horn.

The blaring horn got people's attention. The caravan was speeding by the time they approached the people on the road. Men and women dove out of the way. Some mules by the side of the store started braying and kicking, causing other people to run.

Although Zeth and the others had their weapons in hand and visible through the vehicle's windows, they didn't have to use them. Within minutes, the caravan drove through the shantytown and into the jungle, heading south again.

CHAPTER EIGHTEEN

The Northern Hemisphere of Earth was hell.

Firestorms burned across every continent, caused by thousands of lightning strikes and the eruption of dozens of volcanoes. Earthquakes crumbled mountains and opened fissures that swallowed buildings, roads, and other structures. Hurricane-force winds, driven by the firestorms, uprooted trees, ripped plants from the ground, and flattened every manmade structure. Nothing lived on the lands north of Atlantis.

What nature hadn't destroyed, the debris fall had. For three years, DF meteorites had blasted nearly every foot of the surface. What once had been lush farms raising vegetables, fruits, or grains were now burnt, scorched land devoid of vegetation. Where once life abounded, nothing moved, and only charred bones remained.

The debris fall bombarded Earth along an area the width of Mars, over four thousand miles. From the North Pole, the DF zone extended well within Africa. Dense, black clouds of smoke and ash covered Earth to almost the equator, and less thick, gray clouds covered the rest.

The debris fall was so thick that the fleet's sophisticated systems had difficulty finding one chunk of DF that was many times the size of the next largest. The gigantic chunk, the size of an asteroid, gained speed as it hurtled toward Earth.

At the southern edge of the Arctic Circle, an east-west ridge of low mountains connected the continent on the west side of the Atlantic Ocean with the lands east of the Atlantic. The tallest mountain was only one thousand five hundred feet, and the others were considerably smaller. They were ice-packed pinnacles with rocky foundations and virtually no foliage. Still, they were the bridge that, at one time, over a hundred thousand years ago, allowed primitive men to travel from the East to the West.

Deep in the maelstrom of the debris fall, the gigantic chunk of DF struck the land bridge with the force of an atomic bomb, demolishing it completely. Almost two times the width of the ridge, most of the impact struck the water of the North Atlantic, causing a tsunami over a thousand feet high. The wind became a concussive wave blowing outward from the impact's center at hundreds of miles per hour, turning the smoke and ash in the air into deadly blast projectiles.

The tsunami rushed south, east, and west, while the demise of the land bridge virtually eliminated a tsunami to the north and focused the force to the south. The DF caused every volcano near the Arctic to erupt, spewing millions of additional tons of ash and pumice into the already dense cloud covering the Northern Hemisphere. The toxic mixture armed the hurricane-force winds with destructive content.

To the west, the tsunami swept over the largest island in the Arctic region, burying it in water and dissolving much of its ice. The torrent swept west and south, sweeping across the northeast coast, flooding the northern lowlands, and rushing south into the plains. The mountains and valleys of the western continent channeled the water into their rivers, creating raging torrents and flash floods that decimated everything for thousands of miles.

To the east, the enormous wave hit the mountains along the northernmost coast, carving them into narrower, steeper, and more dramatic shapes while stripping them of the evidence of the debris fall. Simultaneously, the tsunami rushed south into the Atlantic Ocean.

Moving at nearly seven hundred miles per hour, the thousand-foot wave hit the land on both sides of the Atlantic, crushing peninsulas, destroying fragile coasts, and detonating active volcanoes that had not previously erupted. Peninsulas became islands, and what were islands were utterly destroyed. All the debris created by the destruction was added to the tsunami, increasing the wave's destructive capability as it rushed south toward Atlantis.

* * * * *

Rescue 3 flew southwest from ASB toward Atlantis and the southern tip of Nolantis on the western continent.

Still hundreds of miles from Atlantis, as Captain Pad Nedin slept soundly, an announcement over the ship's comm woke him.

"Attention, all ships. A thousand-foot tsunami is heading south in the Atlantic Ocean from the Arctic Circle at over six hundred miles per hour. It extends to the continents on both sides of the ocean. All ocean-going ships are ordered to the nearest port, and people should seek high ground.

"Attention aircraft near the Atlantic Ocean. Two-hundred-mile-per-hour winds accompany the tsunami heading south, east, and west. Watch for ocean-going vessels and be prepared to rescue people. Report sightings of the tsunami immediately. Control out."

"Where are we?" Pad Nedin asked as he studied the pathfinder.

Suddenly, Rescue 3 was shoved to the south. The dark, cloudy skies instantly became streamers of smoke and ash streaking past. Co-pilot Zetu Ordia grabbed the navigation stick and fought to keep flying west, but the ship was forced south no matter how hard he struggled.

"What the hell!" Pad was thrown to his left, along with most of the loose items in the ship. "Now that's gale-force wind." He checked the gauge, and their airspeed was one hundred eighty miles per hour. "Either we just sped up, or the wind's blowing pretty hard out there."

"I can't hold a Western course." Zetu struggled with the stick.

"Take it up. Maybe the wind is less at a higher altitude."

"Good idea." Zetu pulled back on the stick, bringing the ship higher. R3 climbed to over fifteen hundred feet before the wind reduced enough to return to its original course.

"That's better. You got it, or do you want me to take over for a while?" Pad asked.

"Look, that's the tsunami! It's coming straight at us!" The ocean tilted upright, still distant but getting bigger and closer each second.

Pad stared at where Zetu pointed. "Holy Atlan! It's huge!"

"I can't see the end of it, east or west."

He keyed his headset. "Control, this is Pad Nedin, Rescue 3. The tsunami is hundreds of miles north of Atlantis and horizon to horizon. We're encountering gale force winds below fifteen hundred feet."

"Rescue 3, what is your location?" Control asked.

Pad checked the pathfinder. "Approximately one hundred miles northeast of Poseidia."

"Hold, Rescue 3," Control instructed.

"Hey, Zetu, punch it. Let's get to Atlantis as soon as possible."

"On it." He pushed the thrust forward.

"Rescue 3, increase altitude to a safe distance, and get to Poseidia before the tsunami. Hover and keep your video cameras on Atlantis and the tsunami. Control out."

"On it, Control. Will advise when in position. Rescue 3, out." Pad looked to Zetu. "Did I call it or what?"

"Yeah, we're going to have a front-row seat."

"I'll take the controls." Pad took the stick and immediately brought Rescue 3 to two thousand feet of elevation. He pushed the thrust to its maximum, and the red rescue ship jumped forward. "Keep an eye out for ships, as Control said."

"Right. On it." Zetu studied the ocean below them. The wind-driven smoke and ash made seeing difficult, and he strained to find anything on the water. A few minutes later, he pointed to the right of Rescue 3, "Hey, there's something white down there."

Pad took the ship off the pathfinder and turned right. Bringing the ship's nose down, he peered through the window at the ocean. A mile ahead of them, he could see something. He turned on a forward camera and zoomed in. "You're right. There's a white ship sailing east. Try to raise them on the comm." He brought the nose up and turned to fly toward the boat.

Zetu keyed his headset, "Attention, ocean vessel north of Atlantis and heading east. This is Rescue 3. Do you hear us?"

"Rescue 3. Yes, we hear you. Can you pick us up?" a frantic voice came over the comm.

"Can we rescue anyone in these winds?" Zetu asked off the comm.

Pad took a deep breath. "I guess we have to try."

"Ocean vessel, get on top of the boat, and we will pick you up."

"Will do. Thank you!" the voice on the comm declared.

He keyed his headset. "Control, this is Pad Nedin, Rescue 3.

"Rescue 3, this is Control."

"We have spotted an ocean ship heading east northeast of Poseidia. Attempting rescue in the one-hundred-eighty-mile-an-hour wind. The tsunami is north of us and closing fast."

"Rescue 3, good luck. Keep us advised. Control out."

"Rescue 3, out." Off the comm, he said, "Lots of sympathies there."

R3 swooped down toward the ship. Only two hundred feet lower, the gale hit and shoved it south. Pad increased their speed until they slowly made headway against the wind and kept an anxious eye on the tsunami wave that got closer by the second. The lower they went, the more turbulence they encountered. "This is going to be tight." He struggled with the stick.

As R3 approached the boat, the ocean started rising with the tsunami. On the camera, Pad could see the four people on it suddenly grab whatever they could to keep from slipping into the ocean as it tilted sideways. The wind blew ocean spray across the ship, and the people bent over, trying to prevent getting hit in the face.

"We have to angle this just right, or they won't be able to get aboard." Pad fought with the controls to keep it facing into the wind and on course for the ship. "Go back and open the hatch, but keep the deck from extending all the way, or it could break off."

"On it." Zetu stumbled toward the ship's hatch, holding onto the walls and hand grips.

∗ ∗ ∗ ∗ ∗

Rescue 3 was bucking up and down with the wind blasts, and walking was nearly impossible. Zetu arrived at the hatch, hung firmly onto a handhold, and punched commands into the panel next to the door. The door opened, but the deck did not extend. The wind howled into the rescue ship, and wind-driven water drenched Zetu, the floor, walls, and everything within ten feet of the doorway. He took two ropes from a cabinet near the door. He tied a short rope around his waist and the other end to the handhold by the door. Then he tied the end of a long rope to the handhold on the other side of the doorway, keeping the rest in his hand and ready to use.

"We're coming up on them," Pad said over the comm as he flew R3 beyond the boat. "Going to have to go past them to get the hatch facing them. If I turn around, the wind will push us away from them. Advise when close enough."

"On it." Using the hand holding the rope, Zetu shielded his eyes from the wind and water. "Closer…closer…now! Hover!" He keyed the panel again, and the deck extended three feet.

Rescue 3 suddenly seemed to stall, and the wind shoved it away from the boat. "Can't hover! I have to reduce speed until we match their speed," Pad said. Rescue 3 gradually came alongside the boat, although it still bucked up and down in the relentless wind.

Zetu stepped to the doorway and motioned for them to get onto Rescue 3. He threw the rope, and one man caught it as the ship bobbed up and down two feet, and the ocean got steeper and steeper.

"The tsunami is nearly on us! We have to get out of here!" Pad said over the comm, trying to adjust their altitude and speed to stay near the boat yet out of the water, which was quickly becoming vertical.

He held onto the handgrip and extended his other arm to help the man onboard. The man used the rope to get close enough and jumped to the deck. Then, gripping the handhold, the rescued man threw the rope back to the boat. The other man caught it and pulled himself close enough to jump onto the deck.

"It's coming on fast. How are we doing?" Pad asked.

"Two onboard… should have the other two… in a moment." One of the women used the rope to jump but only got hallway onto the deck, landing on her stomach. Zetu grabbed her hand and pulled her across the deck to him.

The rescued man grabbed the last woman's hand and pulled her toward the deck. As she prepared to jump, the boat suddenly tilted upright and moved away, and she slipped. A wave struck the boat, and the woman's legs washed from under her. She fell and disappeared into the water.

"Take it up, now!" Zetu shouted as the ocean was quickly becoming vertical. Pad brought R3 up and away from the boat, causing the passengers to fall to the floor.

Zetu hung onto the handgrip as he pulled the rope inside. Once on board, he keyed the panel to retract the deck and closed the hatch door. Still holding the handgrip, he helped the people into the passenger lounge. The man who had tried to help the lost woman was the last to join the others.

"Taeya's gone," he cried. "I had her, but then she was just gone." He stumbled to a seat. Dropping his head into his hands, he wept.

Catching his breath, Zetu watched the weary passengers. "I'm sorry. There was nothing else we could do. The tsunami was on us." The other two passengers scooted closer, trying to comfort the crying man. Several nodded their understanding as they strapped themselves to the seat and helped the distraught man get strapped down.

He untied the rope from his waist and let it fall to the deck as he got towels from a cabinet near the door. He handed towels to the passengers and kept one for himself. They nodded their thanks and started drying off.

"Hang on, it's a bumpy ride." Zetu walked to the cockpit, from handhold to handhold, as he dried his face and hair with one hand.

* * * * *

Zetu sat on the co-pilot seat and fastened his harness as he turned to Pad. "We lost one woman. She slipped off the deck as a wave washed over the boat, and she disappeared into the water."

"Oh, man, that's bad." Pad kept a sharp eye on the ocean. The tsunami was less than a hundred feet beneath them as Rescue 3 continued to soar up and away from it. "I couldn't wait any longer, or we would have been overrun."

"Yeah, I know." Zetu tried to dry his uniform as he watched the tsunami.

Pad keyed the comm. "Control, this is Rescue 3. We have rescued three people from the boat and are heading for Atlantis at top speed."

"Rescue 3, copy that. Control out."

Quickly rising to two thousand feet, Pad pushed the thrust to its maximum.

CHAPTER NINETEEN

As R3 rushed southwest, Atlantis seemed to emerge from the sea.

The glistening walls of Poseidia formed the boundary of the great city. The fabled concentric harbor was underwater and had been since the ocean rose over two hundred feet when Mars's oceans were sucked off to engulf Earth. Since then, the DF and firestorms across the Northern Hemisphere have melted more ice, raising the ocean another two hundred feet. Only a few large freighters were now anchored near the city as most ships were at sea transporting Atlantians and their belongings to Africa, Solantis, or the South Seas beyond Africa. The harbor, warehouses, and docks outside the walls of Poseidia were underwater. The grand entrances into the city had been sealed, and water covered the bottom half of the walls.

Inside the four-hundred-foot white walls, the fabled city of Poseidia spread up the mountain. From the oldest buildings near the harbor to the three-tiered top of the hill, the diversity of styles, blending of colors, and intricate designs had a fairytale quality. On the first of three tiers, the Imperial Palace's gleaming white marble walls, inlaid with gold, glowed in the dim light. After ten thousand years of artistry in grandeur, the palace had skyborne spires, gleaming pyramids, and sculptured gardens, yet created a breathtaking unity of its many different components.

A hundred hand-carved columns in its colonnade, surrounding an open plaza, connected the palace to Poseidia University, located on the second tier. Occupying the gentle slopes of the hill, the university comprised dozens of buildings dedicated to learning.

Adjacent to the palace, at the climax of the mountain, the Temple of the Church of the One God rose majestically into a tall steeple, whose stained-glass windows cast rainbows in every direction.

On the third tier, a vast, blue-white crystal pyramid rose a thousand feet and dwarfed the other buildings while providing electrical power to the empire. Even in the murky atmosphere, its surface rippled with energy.

The grand houses of the rich and powerful were a little farther down the hill from the palace and had the next-best ocean views. Then, below the houses of the rich, the part of Poseidia that most of its people knew as home covered the area to the walls with condos, apartments, houses, businesses, and parks.

When they could see Mt. Atlan at the island's north end and had a good view of Poseidia at the south end, Pad switched from jet engines to hover engines, turned R3 into the wind, and keyed his headset. "Control, this is Rescue 3. We hover at two thousand feet, about three miles east of Poseidia."

"Rescue 3, turn on your cameras, then record and transmit the tsunami as it arrives at Atlantis. Stay in position until ordered to leave, and then rush to ISB2 to complete your mission before the tsunami reaches it. Control out."

"On it. Rescue 3 out." Pad turned to Zetu. "We'll be broadcasting to the world!"

Pad and Zetu used the ship's two forward cameras, one for close-ups and one for a wide-angle view of the entire island. Using the close-up camera, Pad focused on one part of Atlantis at a time, starting with Poseidia. His hands trembled so much that he had to gently adjust the camera to prevent it from quivering. He noticed that Zetu had the same problem as he shifted the wide-angle camera to view parts of the island.

As they watched, three shuttles launched from the farmland north of Poseidia. "That's three shuttles." Zetu pointed at them as another aircraft took off farther north. "And there goes another ship. Not sure what it is."

"Someone waited until the last moment." Pad focused the camera on the shuttles.

"Here it comes," Zetu muttered as he stared at the tsunami.

To the north, the water rose higher and higher until it hung over Mt. Atlan like the mountain was an anthill. The tsunami rushed forward. Suddenly, all they could see to the north was a wall of water getting closer every second.

"Are you sure we're high enough?" Zetu asked fearfully.

"Yes, pretty sure." Pad focused the close-up on Mt. Atlan.

The vast wave fell on Atlantis. Starting at the beach and moving south at a horrific pace, the tsunami blasted Mt. Atlan. The close-up camera picked up every detail as the revered symbol of Atlan, Atlantis's namesake, exploded and was absorbed in a moment. The decimated fragments became part of the raging water, destroying everything in its path.

Focusing the close-up camera on the forward edge of the tsunami, Pad saw that the island was not deserted. "Oh my God, there are people down there!" Panicking people ran from the disaster but were engulfed within seconds, along with their homes, farms, barns, and fields. Trucks, tractors, and other vehicles became pebbles in the flood. Animals ran but could not outrun it, and even birds in flight were overtaken as the relentless water surged onward.

After Mt. Atlan, the water destroyed the farmlands, pastures, roadways, beaches, bridges, and everything in between. The wave of destruction blew everything away as easily as blowing fluff from a dandelion. One moment, the monuments and creations of a thousand lifetimes were there. A second later, they were gone forever.

Foot by foot, mile by mile, the raging torrent destroyed Atlantis. And its debris was added to the destructive force of the tsunami, battering everything else it encountered.

As it approached Poseidia, the tsunami engulfed the largest farms on Atlantis. Spread out around the capital city like a patchwork quilt, the farms of the oldest families in Atlantis suffered the same fate as the rest of the island. Farms that had taken millennia to build succumbed in seconds.

Then, the tsunami reached Poseidia. Pad thought the massive marble walls of the city could prevent it from being destroyed, but it was impossible. The overwhelming force of billions of gallons of water moving at hundreds of miles an hour produced a destructive power only exceeded by a nuclear bomb, a horror not seen in over fifty thousand years. The last atomic bomb destroyed most of the northern part of Atlantis, turning the continent into a series of unstable islands, most of which had already disappeared into the ocean.

Poseidia's walls burst like they were made of powder, sending pieces flying over the city and into the ocean beyond. The tsunami plunged into Poseidia, reducing structures to debris in seconds and adding it to the wave. The roiling, tumbling mass swept up the hill toward the palace, university, and the Temple.

Pad couldn't tell if the roiling water destroyed everything or if it was a thousand feet of it falling on things. It was all happening so fast that it was impossible to understand more than that everything was destroyed. Nothing escaped the tsunami.

The Imperial Palace and Poseidia University at the top of the hill blew apart like they were models. The marble columns fractured and disappeared in a moment. The buildings looked like a giant hammer had hit them, and they exploded into small pieces and were immediately sucked into the raging water. Hundreds of people were on the plaza, running toward the university or away from the tsunami.

Many more people were already on the ground due to the hurricane-force wind. They all disappeared into the raging water in an instant.

Pad was unsure, but it seemed like the Temple of the Church of the One God suddenly emitted a brilliant flash of light as the tsunami hit it. The steeple toppled away from the building, and then the entire complex burst into shattered pieces and disappeared into the maelstrom.

The crystal tower exploded as the wave hit it, sending jagged bolts of energy in every direction as the glass-like sides of the pyramid shattered. Like lightning from a hell of liquid fury, silver-white streamers flashed into the black clouds, instantly dispelling the gloom. Then, as quickly as it happened, the tower was gone, the dark skies returned, and the tsunami rolled onward.

The instant the crystal tower was destroyed, Rescue 3's power suddenly died. Pad quickly switched from the hover engines to the jet engines. "What a dummy! I should have known we were running on broadcasted power and switched over when we arrived."

Zetu didn't say anything as he stared slack-jawed at the destruction before them.

After the manmade structures were destroyed, the mountain surrendered to the raging torrent of the tsunami. The top of the hill collapsed and shifted toward the harbor below it. Leaning farther and farther, the mountain disintegrated and became part of the relentless mass of churning water. As the tsunami fell on what was left of Poseidia Harbor, pleasure craft and ocean-going freight ships were smashed into shattered splinters and added to the deluge.

After the tsunami devoured Atlantis and moved on, the ocean covered everything. All Pad and Zetu could see was turbulent, fast-moving water to the horizon.

Speechless, Pad looked at Zetu. His cheeks were as wet as his own. "I feel like I've been gut-kicked."

"I'm sick. I can't believe it," Zetu moaned as he held his stomach.

They could hear their passengers moaning behind them as the comm broke through their reflection. "Rescue 3, end transmission, and get to ISB2 as quickly as possible. The coast of Nolantis should slow the tsunami and allow you time to rescue the governor and his people. Hurry. Control out."

"Control, on it. Rescue 3, out," Pad said, turning the cameras off. He keyed the pathfinder to ISB2 and slammed the thrust to the stops.

Rescue 3 shot southwest toward ISB2.

* * * * *

Acton and Cass watched the tsunami on Rescue 1's monitor.

They were approaching New Hope when the broadcast took over their monitor. Since they were already in line to land on the outer bay, they had no time to stop and concentrate on what they saw.

"Oh my God, my family home is gone." Acton watched the tsunami consume Athu Farms. "It's gone! It's all gone." He sobbed as tears ran down his cheeks.

"Mine too, and the university, the palace, the Temple –"

"The palace! Oh God, the Temple, too." Acton could barely see through his tears.

With the broadcast throughout Rescue 1, they could hear their passengers moaning as they watched it in the passenger lounge.

"Rescue 1, approach landing deck. Commence hover mode and enter Spaceport 1," Control said over their comm.

"On it, Control." Acton wiped his eyes, switched to hover engines, and flew into the bay.

* * * * *

In New Hope's Control, Cana, Max, and Ono watched it on the big screen.

"That was Nora! Those shuttles, that was Nora. I thought she left an hour ago." Cana watched in stunned shock as the tsunami laid waste to Atlantis. As the crystal tower went down, the lights suddenly dimmed, then came back to normal as the power switched to the New Hope's internal generators.

"Gone…it's all gone," Emperor Maximus groaned as he leaned on a desk with his head in his hands. "A hundred thousand years to build, ten minutes to destroy. My palace, my garden, my orchids… gone," he cried.

"We are blessed to be alive. Think of all the people still there," Master Ono said. "The Synod of Twelve was still in the Temple. They refused to leave their lifelong home." He started to sing the church's chant to calm himself as tears cascaded down his cheeks.

Emperor Maximus and Commander Athu joined Master Ono's song. Throughout Control, captains, workers, secretaries, and receptionists wept as they watched the destruction of their world and, one by one, sang with the others. Usually, it provided relief, but it didn't seem to help this time. They continued to sing anyway.

✳ ✳ ✳ ✳ ✳

In the Temple auditorium, Genesi watched the end of Atlantis with two thousand people.

The destruction of the Poseidia Temple was like a knife in her heart, and she wept. She loved that Temple and its warm colors and wooden features. She couldn't watch anymore and covered her face to have some privacy. Above her, the big screen showed the end of Atlantis, then went blank and retracted back into the curtains above.

Genesi turned her chair to face the audience and gazed at nearly two thousand people in the theater. They stared solemnly back at her until she dried her eyes and sauntered to the lectern.

Genesi had to clear her throat to speak. "I don't know what to say," Genesi softly said, and her voice was automatically amplified. "Like you, I am in pain." She stood a little straighter as she felt her spiritual strength returning.

"God tells us that He is the source of all love, care, and mercy. He tells us to 'Go with God' as he is always there for us. We are powerless in the face of nature's wrath, but we're not alone. Let us seek comfort, relief from our pain, and solace for our agony by singing our love song to God."

She stood straighter, closed her eyes, and started to sing. The large singing bowls on both sides of the stage picked up her amplified song and added octaves, one higher and one lower. A moment later, nearly two thousand other souls joined her song, and the singing bowls added their tones to its resonating sound.

* * * * *

Nora and her Gen-x AG workers watched the tsunami on the shuttle's screens.

"Oh my God!" Nora exclaimed as the picture of their shuttles came on the screen. "We just barely made it."

Cesa Gen-Athu quieted his grandchildren as they wailed. The Gen-x AG people found it difficult to sit on seats made for standard humans because they had to fold their legs uncomfortably under their bodies or leave them dangling off the cushion. "That was too close."

The captain's voice came over the ship's speakers. "It's all gone, Professor. All gone."

"Thank God we are alive. What of all the people who were still on Atlantis?" Nora cried for all the people who were lost, her home, her farm, and her heritage.

"All dead. All my relatives, friends, and neighbors are gone," Cesa sobbed. He turned to Nora, sitting across the aisle. "What will become of us? What if Cana will not allow us onto New Hope?"

"He will, Cesa. He will." Nora uttered a silent prayer that he would do so.

CHAPTER TWENTY

Magnus Lipo landed the shuttle near the new camp of the girls' tribe.

The camp was close to the largest river in Solantis and wasn't completely set up. Though only a dozen huts were partially erected, the entire tribe turned out to celebrate the girls' return. While the food was being prepared for a feast, Mag gave the chief and his men the blast rifles they had taken from the bandits. Then, because they had never had guns, he had to show them how to use the weapons.

Cat was not happy about being excluded from teaching the men how to use the weapons simply because she was a woman. But instead of making a scene, Cat and Saba helped the girls settle into their parents's hut, where they were lovingly cared for. It looked like the girls would eventually be accepted into everyday tribal life again. Sometimes, after being raped, the victims were shunned and treated like it was their fault. The thought made Cat angry all over again.

After the feast, Mag, Opin, and Saba loaded the tribe's gifts of food and blankets, while Cat made a final visit to give each girl a metal water container with a screw-on top. No one in the tribe had anything like it, and Cat knew it would make them feel special about something positive. Afterward, the entire tribe turned out to see them depart. Magnus flew the shuttle while Cat, Opin, and Saba waved goodbye. Underway, Cat joined Mag in the cockpit.

"I set the pathfinder for home. Do we need to stop anywhere else?" Cat asked.

"No, we need to take a break, get cleaned up, and prepare for our next action."

"I like that. I need to wash all my stuff and work on new clothes."

"It's been a while since we checked on the rest of the world. Let's see if there is anything we need to know." Mag turned on the fleet's comm unit he had taken from a downed aircraft.

As soon as it came on, Commander Cana Athu's voice sounded like he was in the middle of something and announced that Mars would collide with Earth within twenty-four to forty-eight hours.

Mag switched on the monitors throughout the shuttle so they could all listen to the commander's speech. When it was done, Mag turned the comm off. "My God, I never thought it would actually happen. The end of the world –"

"Should we go to the fleet? He said we should get there as soon as possible." Cat stared at Mag, wide-eyed and panicky.

"He's talking about *their* shuttles, dear, not ones they thought had been destroyed."

"But they wouldn't turn us away, would they?"

"I don't know, and I also don't think this ship could get there. It's not airtight, and we don't have enough oxygen anyway. After all, I built it from pieces of half a dozen ships, and I didn't worry about making it safe for space travel." Mag pointed at the crude seams he had welded together.

"Oh, I didn't think of that," Cat admitted. "I guess we better head south then. Do we have time to go home and get our stuff?"

"I think so. The commander said twenty-four hours, and that should allow plenty of time." He checked their location. "Hey, the pathfinder is showing two other ships nearby."

Cat peered out her side window. "I can't see anything."

"Go back and have Opin look. He has good eyes."

"Yeah, good idea." Cat hurried into the passenger compartment. "Opin, the pathfinder is showing two ships behind us. Can you see anything?"

Opin moved to a window on the ship's right side and looked out. The hazy skies made it difficult to see, so he pressed closer to the window to look behind their shuttle. "Yes, two ships. Cannot tell what. Too small. Behind us."

"Keep watching." Cat went back to the cockpit. "Opin sees two ships behind us." She focused the rear camera on the two dots. Minutes crawled by, and the ships got steadily bigger on the screen. Finally, they were big enough to identify. "I think it's two shuttles."

"Damn! Do you think it's the bandits' shuttles?"

"If so, what can they do? They can't force us to land, can they?"

"They can follow us home and attack us there."

Cat leaned closer to the monitor to study the ships behind them. "There's something strange about those ships." She adjusted the camera again to make the image bigger. "Yeah, looks like they have removed a few side windows."

"Let's get out of here." Mag shoved the thrust to its maximum setting. The shuttle jumped forward.

"They're shooting at us! I see muzzle flashes from the side windows."

"We can't return fire while they are behind us." When Mag built the shuttle, he added a blast cannon from a crashed fighter on the front of the shuttle. "Load the cannon. We'll have to outmaneuver them and try to get a shot."

"They have sped up."

"I'd hate to sit in a window seat with no window." Mag grimaced.

Cat rushed into the passenger compartment and stopped at a floor hatch to the storage compartment beneath the passenger area. She climbed down, inserted a belt of five shells into the cannon's magazine, and climbed back up. "Opin, you and Saba move away from the windows and strap in. We're going to have to get away from those guys."

"Yes." Opin sat near Saba and helped her fasten her straps.

Cat returned to the pilot compartment. "Ready."

"They're closer, even though we are near maximum speed. Everyone strapped in?"

"Yes, we're ready for action." Cat primed the cannon.

"I'm going up into the clouds, so watch the monitor. If they stay on the same course, I will loop around so we can get the cannon on them."

"Got it."

As the shuttle flew into the dark clouds, Mag checked the gauge to ensure the filters cleaned the air, as they had very little onboard oxygen. The cabin got darker and darker as the clouds got thicker.

"They are still on our course, so they must have a working pathfinder." Cat leaned over their pathfinder to be sure she didn't miss any deviation.

"All right, I'll do a one-hundred-eighty-degree loop. Be ready to shoot, but only one shot. We don't have enough ammo for rapid fire. Aim straight ahead, and I will head straight for them. That should be the safest place with their guns out of their side windows."

"Got it." Cat slid forward on her seat to get a good grip on the cannon. She wrapped her hand around the stock, put her finger on the trigger, and held herself in place with her other hand.

Mag brought the shuttle upward sharply. With the gravity increasing, he brought the ship vertical and then over, so they flew upside down, causing stuff throughout the ship to fall to the ceiling. Then, when the shuttle was back to its starting elevation, he flipped it sideways so it was right side up again. Unless the bandits monitored their pathfinder very carefully, they wouldn't notice their victim was now approaching them. The clouds were getting thinner as Mag brought the shuttle back down.

"There they are." Mag pointed at their ship.

They swept down toward the bandit shuttle, quickly closing the distance. As they got close enough to ensure a good shot, they saw the second shuttle angling toward them.

"Shoot, Cat!" Mag shouted when he saw the other ship.

Cat pulled the trigger, and the big gun bucked. The moment she shot, the second bandit shuttle opened fire with three or four weapons. Cat's cannon shot hit the first shuttle right where she had aimed, the pilot's cockpit. The shuttle exploded and immediately tumbled toward Earth.

Mag, guessing that the other shuttle would expect them to go up again, dove toward the ground. As he took the shuttle down, one of the bandit's shots hit the side window behind the pilot's cockpit. The shuttle shuddered as the wind suddenly burst into the cabin.

"We're hit!" Mag said. "See how bad, but come right back."

Buffeted by the wind, Cat clung to the walls as she hurried into the passenger compartment. Finding Opin and Saba huddled together with their hands over their eyes, she gave them one of the tribe's blankets, and they covered themselves as she hurried back to her seat.

"The first window is shot out, and the wind is blowing everything all over the cabin, but Sara and Opin are all right. I gave them a blanket to block the wind."

"Good, hang on."

Mag turned sharply to the right, heading north, then steeply up. He watched what the other ship was doing on the pathfinder. The bandit's shuttle followed whatever Mag did only a moment later.

Mag looked through his side window. Below the ship, the blue ocean extended forever. "We're over the ocean, so we must be over the Middle Sea between Solantis and Nolantis. We're heading slightly east of due north, so we should be over Atlantis soon. Keep watch." Cat nodded. "This close to Atlantis, I better put the comm back on."

As soon as it came on, another announcement was in progress, warning of an enormous, thousand-foot tsunami heading south in the Atlantic Ocean accompanied by gale-force winds.

"You got to be kidding! What's next?" Mag checked the pathfinder, and they were flying at a thousand feet. "Watch for the tsunami, especially if strong winds accompany it."

"On it, Dad."

Mag watched their pathfinder. The bandits were still behind them and didn't seem to be getting closer. Suddenly, the shuttle bucked as though hit by an unseen hand. "What the…" He struggled to keep the shuttle flying north with their forward progress cut in half. He glanced at the airspeed gauge and saw it was over one hundred eighty miles per hour.

"The tsunami!" Cat cried as she pointed ahead of them.

It was distant, though it looked closer. Mag studied their monitor and saw the wind was slowing the bandit's shuttle even more than theirs. He had time to act, but they had to get out of the wind and high enough to avoid the tsunami. Mag pulled back on the stick, bringing the shuttle sharply up.

The wind speed at fifteen hundred feet was less than a hundred miles an hour. Below them, still far away, they could see Atlantis and Poseidia, the gleaming white city.

"Control, this is Pad Nedin, Rescue 3," the comm blared. "There is a huge tsunami quickly heading south." They listened to Rescue 3's conversation until it ended.

"Must be another ship close by." Mag studied the monitor again. "Yeah, about ten miles in front of us."

The comm came on again. "Rescue 3, increase altitude to a safe distance, and get to Poseidia before the tsunami. Hover and keep your video cameras on Atlantis and the tsunami. Control out."

"On it, Control. Will advise when in position. Rescue 3 out."

"Those guys will be able to video the whole thing," Mag said.

"I think we better do something about the bandits behind us. I don't think the rescue ship needs more to worry about," Cat said.

The comm came on again as Rescue 3 agreed to rescue the people on a white ship.

"Those guys are nuts," Mag said. "They're going to try a rescue in the face of a tsunami and two-hundred-mile-an-hour winds. They're either crazy or a lot braver than I am." He searched the sky for any sight of the rescue ship.

"Braver, I bet," Cat said.

Mag turned sharply east and watched the monitor for what the bandits would do. They seemed slower than earlier, so Mag checked for their altitude. "Hey, the bandits may be in for a surprise. They're flying about nine hundred feet, so they must not have a working comm."

Cat broke away from watching the tsunami to stare at the monitor. "They better watch out. Here it comes."

Mag turned north, keeping an eye on the wall of water coming straight at them. "That rescue ship better get out of there." Mag could see Rescue 3 close to the boat, and a moment later, it took off nearly straight up.

Mag returned to the monitor and saw the bandit shuttle had also turned north. "I think those guys are about to get a surprise."

Cat flipped the monitor to the rear camera and focused on the bandit's shuttle. The tsunami rose under them as it surged south. The bandit ship suddenly pulled up, trying to escape the tsunami. But traveling six hundred miles an hour, the top of the tsunami curled over the bandit's shuttle, breaking it into pieces, and it disappeared into the water.

"Nasty, way to go." Mag cringed.

"Doesn't bother me. Good riddance."

"Where should we go?" Mag watched the rescue ship head west and away from them.

"South, like the man said."

"Solantis or Africa?" Mag asked.

"You know those weren't the only bandits who would love to get their hands on us. I remember a particularly nasty band of them farther south in Solantis." Cat didn't like thinking about all the bandits they had encountered over the last three years.

"Yeah, you have a point there. And, since the tsunami will destroy everything at home, we better head for Africa. We don't know anyone there."

"My thinking, too."

Mag flew southeast as the tsunami covered everything beneath them.

Cat went into the back, where the wind blew stuff around the passenger compartment. She walked past where Olin and Saba huddled under the blanket to the cabinets near their small kitchen. Finding a roll of sticky tape, she returned to the access door and entered the storage area. She quickly found a large box, cut off its side, shoved it into the passenger area, and then climbed up after it.

"Hey, Opin, help me." Cat shook his shoulder.

Opin pushed the blanket off and stood. "What?"

Holding the cardboard, she pointed at the broken window, and Opin nodded and took the other end. As he held it over the window, Cat taped it firmly over the window. The wind still blew in, but not nearly as much.

Cat, Opin, and Saba started cleaning up as the shuttle flew southeast toward Africa.

CHAPTER TWENTY-ONE

The caravan hurried south, but they weren't going fast enough.

Two hours south of Vandia, the country roads were much worse, with large rocks, deep holes, and brush growing into the roadway. The vehicles had to slow down, and the contents of Zeth's trailer still bounced around hard enough to break things. While X'to, Dimitri, and Perta had no trouble staying close, Kona and his trailer full of animals were a hundred feet behind the rest. As usual, Volf faithfully stayed behind Kona, bringing up the rear. Zeth stopped, forcing the rest of the vehicles to halt behind him.

"We must do something with the animals. They're slowing us down too much," Zeth said as he walked past the three trucks to await Kona and the animal trailer.

"We can't go any faster," X'to said, getting out of his truck. "There isn't a real road in this part of Africa."

"What's going on?" Perta said as he and Dimitri joined the others.

"Let's wait for Kona and Volf." Zeth pointed at them as they drove up.

Kona pulled up behind Perta's vehicle, and Volf stopped behind him a moment later. "What's going on?" Kona asked as he joined them.

"Kona, we must go faster. We should knock the animals out so they will not get hurt, bouncing around in their trailer." Zeth led them back to Kona's trailer.

"Yeah, I guess so. I hate to do it, but it's important, right?"

"Yes, we only have twenty-four hours to get to safety. Do we still have the tranquilizing shots the vet gave us a few months ago?"

"Yes." Kona started looking through his boxes of supplies.

Suddenly, the Eby's horn started frantically honking. They whirled around to see Zuzu standing in the opened roof of the Eby and pointing to their left.

Looking where she pointed, they saw men rushing toward the vehicles. The tall grass hid all but their heads and weapons, bobbing up and down as they ran, and they were within two hundred feet and closing quickly. Suddenly, the bandits' leader opened fire on the vehicles, and the rest of the bandits started shooting, but they were too far away to hit anything.

"Down! Everyone down." Zeth crouched and hurried toward the Eby. "Get behind the vehicles. Women and children under the trucks. Now!" He ran along the far side of the vehicles from the bandits, and the other men returned to their rigs. Grabbing his blast rifle and laser pistol from behind the driver's seat, he handed the laser pistol to Zuzu as she got the children out of the Eby. Better armed, Zeth turned to X'to. "Your family should join mine. Then go into the grass and come at them from their left."

X'to nodded as he helped his family get under the Edy. Armed with the laser pistol, Zuzu joined her children under the Eby. Its rear door was open, and the two large dogs leaped out and ran into the tall grass toward the bandits.

"I'll be right back," Zeth said to Zuzu. "Keep down, and don't hesitate to shoot if they get within thirty feet of you." She nodded as she quieted the crying children. X'to's wife, Saba, and their two children crawled under the Eby to lie beside her.

Zeth ran to Dimitri and Perta's vehicles and waved them closer. "Perta, stay with me, and we'll meet them head-on. Dimitri, go back past Kona into the grass and circle around to come at them from their right. Blast them when you get there. Stop and ask Kona and Volf to stay near their vehicles in case any bandits get close."

"Right." Perta turned to his family, "Stay down, but don't hesitate to shoot if you have to." He handed Geta their laser pistol as she helped their two children get under their truck.

After making sure his wife and children were hidden, Dimitri stopped next to Kona and Volf and told them the plan. As they quickly got behind their trucks, Dimitri crouched down and ran around Kona's trailer into the tall grass.

Zeth and Perta knelt by Perta's vehicle. They could only see the bandits sporadically, mostly their heads bobbing up and down as they ran. "You take the first one on the right. I'll take the first one on the left," Zeth said. Perta nodded as he brought his blaster up to his shoulder. Zeth straightened up for a better aim and brought the blaster snuggly onto his shoulder.

The bandits were less than a hundred feet away when Zeth and Perta fired. The first two shots hit the first two men as they became partially visible through the grass. The other bandits stopped and brought their blast guns to their shoulders. With angry shouts, they started shooting.

As the bandits came within range, X'to and Dimitri opened fire from both sides. As they started firing, Zeth and Perta stood and fired as quickly as they could aim. Further back in the caravan, Kona and Volf began shooting at the bandits from a fourth direction.

Six of the outlaws quickly went down. The rest seemed confused and tried to find cover, but there wasn't any. They made easy targets as they scurried around.

Zeth and Perta started toward the bandits while X'to and Dimitri closed in from both sides. Zeth knew the outlaws would be much deadlier if they could stop and aim. So, as soon as they hesitated, he rushed forward and started shooting as quickly as he could pull the trigger. Next to him, Perta did the same.

Suddenly, six more bandits went down. As they fell, one of the Mercu's dogs attacked another by leaping for his throat. The bandit fell backward, trying to keep the two-hundred-pound dog from ripping out his throat. Another bandit aimed at the dog, but the second dog leaped on him before he could fire, knocking the bandit over. As they fought with the dogs, Zeth shot one, and Perta shot the other.

With eight more outlaws quickly killed, the tallest of the remaining four lifted his blaster overhead and shouted, "Don't shoot! Don't shoot!"

Zeth saw them surrendering and shouted, "Stop firing!"

Another bandit, somehow ignored because he was away from the remaining four, crept closer and kneeled to aim at Zeth. As he did, both dogs attacked him. He fell back, and his rifle discharged as he tried to fend them off.

Zeth hurried to where he fought with the dogs while Perta, X'to, and Dimitri guarded the other four bandits. As soon as Zeth disarmed him, he turned back to the others. "Stop, or everyone is dead! Drop your guns."

The last four bandits dropped their guns, and Zeth called off the dogs, allowing the bandit to join his comrades.

"Now what?" The tallest bandit asked.

"Get out of here and never come near us again," Zeth said.

"We'll die without our guns!" The man shouted angrily.

"You'll die before you get any of these guns," Perta shouted, stepping forward. He was taller than the tallest attacker and much more muscular. "Leave while we are feeling generous."

The remaining bandits ran back the way they came.

"Watch them! Make sure they don't pick up any weapons," Zeth shouted.

X'to and Dimitri walked through the field of fallen men, making sure they were dead and picking up weapons and ammunition. As X'to approached one of the "dead" bandits, he raised his blast rifle and aimed at him. Dropping what he had collected, X'to dove to the side and shot the man from a few feet away. As his friends ran toward him, X'to got to his feet. "One of the dead ones was aiming at me."

Zeth and Perta joined them, carefully made sure of the dead, and collected their weapons and ammunition. When they returned to their vehicles, they found the women and children gathered on the far side of the Eby, and the children were starting to calm down after all the noise and confusion.

"Everyone all right?" Zeth asked as he dumped the bandits' weapons and ammo into the trailer, and the others added what they had collected.

"Yes." Zuzu hugged him.

"I got a bit of a scratch." Kona hobbled up and sat on the bumper of the Edy.

Zuzu and Shea found a bloody hole in his right thigh, bleeding freely through his pants, and Shea immediately got the medical kit from the trailer.

"A shot shattered my truck's headlight, and a piece punctured my leg." Kona tried to stop the bleeding with a handkerchief.

"We better keep watch while he's getting patched up," Zeth said. Perta joined him, and they climbed onto the Eby to watch for returning bandits.

Zuzu and Shea cut his pant leg open to reveal a bloody wound from glass buried deep in his thigh. Shea, his wife, gave him a shot to numb the pain, then dug the glass out. Afterward, she applied disinfectant to the wound and bandaged it. By the time he was taken care of, X'to and Volf had the animals knocked out and tied so they wouldn't hurt themselves if they came to.

While Kona was being doctored, the other women prepared food for everyone. Zuzu got the jug, poured a bowl of water for the dogs, and fed them from a bag of last night's leftovers.

"Let's eat on the way. We only have a few more hours of daylight and must get as far south as possible." Zeth walked over to Kona. "Are you able to drive?"

"Yeah, I think so. If not, Shea can drive."

"Good, honk if you need anything." Zeth returned to his Eby and put the blaster behind the seat before starting it. He made sure Zuzu and the children were strapped in, then glanced back at the other trucks. Assured everyone was ready, he pulled forward.

Minutes later, only the dead remained at the site of the battle.

CHAPTER TWENTY-TWO

Rescue 1 and Shuttle 15 entered Spaceport 1 of SS New Hope.

As soon as they touched down, four tractors, driven by people in spacesuits, raced out and moved the ships into the inner bay. The tractors returned to the outer port, and the hundred-foot metal doors closed behind them with a loud bang. When the doors were sealed, air flooded the inner bay, and other tractors driven by uniformed workers positioned the ships in their respective stalls. Once in place, magnets on their landing gear secured the two ships to the metal floor with a distinctive clank.

Rescue 1's hatch opened, and stairs with handrails lowered from the ship to the floor. "So, you understand, right?" Acton said to Trice as they stopped at the door. "I will meet you at the Flight Club when I get permission for a shuttle. Wait for me there."

"No problem, I will tell Cass and Farl. You go ahead."

"Thanks, Trice. I appreciate it."

Acton stepped onto the stairs and jumped up. A latticework of multicolored ropes throughout the inner bay crisscrossed the area above the parked ships. He grabbed the green rope and pulled himself hand-over-hand toward the lobby, the easiest and quickest way to cross the bay in zero gravity. As he neared the lifts, he glanced back and saw Trice helping people down the stairs, and Shuttle 15's passengers carefully used the stairs. Standing was difficult for people not used to zero gravity, and going down the stairs was worse. As the medical team arrived at R1, he refocused on arriving at the lifts.

He used a vertical rope to pull himself to the floor. Grabbing a handrail near the bank of lifts, Acton joined five other people as one arrived. When it opened, they each selected one of the ten seats. No one could stand because the lift rotated around the inside of a shaft, spinning until it matched the revolutions of the habitable part of the ship. The process was the only way to go from zero gravity to a level of gravity nearly equal to Earth's. Acton pressed himself into a snug, over-padded seat, and it wrapped around his body and held him firmly in place. The lift launched as soon as sensors confirmed all the passengers were snugly in place.

A few minutes later, it reached the central lift lobby. The doors opened, and Acton hurried past the bank of lifts going to the lower half of the ship to the lifts that could take him up to Command. Once everyone had entered, it went up but seemed slow. After traveling from the port bay to the lift lobby – halfway across the spaceship – at speeds matching the revolutions of the sphere, the internal lift seemed to take much longer. Traveling a hundred and fifty floors in less than two minutes, the momentum pressed him down and made him feel like he had gained weight.

The lift arrived at Command, the top floor of the ship, and Acton jumped up due to the sudden release of pressure and loss of the phantom weight. After a moment to regain his balance, he hurried toward Control in the heart of Command.

Command was on the top floor and, therefore, the smallest inhabitable floor of the sphere. The level above it was heavily shielded to protect against harmful elements encountered in space. The wide aisle from the lifts to Control was lined with cubicles and desks for human and Gen-x workers, offices for managers, and waiting areas.

Many people who worked at desks along the aisle were Gen-x AD and, having four arms and two legs, routinely worked on two computers and two comm units. Most of the cubicles and offices had transparent, unbreakable, glasslike walls to easily see who occupied each one. Acton had been to Command and Control many times and knew most people by sight, if not by name. He acknowledged people with a wave, a brisk hello, or a head nod as he rushed toward his father's office. At the entrance to Control, he was stopped by a guard, a hoops teammate from his university days.

"Identification, please." Sergeant Herzer said, trying to sound official while grinning.

"Captain Acton Athu to see Commander Athu," he said as he came to attention.

"Yes, thank you, sir!" Herzer executed a crisp salute as he came to attention.

Acton grinned, then gave him a shoulder nudge as he went by. "Not a problem, Herzer."

Entering Control's lobby, he urgently scanned the room for his father, seeing the wall of monitors, the big screen showing Mars and Earth, and captains and other officers hurrying in one direction or another. Acton recognized the receptionist immediately. Alsa Gen-Aga, a blue-eyed, voluptuous female Gen-x AD, was engrossed with two computers, keyboards, and comm units.

"Hi, Alsa. Is my father here?"

"Hello, Acton," she said sensually. Using her upper right arm, she pointed at a group of people in an animated discussion in front of Cana's office.

"Thanks." He walked a few feet toward the group, then stopped. Pretending to study the wall of monitors, he watched for an opportunity to interrupt his father. A minute later, he saw Cana break away and hurry toward him.

"Good to see you." Cana shook his hand.

"Thanks, Father. I'm glad to see you, too. Is Mother here?"

Cana's smile disappeared, and he frowned. "Should be here any moment. Her shuttles left Atlantis just moments before the tsunami. For a while, I thought I had lost her."

"My God, I didn't know. She's safe, right?"

"Yes, she's safe.

"I'm so glad to hear it. Father –"

An officer rushed up. "Just a minute." Cana turned away to listen to the officer.

Acton stepped back and waited impatiently. A minute later, Cana finished speaking by giving the officer instructions. Acton stepped closer. "Father, I have a favor to ask."

Cana studied the wall monitors, distracted by whatever news he had received. "Hmm, yes, what is it?"

"Mya is still at Aswanga Mine. I need a shuttle to rescue her."

Cana stared at the monitors as if not hearing him. "They have shuttles they can use."

"Their shuttles are damaged and won't make it. I need to go get them."

Cana turned back to Acton. "Impossible!" He loudly declared. "There are no more rescue missions because the fleet is moving away from the planets. There's no time!"

"Father, I have to rescue her!" Acton said urgently and louder than he intended. "I love her. I can't leave her there to die!"

"Don't raise your voice to me!" Cana shouted, his angry face only a few inches from Acton's. "I cannot allow you to risk your life. Things are getting worse by the minute, and if you leave, you won't be able to get back."

Another officer came to attention a few feet away. Cana immediately turned to the officer, leaving Acton sputtering. A minute later, he returned. "I must attend to another emergency. Report to periphery defense." Cana turned away and rushed toward his office, leaving Acton stunned and staring after him.

"Father!" Acton waited for him to look back, for an opportunity to beg him for a shuttle, but Cana quickly disappeared into the group of people in front of his office. "Damn! Damn! Damn!" He turned away and stormed from Control.

* * * * *

Pushing through the group of officers, Cana entered his office, closing the door behind him.

He lifted the comm unit on his desk. "Nora?"

"The shuttles landed a few minutes ago, but the port manager won't let us leave the port," Nora said.

"Why not?"

"Because I brought Cesa and the others with me. I couldn't leave them there to die."

"For God's sake, Nora! You know we can't bring AG workers to the fleet ships. They're just not designed for it."

"Nonsense, I told you that rule was wrong when you told me about it. It's just plain wrong. You have Gen-x office workers, and I remember a pretty one in your offices, Alsa, or something."

"That's not the same, and you know it. AG workers are too big and clumsy to be on the fleet ships. There's no way to bring them into the habitable part of the ship because the lifts aren't built for their bodies."

"Nonsense. They can enter the ship and will be invaluable in the agricultural program. My program. They're here, and you said there would be no more missions, so they stay. Send me someone to figure out how to get them to the AG deck." Nora watched Cesa's Gen-x family try to climb down the steep shuttle stairs on four legs in zero gravity. If the situation weren't so urgent, their antics would be comic. The young Gen-x children had fun trying to stand, walk, stop floating, stay upright, and not bump into each other.

"Damn it, Nora! How come no one in this family does what they're supposed to do?"

"What's that supposed to mean?"

"Never mind. Oh, damn it to hell! Have the port manager call me!" Cana slammed the comm unit down.

✳ ✳ ✳ ✳ ✳

Nora motioned for the port manager to come to her. She wasn't used to zero gravity and constantly had problems moving around while maintaining any semblance of dignity.

Kensa Storn, the port manager on SS New Hope, easily walked across the bay as though natural. "Yes, Professor?" He was a large man in his forties with short, graying hair.

"Commander Cana Athu, my husband, said to tell you to call him. But before you do so, get some carts to the shuttles so we can unload."

Storn stared incredulously at her for a moment, then returned to the flight desk. He had been the manager for several years and knew when he was beaten. He sent a crew to the shuttles and then called the commander.

Cana answered abruptly. "Yes?"

"Commander, this is Port Manager Kensa Storn. Professor Athu said you wanted to talk with me."

"Yes, Kensa, the Gen-x AG workers will join us onboard New Hope. Please help them deplane and maneuver the lifts to enter the ship."

"Hmm, how do I do that, sir?"

"How the hell do I know!" Cana shouted. "Call engineering or someone to get it done." He slammed the comm down.

"Yes, right away, sir." Kensa chuckled as he ended the call. Grinning, he placed another call to engineering. Apparently, he wasn't the only one taking orders.

✳ ✳ ✳ ✳ ✳

Leaving Control, Acton rushed through Command toward the bank of lifts.

He couldn't remember a time when he had been refused something important. Even as a child, he always got what he needed. He tried to remember how he made that happen but couldn't think of anything specific he had done. All he did was ask his parents, relatives, officers, instructors, or whoever, and someone always stepped up and made sure he got it. How could he do so now? Who could he see?

Acton arrived at the lifts and cut off other people to get on the next one. Facing the back corner so others couldn't see him wiping tears from his eyes, he clenched and re-clenched his fists. His whole body twitched as he angrily swore under his breath. Acton ached to hit something, yet he was crying.

The Flight Club was near the central lift lobby and the middle of the ship. Acton was so immersed in contemplating what to do that it only seemed to take a minute to arrive. He hurried to the club's entrance, spotted Cass, Farl, and Trice at the bar, and rushed through the busy room to join them.

"Uh oh, you look mad enough to charge a crazed bull," Farl said as Acton threw himself onto a stool next to Cass.

"You didn't get permission, did you?" Cass asked.

Acton shook his head and mimicked his father, "No new missions. It's too dangerous. There's no time." He flounced, staring at the floor as his mind raced.

"Now what?" Trice asked from the next stool.

Acton's eyes suddenly opened wide, and he jumped to his feet. "Now, we try something different." He raced back toward the lifts. "Wait for me. I'll be right back."

"Well, I guess we'll wait. Barman, another beer." Cass signaled the man behind the bar.

Acton arrived at his parents' apartment and keyed the panel by the door to enter. No one was home, so he decided to try his mother's office on the AG deck. The only food raised in New Hope was fruit, herbs, and spices. All the rest was grown on the agricultural ship, Grand Poseidia, one of the three spaceships in the New Hope triad. Since the agriculture levels were in the bottom half of the ship, he took the lift to the center lobby, walked across to the lifts to the lower half of the ship, and took the next one. A few minutes later, he arrived at the first AG floor.

Acton stepped off the lift and abruptly stopped when he saw a Gen-x AG person. "Cesa? Is that you?"

"Acton! Yes, it's me." Cesa wore his overalls and work shirt as though still on the farm.

"What are you doing here?" Acton stared at him like he was an apparition.

"Your mother insisted we come with her to New Hope. When we got here, they nearly arrested us, including your mother. Your father had to use an imperial command to prevent it," Cesa chuckled. "Your family has great power."

Acton nodded. "Yeah, it never hurts to have an uncle who is the emperor and a father who is the fleet commander."

"They're making room for us on this floor. Nora sent me here to find a place for all the boxes we brought from the farm. The rest of my family will be here soon."

"Is that where Mother is?"

"No, she went to see your father."

"Well, that doesn't help."

"Sorry?" Cesa asked.

"I needed her help with father. If he's upset with her, she won't be any help, that's for sure." Acton placed a hand on Cesa's shoulder. "It's good to see you here. You've always been part of the family."

"It's good to be here, Acton. Thank you."

"Tell my mother that I'll see her later."

"Yes, of course."

Acton retraced his steps to the lift and took it back to the central lift lobby. Then, he took another one to the level of the royal family's apartments. Walking toward his parents' suite, he spotted Master Ono walking toward him. "Uncle Ono," he called, spontaneously smiling.

"*Uncle*? I'm an uncle now? When did that happen?" Ono chuckled.

"Well, I have always thought of you as an uncle. I've seen you around the house more than my real uncle, so I think you qualify."

"I'm moving up in the world." He puffed his chest up and grinned. "Now, I'm a member of the royal house. I'll try not to let it go to my head."

"Good to see you, *Master* Ono. Is that better?"

Ono chuckled. "I think I like uncle better. Where are you going?"

"I'm trying to find my mother."

"Hmm, not a good time to pop in on them. Why don't you come to visit me instead?"

They walked toward Ono's apartment. "Okay, but just for a few minutes. I have to get them to let me rescue my… girlfriend." He stumbled over what to call his lover to the head of the church.

"You mean Mya?"

Acton stared wide-eyed at Ono. "You know who she is?"

"Of course, I keep track of people I may someday get to marry." Ono chuckled at Acton's bewilderment.

"Not if I don't go rescue her!" Acton blurted. "Oops." They stopped walking.

"Where is she?"

"At her father's mine in Africa. Uncle Ono, I must rescue her. I can't let her die there."

Ono took Acton's arm and led him the few remaining feet to his apartment. He escorted Acton across the living room to a sofa against the wall. "Sit. We better discuss this."

"There's nothing to talk about. Father refused to let me take a shuttle to rescue her." He mimicked Cana, "It's too dangerous. There's no time."

"He loves you, Acton. He just wants to protect you."

"I know, but I love Mya. I can't live without her."

"I know. I know. I'll make some tea, and you will feel better after you have some." Ono walked toward the kitchen as Acton fought back his tears. "Try to relax for a few minutes, and we'll see what we can do. Sing the chant if nothing else." Ono grinned as he entered the kitchen.

"Thank you. I appreciate it." Acton leaned back on the sofa and took a deep breath. The apartment was dimly lit but comfortable. Somehow, it seemed suitable for a man of God to have a dimly lit living room. He gazed at the religious symbols on the walls and the sacred texts on the tables and bookcases. Somewhere, a flute played soft, calming music. He yawned. The day was already quite long.

Out of the corner of his eye, he saw what looked like military orders on a small table nearby. Acton glanced at the kitchen but couldn't see Ono. He tiptoed to the table and picked up the papers. They were transit orders for two shuttles to bring thirty-four clergy members to New Hope from SS New Venture.

Startled, Acton glanced around the room again. It was too good to be true. Somehow, he had precisely what he needed in his hands, access to two shuttles today. He didn't hesitate. He took the papers, quietly walked to the door, opened it, and left, closing it behind him.

✱ ✱ ✱ ✱ ✱

Ono stepped out of the kitchen. He saw the empty table where the orders used to be, the unoccupied sofa where Acton used to be, and smiled knowingly. "Go with God, Acton." He re-entered the kitchen as the kettle started to boil.

CHAPTER TWENTY-THREE

Acton arrived at the Flight Club, but his friends were no longer there.

He keyed his wrist comm and called Cass. No answer. He called Farl next, but still no response. Angrily, he tried Trice, and no answer. "Where are those guys?"

Maybe they found an available aircraft and went to the port, not that it made much difference now. Acton hurried to the lifts and took one to the port level.

Arriving at the port's lobby, they were not there, and the airlock was sealed. Where else could they have gone? Because he had taken the orders, he had to act quickly. If Master Ono reported the missing papers, he could spend the following year in lock-up.

Stabilizing himself in zero gravity, Acton keyed his wrist comm and tried them again. No one answered. He moved to the far side of the lobby, away from the steady flow of people to and from the entrances to the five levels of spaceports.

Acton had to get two shuttles; the orders were specific. To get two shuttles, he had to have four pilots. If he couldn't find his friends, he would have to locate three other pilots, but he didn't know which pilots were off duty, so it would take time to find different pilots. Time was his enemy. He had no time.

While Acton stared at the entrance to the entrance to Spaceport 1, unconsciously watching people coming and going as he tried to figure out what to do. He suddenly realized he could find out if they went inside. He only had to ask. It would be logical to go to Port 1 as most shuttles were stationed there.

The green light above Spaceport 1's entrance indicated the port had an atmosphere. Entering through its airlock, Acton looked around the vast inner bay. To his right, men in tan overalls worked on a shuttle. The flight desk was one hundred twenty feet in front of him, a square booth with a chest-high counter surrounding it. One side faced Acton, and one faced the opposite way.

On the other side of the flight desk, shuttles and rescue ships filled both sides of a wide center aisle. On the right, the noses of blue shuttles faced the aisle and their engines toward the wall. On the left, closest to the booth, Rescue 1 was the first rescue ship in four rows of eight ships each. Tractors awaited orders in the wide center aisle. To the far right, huge doors with warnings painted on them led to the outer bay and were closed, allowing the inner bay to have an oxygen atmosphere. He couldn't see them anywhere in the million-square-foot inner port.

Searching for someone who might have seen them, he found a man in a tan uniform supervising two others working on a shuttle to his right. "Excuse me. I'm looking for the rest of my flight crew: three Rescue pilots in dark blue uniforms, one guy my size, and two women, one redhead and one blonde. Have you seen them?"

The man thought for a moment as he continued to watch the workers. "Yeah, sounds like some pilots I saw a few minutes ago." He grabbed a bracket on the ship and leaned closer to the guy welding a landing strut. "You gotta weld all of it. See?" he shouted over the noise of the welder, pointed to the spot, and then got out of the way as the welder worked on it.

"Do you know where they went?" Acton shouted.

"No, but I thought they went to the flight desk." The worker was so focused on his work that he didn't look at Acton.

"Thanks." Acton jumped up and grabbed the rope leading to the flight desk, the checkpoint for all flights using the port. Then, he used a vertical rope to get down to the desk.

When Acton arrived at the counter, the attendant looked up. "May I help you, sir?"

"Yes," Acton handed the orders to the man, "I have orders to take two shuttles to New Venture and return with thirty-four clergymen. But I can't find my co-pilot or the pilots for the other shuttle. Have you seen three pilots wearing Rescue blue in the last half hour?"

The attendant took the orders and studied them. "Yeah, I saw three pilots in blue, but they didn't report to the desk."

"Hmm, they must have gone directly to the ships since they didn't have the orders." Acton turned away from the attendant to minimize the possibility of being recognized.

"Possible." The attendant looked at his monitor more than Acton.

"Can you sign them out? I will give them their copy when I see them at the shuttle."

"Normally, but not under the lock-down status we've been operating under since the commander's announcement. I'll have to see the pilots myself to sign them out. You can go ahead and sign for your shuttle. Send the other pilots back to the desk for their orders. I will need to see your co-pilot, so send him back with a copy of these orders." The flight officer returned one set of orders to Acton and stamped the other. Then he looked up some information, wrote on the papers, and gave them to Acton. "Here you are. I assigned you Shuttle 6122." He pointed at the first shuttle next to the desk.

"All right." Acton took the orders, signed both pages and returned one signed copy to the attendant. "Thanks, I will send them over."

Acton tried to appear calm, even whistling a tuneless melody as he half walked, half floated toward the shuttle with the number 6122 stenciled on its nose. The shuttle was near another shuttle with the number 6756, probably the next two shuttles available for duty. As he inspected shuttle 6122, he remembered that shuttles were much larger than his rescue ship.

Shuttles were fifty-one feet long and fifty-seven feet wide. Each was large enough for thirty-two passengers to sit comfortably on the top level and had a cargo bay below the passenger compartment. The pilots sat in a cockpit in the rounded, aerodynamic nose of the aircraft. The ship's body was conical with swept-back wings, each wider than the shuttle's body. The jet engines at the rear were almost twice the size of the ones on a rescue ship, making take-offs and landings easier on Earth. The shuttle also had lighter-than-air engines for hovering.

When he arrived at its entrance, between the rear engines, the door was open, and the stairs were down. He grabbed the stair rail and pulled himself onto the ship. Walking through the entry landing, he entered the passenger lounge and continued down the broad aisle, separating two seats on each side until he arrived at the pilot's cockpit. He slid onto the pilot seat on the left side. The panels of gauges, switches, and buttons spread across the shuttle's dashboard, the pathfinder and avoidance system were in its center, and the co-pilot's seat was on the right side.

Acton studied the controls and gauges. He had flown shuttles before, as pilots learned to operate all the different ships while in flight school, but he hadn't flown one in years. Acton studied the switches and settings and tried the navigation wheel while he located the most frequently used gauges and noted the readiness of the shuttle.

"We thought we would find you here." Cass stood in the doorway.

Acton whirled around and saw his friends at the cockpit door. "Where have you guys been? I looked all over for you. Even called you with no answer."

"The guy at the flight desk was acting weird, so we boarded the next available shuttle to wait for you. We figured that one way or another, you would get one. I guess the comm doesn't work in the cargo hold," Cass explained.

"Thanks for your vote of confidence." Acton shoved the papers at Cass. "Now, get your butts to the flight desk and get cleared for your shuttle. I got two of them. Master Ono ordered two shuttles to go to New Venture to pick up some people, and I borrowed them."

"Uh-oh," Farl said. "We're serving time when we get back, huh?"

"You should be worried about getting back. If we do, we can worry about serving time, but at least Mya will be alive while we serve it. Now, get going. We can't take a chance of them questioning the orders. If Master Ono notices they're missing, we'll be locked up in a heartbeat." They hurried out of the shuttle toward the flight desk.

A few minutes later, Cass returned to Acton, and Farl and Trice were seated in the shuttle parked next to Acton's. As Cass sat on the co-pilot seat, Acton keyed his wrist comm. "Farl, are you ready?"

"Yes, we're ready," Farl said over the comm.

"All right, let's do it." Acton keyed the shuttle's comm. "Control, this is Shuttles 6122 and 6756 requesting departure for New Venture."

"Shuttle 6122 and Shuttle 6756, permission to position for departure. Control out."

Two tractors attached the shuttles' linkage and towed them six hundred feet across the inner bay to the launch area in front of the huge outer doors. With the shuttles positioned, the tractors moved out of the way, and the port's workers entered the preparation room to the right of the doors. Giant suction pumps removed the oxygen from the inner bay before the outer bay doors opened.

Two other tractors, driven by people in space suits, towed them into the outer bay and aligned them in front of the space doors for take-off. After the tractors left the launch area, the metal doors banged down, sealing the bay, and the external doors opened into space.

"Control, this is Shuttle 6122, requesting departure," Acton said over the ship's comm.

"Shuttle 6122, you are cleared for departure."

Acton took the navigation wheel in his left hand, started the hover engines, and slid the thrust control to flight level. "Here we go." Acton flew the shuttle through the massive door and into space. Switching to the jet engines and pressing the thrust slowly forward, the shuttle moved away from New Hope.

"Control, this is Shuttle 6756, requesting departure," Farl said over the comm.

"Shuttle 6756, you are cleared for departure."

Shuttle 6756 used its hover engine to exit the ship and, once outside, slowly caught up with Shuttle 6122.

"All right, New Venture is one-hundred-twenty-degrees to the left," Acton said to Cass. "Let's head toward it until no one can do anything when we change course."

"Won't take long for them to notice we are not on the scheduled flight path."

"I know." Acton looked to his right, through Cass's window, and saw Farl and Trice's shuttle flying alongside his. "Farl is following us."

"Life is an adventure."

"Philosophy from you?" Acton chuckled.

"More like resolution."

A few minutes later, getting closer to New Venture but not yet within hailing distance, Acton glanced at Farl in the other shuttle. He gave her a thumbs-up gesture and nodded.

Farl returned the thumbs-up and nodded back.

"Here we go." Acton took a firm hold of the controls.

"Kiss your ass goodbye." Cass grimaced.

Acton brought the nose around, facing Earth, and pushed the thrust forward to maximum velocity. Shuttle 6122 rushed forward and swung into a new flight path toward Earth. Behind them, Shuttle 6756 followed, matching their speed.

Moments later, the comm blared. "Shuttle 6122 and Shuttle 6756, this is Control. You are off course. Return to your flight path for SS New Venture."

Acton ignored them, and Farl did too, as the comm was silent.

"Shuttles 6122 and 6756, this is Control. Return to your flight path to New Venture."

Acton shook his head at Cass. "Won't be long now."

"Sometimes, I am very happy that I am *not* you," Cass said.

"Shuttle 6122, this is Control. Respond, please."

"Are you going to respond?" Cass asked.

"Not until my father calls."

The following minute of silence seemed a lot longer.

"Shuttle 6122, this is Fleet Commander Athu. Acton, are you receiving this transmission?"

"Control, this is Shuttle 6122, Captain Acton Athu, receiving you."

"Acton, I thought I made myself clear. You are *not* to go to Earth. You will not be able to return to New Hope or any other fleet ship if you continue this lunacy."

"Father, it's not lunacy. I must rescue Mya. I cannot live with any other possibility. I'm sorry you do not understand that."

"I understand, but it's juvenile. I thought you were more responsible than this. I'm not going to explain what will happen because of your actions, as I doubt you will survive to find out. Control out." The comm went dead.

"Shuttle 6122, out," Acton replied.

"Ouch, even if we survive this, we won't survive that," Cass said.

Acton cocked an eyebrow and nodded, too late to do anything else. He keyed the ship's comm. "Mya Moriset."

The comm unit buzzed, then no answer. As usual, when no one answered, it tried again and would continue trying every twenty seconds as long as it was engaged. After one more try, Acton shut it off.

"Where can Mya be?"

CHAPTER TWENTY-FOUR

Cana slammed the comm unit down and stormed from his office.

He had won victories over age-old rivals, negotiated peace treaties with Zu, established colonies on Mars, and created the Atlantian Fleet. Yet, he couldn't get his family to follow orders. His clenched fists turned white as he stormed toward the communications desk.

Nora had brought forty-two Gen-x AG workers onto his ship. He must be the laughingstock of the entire fleet. Ridiculous. The whole purpose of the fleet was to save Atlantians, not Gen-x. For thousands of years, the Gen-x people were the divisive issue between the royal family and the Sons of Belial. The problem was whether Gen-x were people or property. Whether they were primarily human was not the point. The argument was whether genetically created creatures had the same rights and privileges as ordinary people. When he began the program to build the Atlantian Fleet, the Council of Nine and the royal family had decided that Gen-x AG people, with their centaur-like bodies, did not have the same rights as standard humans. At the same time, Gen-x Admin people with four arms and two legs were enough like ordinary humans to have equal rights. Now, because of Nora, he would have to deal with the issue again. The more he thought about it, the angrier he became.

And if that wasn't enough, Pal disappeared without telling anyone. The boy had never behaved like a member of the royal family. One would think he would follow Acton's example and set the standard for how Atlantians should be. But not Pal. No one even knew what he was doing since he went to the university; worse, not even his girlfriend knew where he was. Now, the police were investigating a royal family member – something unprecedented in the empire's history. The royal family was above the law because they made the law. In fact, they were the law. As he wondered what the boy could be thinking to put us in a position where outsiders investigate the royal family, Cana clenched his fists even harder at the idea of being subject to the police or anyone else.

And then Acton disobeyed orders, stole two shuttles, and deliberately went to Earth when he knew the fleet was moving. How dare he? If it had anyone else, they would have been shot down. Not only did they ignore the chain of authority, but he and three other officers violated an Imperial Command. And, even if none of those things made any difference, he disobeyed his father. Never in his entire life had Acton done anything so ridiculous. No one in his ten-thousand-year family history had ever done something like this. The royal family was about duty. The Empire First had always been their motto. Now, Acton's girlfriend was more important than the empire. Ridiculous.

When he arrived at the comm desk, Cana was ready to explode.

Captain Thegan looked up from his monitor as Cana stopped abruptly beside his desk. "Commander?"

"Orders! Except for New Venture and Grand Poseidia, all ships must go fifty thousand miles at full speed. We must move farther from Earth. Now!"

"But sir…" Captain Thegan said.

"Don't 'but sir' me, Captain. Just issue the orders. Now!" Less than a foot away, Cana leaned over and shouted at him.

Thegan reached for the mic, looked up at the big screen, and then back at the monitor showing their guidance system. His hands shook, and he hesitated, unsure how to act. "What heading, sir?"

"The same heading we're on now."

"Yes, sir." Captain Thegan grabbed the microphone and pressed the red button, routing the call to all ships, all operators, and all personnel in the fleet. "New orders! All ships, except New Venture and Grand Poseidia, go to full speed on the present course for fifty thousand miles. Now!"

Before Captain Thegan could put the mic back on the desk, the massive engines on New Hope fired. The spaceship accelerated from a hundred miles an hour to over a thousand miles an hour in a few seconds. Inside the ship, everything not firmly attached was airborne. Comm units, monitors, computers, pens, papers, and other surface items hit the floor and scattered. Standing people fell to the floor, and others were thrown against their desk, walls, or other objects. People sitting on chairs with rollers were flung across open spaces or into things nearby.

On the agriculture floors, planters slid off their raised stands and spilled plants and soil across the floor. In the port bays, tractors tumbled across the floor and crashed into ships, walls, and other equipment. Kitchen workers fell, and the food they were preparing flew from the stove or table to land on the floor and often on the workers. Doctors, nurses, and patients in the infirmary plunged to the floor, and gurneys crashed into nearby objects.

In Control, Cana tumbled across the floor and into his office wall. Captain Thegan fell on the comm desk, sweeping everything off. Salia, who was walking to her desk, fell and rolled across the floor to land on Cana. Throughout Control, people suddenly found themselves on the floor, dodging falling items they had been working with a moment before. Alsa tried to catch her comm units, monitors, and keyboards at the reception desk as her chair rolled across the floor and into the wall.

As the comm board lit up with incoming emergency calls, Captain Thegan climbed to his feet and helped comm workers get to their stations. Together, they found the comm units that were still functional and started answering calls.

Salia pushed herself up and found she was on top of Cana. She got to her knees and checked on the commander. "Are you okay, sir?"

"Ah…" Cana tried to sit up and then settled back down. "I think so." He gazed at the chaos around him. Captain Thegan ran over to them and, with Salia's help, got Cana to his feet. "Better cancel that order, Captain." He leaned on Salia, too embarrassed to say more.

"Yes, sir." Thegan hurried to the comm desk and pressed the red button again, "New orders. All ships *gradually* return to normal cruising speed. Repeat, cancel the orders to go to full speed, and gradually return to normal cruising speed." A moment later, the spaceship began to slow down.

Salia helped Cana into his office, where he dropped onto his chair and slumped over his desk, still dizzy and breathing heavily. She rushed back out to the office to help get things operational again.

✳ ✳ ✳ ✳ ✳

Several floors below Control, Emperor Maximus pushed himself up from the floor. His lapdog was barking and trying to help him as he stared groggily around his spacious suite. Items from his desk were spread across the floor, mingling with the contents of his shelves and planters. His assistant hurried to his side and helped Max to his feet.

"What happened?" Max asked.

"The ship moved."

Max keyed his headset, "Cana." No answer, so he tried Salia.

A moment later, Salia answered the call. "Yes, Your Majesty?"

"Cana doesn't answer. Is he there?"

"He fell. I will check and have him call you back."
"Yes, right away." Max disconnected.

* * * * *

Salia returned to Cana's office and found him at his desk, still groggy and confused. "Commander, are you okay?"

"Yes, I think so." Cana didn't sound convincing.

"Where's your comm unit?"

Cana reached for his headset but didn't find it. "I don't know."

"It must have come off when you fell." Salia went to look for Cana's headset, but a comm worker handed it to her before she arrived at where he had fallen. Salia thanked her and returned to his office. "Here it is, sir. The emperor wants you to call him." Unsure he was fully functional, she waited until he called.

Cana put the headset on and keyed it. "Max."

A moment later, Max answered. "Hello? Cana, is that you?"

"Yes, what can I do for you?"

"What happened? I fell. Everyone fell."

"We started moving away from Mars and Earth."

"Without preparing for the move?" Max asked incredulously.

"Ah… no," Cana said, "I mean yes, without preparing for it."

"I see. I want to know what damages we sustained. Get reports on it, now." Max killed the connection.

"Yes, sir, of course," Cana said as the comm went dead. He turned to Salia. "Order status reports from all departments."

"Yes, sir." Salia rushed from his office.

Cana slumped over his desk and held his head with both hands.

* * * * *

Emperor Maximus paced in his suite, carrying his small dog.

He stopped petting the dog to tenderly touch a bruise on his forehead. To his right, the wall behind the sofa displayed a scene of the impeccable gardens full of orchids of a dozen colors at the Imperial Palace in Poseidia. Behind him, his assistant picked up fallen items from the carpet. The wall behind his desk had a view of the ocean and concentric harbor below the palace. The kitchen and dining room were to his left, and the bedroom to his right.

He stopped pacing and keyed his comm unit. "Ono."

"Hello, Max. Are you okay?" Ono answered.

"I took a nasty fall, but I'm all right. How about you?"

"I'm fine. I was having tea. I spilled the tea, but nothing worse."

"I am concerned about Cana. I have never known him to make an error like this in thirty-plus years."

"What happened?"

"He just moved the fleet without making sure we were prepared to do so. People may have been killed. I asked for damage reports, so we'll see." Max resumed petting his dog.

"Not good. Sounds like that would be fairly basic."

"Absolutely. What if ships were landing when we moved? It could easily have resulted in fatalities. Do you think we should relieve him of duty? At least for a little while?"

"No," Ono said immediately, "I think that would be the worst thing we could do. Cana is under a lot of pressure. His son Pal is missing. Acton disobeyed orders and stole two shuttles to go to Earth. Nora brought forty-two Gen-x Ag workers onto New Hope. All he has right now is his position, reputation, and honor. If we threaten any of those, Cana may not recover. He is still the best commander – the only commander – of the fleet we have ever had."

"Yes, I agree, but we cannot tolerate any more mistakes. We need someone who can intercede."

"How about Salia, his assistant? She is close at hand and can easily keep us informed of questionable actions."

"Good idea. I will speak to her. I don't want to overrule any orders publicly. Still, I may need to do so if he does something crazy."

"Let me know how it goes."

"Thanks, Ono." Emperor Max disconnected. He sat on his sofa and keyed his comm unit, "Salia," he said.

* * * * *

A few minutes later, Nora entered Cana's office.

Seeing him sitting at his desk, confused, and with his hair disheveled, she closed the door and crossed the office to him. He stared at her blankly as she stepped between his desk and credenza and leaned on the edge of his desk. "Are you okay?" Nora asked calmly.

"Of course," he said. His deep red complexion wasn't healthy, his hands shook like he had palsy, and he stared at things like they were strange.

She keyed her wrist comm, "Dr. Coomly." The comm buzzed.

"Hello, Nora. I haven't spoken with you in a long time. Are you well?" Dr. Coomly said over the comm.

"I'm fine, Jorg, but I'm not so sure about Cana. Can you come up to his office as discreetly as possible?" Cana frowned at her but didn't object.

The doctor didn't hesitate. "Yes, I will be there in a few minutes."

"Thank you." Nora ended the call.

"You shouldn't have done that," Cana said. "I'm fine."

"Good, but your body may disagree. You're a deep red color, your eyes are bugging out of your head, and you're shaking all over. I think your blood pressure just went off the charts, and the last thing we need right now is for you to have a heart attack or something."

CHAPTER TWENTY-FIVE

Over two thousand people attended the five o'clock Temple services, many more than usual.

Genesi waited patiently near the lectern for people to walk down the long center aisle and find seats close to the front. Due to the loss of Atlantis, most people were solemn, and many openly wept and wiped their eyes, so she smiled to cheer them up.

With its destruction today, she looked around the large auditorium, remembering the Poseidia Temple. It had a tall steeple of stained glass that let in multi-colored light. This one had ornate light fixtures throughout the room. The interior of the Poseidia Temple was made of rich, warm hardwoods. This one was made of metal and molded plastique. In Poseidia, the Synod of Twelve had built-in seats along the side, whereas, in New Hope, there were twelve alcoves featuring pictures of previous masters on the walls above the seats.

She was ready to begin the service when a man entered the Temple and hurried down the aisle. As he got closer, Genesi grinned. Still wearing his red shirt with yellow bananas, Harcu nodded to her, and she nodded in return. He sat in a row behind the other people.

"Thank you for attending the five o'clock service today. This has been one of the most traumatic days in the history of the empire. The loss of Atlantis weighs heavily on our hearts and minds. So, let's take that burden to God. He is our refuge, our salvation, and our support. We will sing our love song to God for as long as needed to find the peace and comfort we desperately need. After the song ends, we will spend ten minutes in silent meditation, where you can inwardly seek relief from God for your pain and sorrow. I will end it by saying, 'Go with God.' Let us begin."

Genesi closed her eyes, took a deep breath, and started chanting on her outward breath. "Yuuuuu." Slowly taking a breath, she sang it again. The singing bowls at both ends of the stage picked up the sound and added an octave above and one below, filling the auditorium with sound. Two thousand people joined in, adding their chant to the reverberating sound, and the singing bowls added to their sound in an endless loop. She sat near the lectern, closed her eyes, and sang from her heart.

Forty minutes later, the chant slowly stopped. Not because Genesi ended it but because, collectively, the people attending the service gradually stopped singing. In silence, everyone looked inward for God's guidance, solace, or inspiration. Genesi watched the time and after ten minutes, returned to the lectern. "Go with God."

She allowed a few moments for people to return from their meditation. "That concludes our five o'clock service. For those interested, we have another service at six o'clock. You are welcome to stay or return for it, and please let others know. Go with God."

She went down the center-stage stairs to greet people. Smiling warmly, she received people who wanted to shake her hand or chat quietly, and many simply wanted to thank her.

Harcu was the last in the line of people greeting her. "Hello, I haven't attended a service for a while. That was amazing. How often do you conduct a service?" he quietly asked.

Genesi grinned. "Six to eight times a day."

"Really? That often? Isn't that exhausting?"

"No, quite the opposite, actually. Joining spiritually with God is invigorating. I often take long walks to use the energy I get from the services." She turned toward the stairs. "I'm sorry, but I need to let others know I am done so the next person will be ready to start another service. If you wait for me, I'll walk out with you."

"Sure, take your time. I'll wait here."

Genesi hurried up the stairs, across the stage to the door at the curtain, and entered the office. A minute later, she returned carrying her shawl and bag. "Thanks for waiting."

"My pleasure." He walked up the aisle with her. "Are you done for the day?"

"Yes, I'm off until tomorrow morning."

"Did you hear from Captain Ketsu?" Harcu asked.

"No, I imagine he is quite busy."

Harcu held the Temple door open for her, and they stopped at the lifts. He stepped closer to her. "Hey, do you eat?"

Genesi stared at him incredulously, then burst out laughing. "Yes, of course."

"Well, how about you and me getting something to eat? After all, I eat too."

Genesi couldn't help but smile. "Oh, I don't know. It's been a long day, and I'm tired."

"But even tired people need to eat, right?" Harcu did his best puppy-dog-eyes.

"Yeah, but–"

"Come on, let me take you to the Flight Club. My friend works there and will let us in, even if we're not in uniform. And I know some of the band members performing tonight. I'm sure a pretty girl like you must like music, right?"

"I'm not exactly dressed to go out." She held out her acolyte robe away from her legs to demonstrate.

"No problem, you can go back to your apartment and change clothes. Then I'll pick you up in thirty minutes to go eat." Harcu's grin seemed to cover his face.

"You're a hard man to say no to, so okay." She recognized that it meant a lot to him. "Do you know where my apartment is?"

"I will when I take you home. Then I'll change into something a little more appropriate than bananas and return for you."

The lift arrived, and Genesi ignored it. Confused, Harcu motioned for her to enter. "I was just accompanying you to the lift, and my apartment is down there." She pointed at the hallway beyond the lift, and they walked past a few alcoves, arriving at her apartment within a minute. Genesi keyed the entry pad, and the door slid open.

"All right, I'll be back in thirty minutes." Harcu gave her a big smile.

Genesi stepped inside and then turned back with a big smile. "I'll be ready in sixty minutes." She started to close the door.

"Like I said, I'll be back in sixty minutes." He stepped back.

"Bye, silly." She chuckled and closed the door.

Harcu jumped up and almost let out a victory whoop. Skipping toward the lifts, he saw a short woman in an acolyte robe like Genesi's walking toward him. Taking her hands, he waltzed her around the hallway for eight beats while singing a la-ti-da tune. Then, as she stared at him in absolute astonishment, he kissed her cheek and ran the last few feet to the lift. He glanced back, motioned he was crazy, and laughed as he got on the lift.

Marlenel dashed to her apartment and let herself in. "Genesi, you'll never guess what just happened."

Genesi stepped out of the bathroom, where she was running bath water, dressed only in her underslip. "You met a crazy person in the hallway wearing a red shirt with yellow bananas, right?"

Marlenel came to a sudden stop in the middle of the room. "Hey, how'd you know?"

"He left here a few seconds ago and will return in an hour. He's taking me out to dinner at the Flight Club." Genesi returned to the bathroom.

Marlenel sighed. "Well, good for you. You need to get out." She didn't mention that Genesi hadn't been out since Pal disappeared. She smiled as humming came from the bathroom.

* * * * *

Precisely sixty minutes later, Harcu knocked on Genesi's door. He wore a dark blue silk jacket, an iridescent blue shirt, trim black pants, and black dress shoes.

Marlenel opened the door wearing a light-pink housecoat.

Harcu did a double take, staring at her. "Oh, hi."

"Hi," Marlenel said seductively. She batted her eyelashes at him and gazed adoringly into his green eyes as she cozied up to the door frame.

"Mmm, is Genesi here?" Harcu asked loudly in case he might be at the wrong apartment.

"I'm here," she called from somewhere inside the apartment.

"Oh, good. For a moment, I thought I was at the wrong apartment."

Marlenel stopped flirting and stepped back. "Come in."

"Thank you." Harcu stepped inside. "And you are?"

"I'm Marlenel Nete, Genesi's roommate." The door closed.

"So nice to meet you," he said loud enough for Genesi to hear. He stepped closer to Marlenel and whispered, "I hope you have forgiven me for the little whirl around earlier."

"Oh, yes, of course. Happens all the time." Marlenel sat on the sofa.

Surprised, he laughed out loud. "Hmm, I'm sure it does."

Genesi entered the living room wearing a sleeveless blue dress that flowed smoothly over her trim body, accenting all the right places as it glided to the floor. As she walked, luminescent trickles of light moved up the dress and dissipated over her breasts. She also wore a stunning blue sapphire on a silver chain at her throat. Her long brown hair was smooth and hung loose to her shoulders. "I'm ready."

"Whoa, I'll say you are. You're beautiful!" Harcu could barely contain himself.

"Well, thank you." She blushed and grinned at him. "You're very handsome. I almost didn't recognize you without the yellow bananas."

"Once in a while, I actually have a reason to dress up. Otherwise, bananas or something else are more than adequate."

He took her hand and walked toward the door. "Let's go eat. Bye, Marlenel. It was a pleasure meeting you. Don't wait up." Harcu chuckled.

Genesi laughed and returned Marlenel's wave as they exited the apartment.

Harcu didn't have to use any favors from his friend at the Flight Club. The host couldn't look away from Genesi long enough to notice they didn't wear a uniform and probably shouldn't be there. Harcu asked for a table near the band. Seeing several band members respond to his wave, the host sat them at a table near the dance floor.

Their waiter appeared a moment later. "Would you like something to drink?"

"Iced tea, thank you," Genesi replied.

"Make that two, thanks," Harcu instructed. The waiter handed them menus and left.

Genesi glanced around the room. Over a hundred people were in the Flight Club, and most wore uniforms. "Do you feel a little out of place?" she quietly asked Harcu.

"Nope. Secretly, we're the envy of everyone here. They all want to wear something nice instead of the uniforms they must wear every day." Harcu couldn't take his eyes off her.

"Is that why everyone is staring at us?"

"No," he paused for emphasis, "that's because you are the prettiest girl in the place."

"Oh, stop. You'll make me blush again." She blushed.

"You are even more beautiful when you blush."

"Who's that?" Genesi nodded at a striking woman with blonde hair walking seductively toward them.

For the first time since they sat down, Harcu tore his eyes away from Genesi to see who she was talking about. "Oh, that's Patel."

"Hi, Harcu. How are you?" Patel's ample endowment strained her low-cut gown.

"Hi, Patel. I'd like to introduce Genesi Forcu. This is Patel... I never did get your last name," he said to Patel.

"Derna. Patel Derna."

"Patel sings with the band." Harcu finished the introduction.

"Nice to meet you." Genesi nodded to Patel.

"Same here." Patel turned to Harcu. "Titu said he would be by later to say hello. Well, I better get back to work. See you." She walked back toward the band. She wore a tight, backless, floor-length gown that left little to the imagination.

"Striking girl, known her long?" Genesi asked coolly.

"I don't know her other than she is the singer with the band." Harcu pointed at the band members. "See the guitar player with the beard on the right?"

"Yes." As she followed his aim, the band played a lilting melody, light and romantic.

"He's my brother's best friend, Titu. He practically lived with us back in Poseidia while at the university, and he's a super nice guy."

The waiter returned with the drinks. "Do you know what you'd like to order?"

"Do you like steak?" Harcu asked Genesi.

"Yes, sounds good."

Harcu looked at the waiter. "Two orders of Steak Du Kango, salads au prov…" He turned to Genesi, "Do you prefer noodles or potatoes?"

"Noodles, please."

"One order of noodles, one of potatoes, and bread, of course."

"Thank you." The waiter picked up the menus and walked away.

"That sounds really filling. I don't think I've eaten that much in a long time. I might fall asleep on you."

"Oh, I'm not worried. Dancing will keep you awake. Shall we help get people started dancing?" Harcu took her hand and stood.

"Yes, all right." Genesi followed him onto the dance floor.

They walked closer to the band, and Harcu took her into his arms. After a few steps to get into the tune's rhythm, he whirled her around in a majestic flurry. Genesi followed effortlessly as his arms and body language told her what direction he would take. Since they were the only dancers, Harcu could use his most grandiose movements to sweep them around the dance floor. His body language was precisely what she needed to keep in step with him. They danced smoothly across the floor as though the dance was choreographed for them alone, and they had practiced for years.

"You dance divinely," Harcu cooed.

"So do you." Genesi sounded as surprised as he was. "Where did you learn to dance like this?"

"I'm an art and theater major. I have taken dance, voice, and acting lessons for years."

"I'm impressed." Genesi's eyes sparkled as she enjoyed being expertly swept around the floor. The luminescent trickles of light that moved up her dress seemed to do so in sync with the music and provided a light show for those watching from the other tables.

"Good." Harcu smiled.

The song ended, and most people applauded, probably thinking their dancing was a part of the performance. Even Titu and the rest of the band applauded. Harcu held her hand firmly as he bowed to the audience, and Genesi blushed but bowed gracefully.

The band immediately struck up a similar song. By the time they danced to the second song, their food was on their table, and they talked quietly as they ate. Then afterward, they danced. The hour was getting late when they returned to their table.

"I haven't had so much fun in a long time." Harcu took a drink of his iced tea.

"Me either." Genesi laughed. "Not since Pal and I went out a month ago." Her voice suddenly became melancholy.

"I'm sorry."

"Don't be sorry. You have been wonderful, and I feel better than I have since Pal's disappearance."

"Good, that is the purpose. I just want you to be happy." He noticed someone approaching and turned to see who. The waiter stopped at the table and presented the bill. Harcu gave him his ID card, and the waiter went to process the payment. As he left, Harcu's eyes were drawn to movement at the front of the room near the entrance. Several people dressed in black were getting up from a table.

"Hey, see the six men by the front wall?" Harcu asked.

"Hmm, yes, I see them."

"They are not wearing uniforms either."

"Hey, you're right," Genesi said.

"I think they're students, but I can't tell if they are the ones we want. Can you?"

"No, they're too far away."

"I think I better find out more about them." Harcu began to get up from the table.

"I'm coming with you." Genesi started to get up.

"No, either go back to your apartment or stay here. I don't want to take a walking light show with me as I try to follow them." Harcu smiled. "And you're pretty noticeable right now."

"Are you going to follow them?" Genesi asked in a concerned tone.

Harcu nodded. "Are you staying here or going to your apartment?" He glanced back to make sure the students were still at their booth.

"Go to my apartment, I guess."

"Most of them are leaving. Can you wait here long enough to get my ID card for me? The waiter has it."

"Oh, certainly. I can do that."

"All right, I will follow the students if that's who they are. I don't think you should be alone with them. If any of them stay here, you should also stay. I will come back when I find out where they're going. If the band leaves before I get here, go with them and explain to Titu that I asked you to do so. Then, go back to your apartment. I'll get your comm number from Duc and call you." He walked toward the door.

"Be careful, and be sure to call me tonight so I won't worry."

Harcu nodded and walked calmly toward the door where four of the six men in black were leaving.

CHAPTER TWENTY-SIX

Four of the six students, talking among themselves, walked out of the Flight Club.

Harcu strolled over to the host's stand. While the other two students returned to their table, Harcu got the host's attention. "Excuse me, where's the men's room?"

"In the hall, go right, and it's on your right about forty feet."

"Thank you." Harcu walked into the hallway, glancing at the two students seated in the booth nearby. They looked like some of the Belial students he saw in the L.E.T.'s pictures.

The hallway was empty, but voices came from his right. He quickly walked toward the men's room in the same direction as the voices. Forty feet from the club's entrance, a pair of double doors on his right still moved as if someone had gone through them. Harcu quietly approached the doors and peeked through a narrow slit between them. The last of the four students went through another pair of double doors on the far side of a small room full of laundry tubs and trash receptacles.

Harcu pushed through the double doors and silently dashed across the trash room. He peeked through the slit in the second set of double doors to see a stairwell landing. Pushing one of the doors open a few inches, he heard the students' voices coming from the stairs and slipped onto the landing. He stooped low and approached stairs that went up or down.

"Nah, Evvan, he wouldn't do that." One student's voice came from down the stairs and had a thick foreign accent, not one Harcu could recognize.

"Course, he would. It has to be then. That's the only time they are all together," a different voice said.

"But that's tomorrow. That means we have to do it tonight then–" the first voice said and was cut off.

The way the sound ended, they must have left the stairs. The stairwell was scary. He peered up and couldn't see the top, and looking over the banister, it descended out of sight as well. The center space of the stairwell carried strange sounds like moans mixed with machinery. Harcu quickly but silently went down two floors and then slowly approached the landing to see if anyone was there. No one was, so he bounded down to the next floor.

Stopping, he strained to listen. No voices came from farther down the stairs. Pushing open one of the double doors on Floor 276, he heard voices, but he was too far away to tell what they said, so he entered. The room was a vast, dark space full of pipes, electrical conduits, vent shafts, and other mechanical equipment. Faint voices came from his right, so he carefully crept around engineering devices, ducked under low-hanging pipes, and tried to find the students. The farther he went from the stairwell, the darker the room became.

Rather than walk into something dangerous or stumble into the students in the dark, Harcu turned back to return to the stairs and nearly banged his head on some pipes. When he ducked under them, he saw a shoe on the floor and squatted to pick it up. In the faint light, he could see the lettering on the back of the athletic shoe, which read Pal Athu.

Harcu surged back to his feet and nearly let out a victory whoop but stopped in time to prevent trouble. He zig-zagged back through the labyrinth of engineering fixtures to the stairwell without damaging anything more severe than bruised shins. At the stairwell doors, he paused to hear if someone was on the stairs, but no one was there.

Bounding up three floors, he peeked into the trash room again. It was empty, so he rushed through the small room and glanced uneasily into the hallway for the other students. Seeing no one, he returned to the Flight Club, sticking the shoe under his jacket.

Stopping at the host's stand, he saw the students' booth was empty. Harcu quickly looked for Genesi, and their table was vacant, too. The band was playing with Patel singing.

He got an awful feeling in the pit of his stomach and hurried to the lifts. One arrived a moment later, and he went to the floor where Genesi's apartment was located.

When the lift doors opened, three men, the two students from the club and a man with a gray hood over his head, struggled with Genesi. The hooded one had her feet, and the others held her arms as they carried her toward a hallway. Kicking and fighting to get free, she seemed to be weakening.

When the lift doors closed, they saw him. Harcu dropped Pal's shoe and assumed a fighting stance he had learned in military classes. Jumping up, he kicked the two students in the middle of the back who were holding her arms. With all his weight landing on them, they flew across the hallway and hit the wall hard. Genesi fell to the floor, forcing the hooded man to let go of her feet. Harcu jumped to his feet first, turned to the hooded man, and dropped into a crouched, aggressive fighting stance, focusing all his energy on his hands and arms. He moved to draw the hooded man to his right so he could attack with his left, but the hooded man took one glance, turned, and ran down the hall.

Harcu let him go and turned back to the two men he had kicked. The tall, wiry student was already in a similar fighting stance. Harcu straightened a little, bringing his fists up like he would hit the man in the face, but only shifted his weight onto his left leg. Harcu moved to punch the man with his left fist but instead kicked him in the stomach with his right foot. The man fell to the floor as the air exploded from his lungs. Harcu was ready to knock him out with a punch in the face when the other student tripped him from behind.

Harcu fell to the floor next to Genesi. He sprang back up, but the third man had already helped the other student to his feet, and they half ran, half stumbled down the hallway in the same direction the hooded man had gone. Harcu let them go. Breathing hard, he turned to Genesi, who was trying to get up. "Are you okay?"

When he helped her up, she was a little shaky. "Yes, I think so. Thank you."

"You're very welcome. Let's get you into your apartment."

Genesi leaned on Harcu as she hobbled to her door and went inside. "Come in."

Harcu helped her to the sofa, and she sat, rubbing her arm. "Why did you leave the club?"

"The men left, so I thought I could go. When I got off the lift, they attacked me."

"So they know where you live."

"Oh… Yes, I guess they do. What do they want?"

"No idea. Wait a minute, I left something in the hall. I'll be right back." Harcu entered the hall, and before her door could close again, he returned with the shoe and handed it to her. "I'm sorry. I found this on an engineering floor, three stories below the club."

Genesi took the shoe from Harcu like it might be a deadly viper and turned it over as she stared at it. "Oh my God… It's Pal's." Her eyes watered. "It's his shoe. Oh my God, he might be dead."

"Calm down. He just lost his shoe. The real question is, why didn't he pick it up?"

"What's going on?" Genesi muttered as she wept.

"And that's not all. I heard them planning something for tomorrow. We have to call Captain Ketsu and tell him that Pal is definitely in trouble. And these students are plotting an assassination or something like that for tomorrow." It took a few minutes to find Nortin's number, then Harcu keyed his comm.

"Hello..." Nortin sounded half asleep.

"Sorry, Captain. This is Harcu. You said we should call you if we saw any Belial students. We not only saw them but fought with them," Harcu said while Genesi quietly watched.

"What? How did... Wait, it's after midnight. Can you meet me at my office in thirty minutes?" Nortin said.

"Yes, sir, we can meet you in thirty minutes." Harcu looked at Genesi to see if she disagreed, and she nodded. "We'll be there, thanks." He ended the call and sat next to Genesi. "I think I woke him up." He grinned.

"I'm not surprised." She gazed into the dark bedroom where Marlenel was hopefully sleeping. "Let's go before we wake Marlenel."

"Yes, let's do that." Harcu helped her stand, and they left, taking Pal's shoe with them.

✳ ✳ ✳ ✳ ✳

Genesi and Harcu were waiting in the L.E.T.'s lobby when Captain Nortin Ketsu arrived.

"Whoa, you both look different from..." He glanced at his wrist comm. "...yesterday." He raised his eyebrows at Genesi's dress and smiled.

"We went to the Flight Club for dinner and dancing," Harcu explained as Genesi blushed.

Nortin glanced at his wrinkled uniform and exhaled loudly. "Let's go to my office." They quickly walked to Nortin's large office. "Have a seat." He pointed to chairs across the desk from him. "So what happened?"

Harcu summarized everything that happened after dinner at the Flight Club and Genesi's apartment. When he finished, Nortin stared silently at them for a few moments.

"Incredible," Nortin said. "Genesi, why did you leave the club?"

"The other two students left, so I thought I could go to my apartment. But when I got to my floor, they jumped me."

"They know where you live and who you are." Nortin frowned.

"That's what I said," Harcu exclaimed.

"This is very bad." Nortin paced to the far side of the office and then back again. "Tomorrow. Why tomorrow?"

"Tomorrow is Atlan Day," Genesi said.

Nortin stopped, surprise registering on his face. "Of course! That's why tomorrow."

"The Atlan Day celebration will be in the Temple this year," Genesi said.

"Right, Emperor Maximus, Commander Athu, and Master Ono will be on stage. That's what they meant when they said it's the only time they will all be together." Nortin rushed back to his desk. "Anything else?"

Genesi and Harcu looked at each other and then shook their heads. "No, that's all," she said.

"All right, I will need both of you to meet me at Commander Athu's office in the Control Center at eight in the morning. Can you do that?" Both nodded. "Good, you better go get some sleep. I have a lot to do between now and then." Nortin stood. "Thank you. If you hadn't discovered this, things could have been terrible. Now, we have to stop whatever they have planned. Bring Pal's shoe with you in the morning." Nortin handed the shoe to Harcu.

"You're welcome, Captain," Genesi said as she turned to go.

Harcu shook Nortin's hand. "Captain, let me know if I can help in any way." Nortin nodded as Harcu followed Genesi from the office. "Come on, I will take you home."

"Thank you, Harcu. What would I do without you?"

"Hopefully, you'll never have to find out." He smiled warmly.

They hurried to the lifts. One arrived less than a minute later, and they reached Genesi's apartment without seeing anyone else. Genesi stepped close to Harcu at her door. "Harcu, thank you so much. I really appreciate your help." She lightly squeezed his arm.

"Genesi, I cannot think of anywhere I'd rather be or anything I would rather be doing. You get some rest and don't leave your apartment in the morning until I am with you. I will meet you here a little before eight."

"Unfortunately, I have a six o'clock service in the morning."

"Then, I will be here a little before six and take you to the Temple."

Genesi smiled. "Thank you, Harcu. Good night. You sleep well, too." She opened the door, entered, and closed it behind her.

Harcu waited in her door's alcove. A few minutes later, an L.E.T. officer arrived and stopped a few feet away. "I thought an officer would be here."

"You must be Harcu Simoon," the officer said with a smile.

"The one and only." Harcu nodded, then walked to the lifts.

CHAPTER TWENTY-SEVEN

The tall grass was so thick that Zeth felt he was driving in a tunnel.

Zeth drove through a grass-lined corridor filled with shadows that grew darker each minute. He couldn't see more than two feet outside on both sides of the Eby, and what he could see was a dark blur.

"I guess we will have to stop soon. I can't see where I'm going anymore." Zeth turned to Zuzu and shrugged.

"As soon as we can. The children are exhausted, and we all need to rest." Zuzu checked on Feri, Marta, and little Ollie in the backseat. Sitting between his brother and sister, Ollie was already asleep. Marta made clothing for her stuffed bear out of old dishtowels, and Feri tossed a small ball to the dogs lying on the floorboard and then wrestled it away from them to do it again.

"I'm not sure we've gone anywhere. Everything looks the same as two hours ago."

The grass thinned out and became shorter over the next mile. Then, they emerged into an open area with only a few shrubs and bushes to find that the last of the dark orange sunset was fading into darkness.

"Hey, what's that?" Zuzu urgently pointed in front of them.

"What? I can't see –" Zeth saw a tall African standing twenty feet in front of the Eby, waving a flaming branch back and forth. He slammed on the brakes, and the Eby suddenly stopped.

Zeth, Zuzu, and the children were thrown against their seat restraints, and all the loose stuff fell to the floor. All their boxes, containers, and other personal items in the trailer slid forward and crashed into the front wall. Rudely awakened, Ollie started to cry, and the dogs tried to get on the seat with the children.

Behind the Eby, Perta, X'to, and Dimitri suddenly stopped, while Kona and his trailer full of animals were far enough behind to stop more gradually. Volf stopped behind Kona.

"Stay here." Zeth stepped out, leaving the Eby running and its lights on so he could see the man in the middle of the path. He leaned back into the Eby. "Feri, keep the dogs inside the truck."

"All right, Papa." Feri grabbed their collars and held on.

Zeth wondered if the African was a Bantu Chieftain as he walked toward him. He had never met one but had seen pictures in school.

The man was tall, at least six inches taller than Zeth, and strikingly dressed. He wore feathers in his elaborate hairdo, metal rings on his upper arms, and another inch-wide metal band around his forehead. A lion skin draped off one shoulder and wrapped around him halfway down his thighs, and he wore intricately woven leather sandals. He was waving a four-foot flaming branch.

As Zeth got closer, Perta and X'to ran up and joined him.

"Is he Swahili?" Perta said as he came up beside Zeth.

"I don't know. I don't speak it." Zeth stopped ten feet away.

"Me either," X'to said as he fell in beside them.

The man spoke emphatically as he shook the flame at something hidden in the darkness in front of them, but no one understood.

"From his tone, he's warning us about something." Zeth and the others stepped closer and peered into the dark. As they approached the chieftain, he stopped them by putting the flame directly in front of them. Blinded by the firelight, they stepped back.

The native took the fiery branch away and used it to point at an area as he spoke eagerly, then pulled the flame farther away. Their eyes became accustomed to the darkness again, and they saw what the chief was trying to tell them. Six feet away, the road plunged into a jagged ravine, at least twenty-five feet across, and its bottom was lost in darkness.

"Whoa! That would have been the end of us." Zeth stepped away.

"You can't see it from more than a few feet away." Perta leaned forward to stare into the ravine. "Did an earthquake do this?"

Zeth turned back to the chieftain, offering his hand to shake. "Thank you, thank you! You saved our lives."

The man shook Zeth's hand, bowed, and said something more that no one understood.

Zeth and the others bowed, and each shook the chieftain's hand and thanked him repeatedly. The rest of the men joined them and peered into the ravine. As they watched, a significant section of the edge ten feet to their right broke off and fell into the abyss.

"Whoa, not safe to be so close." Dimitri backed away.

Zeth stepped back to introduce the chieftain to the other men, but he was gone. "Where did he go?"

Perta looked around. "I don't know. He just disappeared."

"You'd think we could see his fire anyway. He sure saved us, and we owe him." Zeth stopped and listened. "The warning drums are very loud."

"And all around us, too." X'to stared into the darkness.

"We know one reason for them to be so loud." Perta gestured at the ravine.

"Let's move back as far as we can. I don't want to be close to this… What is it? Did an earthquake do that?" Perta walked toward the vehicles.

"I agree. Let's move back as far as we can. Zuzu and I were talking about stopping for the night, and if we didn't see something this big, we could run over anything."

"Lead the way, and we'll follow." Dimitri followed the others.

They went back to their vehicles, carefully turned around, and drove back as far as they could and still had room to pitch their tents for the night. They formed a big circle and used their headlights to see as Dimitri and Volf scraped a six-foot area free of brush, got several large pieces of wood from the trailer, and built a fire. Zeth, Zuzu, and three others gathered the food and cooking utensils and started making supper. Perta, Kona, and X'to took the animals from the trailer, put lead ropes on them, and staked them inside the circle of vehicles for the night with fresh food and water. The chickens remained in their cages with their feed.

While supper was cooking, they set up their tents for the night, and the children helped by getting blankets, sheets, and other items from the trailer. They were nearly done when dinner was ready.

One by one, each family visited the cooking pot for the savory stew and hard rolls. Dinnertime was family time. Each family sat together to eat, spending time with their children. Afterward, by the firelight, the children showed their parents things they had made during the day, tossed a ball to one another, or played games. Parents put their children into bed as the fire burned low, then sat around it. The dogs had chased back and forth as the children played their games and were content to rest near the Mercu's tent, only a few feet from where the animals were staked.

"We'll have to find a way around the ravine in the morning." Zeth took another swallow from the water bottle. "It may run for miles in both directions."

"Yeah, I was thinking the same thing." Perta moved closer. "At first light, I will go east to see if we can get around it."

"Then, I will check on the west side." Dimitri leaned against the bumper of his truck.

"Sounds good. The rest of us will load everything, so we'll be ready to go when you return." Zeth stretched and yawned.

"It sounds like I'll miss breakfast again." Perta chuckled.

"I'll make you a sandwich you can take with you." Geta went to the food chest.

"Make that two, please, Geta," Dimitri asked.

"No problem."

They sat and watched the lightning in the northern sky. With the dense cloud cover, the rest of the night sky was pitch black.

Zeth remembered sitting outside at night on his parents' farm in Atlantis. Back then, the stars were amazingly bright from near Mt. Atlan. He sat for hours daydreaming about what he wanted to do. He wiped his eyes and wondered what the future would be like now.

What would the rebel camp be like? Were they good people who somehow couldn't get to the fleet, or were they outlaws who wouldn't be allowed on the spaceships if they got there? He had no idea, and the thought worried him.

He walked away from the fire. On the other side of the Eby, he stopped and looked south, where the rebel camp should be. He could see hills a mile to the east and others to the west, possibly farther away. A small fire burned brightly on the one to the west. Was it part of the rebel camp or a native fire? He didn't know, and that was a problem.

"What are you thinking?" Zuzu joined him.

"Wondering if that light is part of the rebel camp or a native fire."

"No way to know. We'll have to go find out."

"It's the not knowing that bothers me."

"I know." She took his hand and tugged him toward their camp. "Come on, we need to sleep. The morning will be here soon enough."

"Yes, you're right." They walked back to the camp. Most others were in bed already, and the rest were in their tents. Someone had put another log on the fire, which burned brightly in the night.

CHAPTER TWENTY-EIGHT

The gale-force wind shoved their homemade shuttle south.

Cat settled into the co-pilot seat and stared at the ocean. Nothing had changed; dark clouds covered the sky, and the wind kicked up tufts on the ocean waves as far as she could see. It only took a few minutes of staring at it for Cat to decide any conversation was better than none. "Were you ever in Africa?"

Mag glanced at her, recovering from whatever he was thinking about. "Many years ago, before I met your mother, I had left the air corps and went to work for a company that developed areas rich in natural resources. I told you about it."

"Yeah, but where were you located in Africa?"

"Oh, I was near the Middle Sea on this huge river with beautiful delta farmland and rich soil for palm trees, dates, olives, and other food. Probably in the middle of the debris fall now."

"And the tsunami will destroy most of the area around the Middle Sea," Cat said.

"True –"

The comm unit suddenly announced, "Control, this is Rescue 3. We are hovering at two thousand feet about a mile northeast of Poseidia."

"It's that rescue ship we saw. Sounds like it arrived at Atlantis," Mag said.

The broadcast continued, "Rescue 3, turn on your cameras and record and transmit the tsunami as it arrives at Atlantis. Stay in position until advised to leave, and then rush to ISB2 to complete your mission before the tsunami reaches its location. Control out."

"On it. Rescue 3 out."

The monitor winked and then showed the video from the rescue ship. As the tsunami got close to Atlantis, three shuttles took off from near Poseidia, and then a moment later, another craft departed from farther north.

"Did you see that? Four ships took off from Atlantis." Cat flipped a switch so Saba and Opin could watch on the monitors in the passenger compartment.

"Yeah, talk about just in time." Mag let the pathfinder and avoidance system fly the shuttle and watched the monitor.

The picture switched between close-ups and wide shots. Stunned by the sheer destruction caused by the tsunami, they watched in shock. Mt. Atlan, the farmlands and cities, and the homes of the oldest families in Atlantis were all destroyed and sucked into the raging waters. It crushed Poseidia's walls, the palace, the university, the crystal tower, and the Temple, then devastated the rest of the island. Within minutes, nothing was left.

A new announcement startled them out of their shock. "Rescue 3, end transmission. Get to ISB2 as quickly as possible. The coast should slow the tsunami down and allow you time to rescue the governor and his people. Hurry. Control out."

"Control, on it. Rescue 3 out."

"Holy Atlan! That was horrible," Mag said. "I haven't been to Poseidia in years, but it was the most beautiful city in the world. I doubt if there will ever be another one like it."

Cat sniffled and wiped the tears from her cheeks. "The world's ending, Dad. Of course, there won't be another one like it."

"I know, dear. I'm afraid we will not see another city. We'll probably be lucky to find a camp or small town where we can live."

Opin stepped into the cockpit and held the handhold at the cabin door. "Where go? Now, Atlantis gone," he asked, his jaw trembling and eyes brimming with tears. His command of the Atlantian language was always worse when he was upset.

"I'm sorry, Opin. I should have come back. How are you and Saba doing?" Mag turned and studied the young man.

"We scared. No more home."

"I know. Mateveco has been destroyed, and now Atlantis." He motioned at the tsunami, now extending to the horizon. "So, we're going to Africa to build a new home." Mag took a deep breath and tried to get past his pain as Saba squeezed past Opin and into the pilot compartment.

Pulling Saba onto her lap, Cat hugged her. "We'll be all right. Don't worry."

Mag smiled as she comforted Saba, but he was concerned that Opin kept everything inside. This was his family now. He glanced at his wife's picture. They couldn't continue to dwell on the past, or nothing would ever be good again. Already, they had spent nearly three years rescuing people from bandits, pirates, and bad guys. For what? Revenge? Whatever the reason, the pain and loss didn't stop. "You guys better go in the back and finish picking up everything. After all the crazy flying, things must be a mess." Mag grinned at Opin.

Opin snorted. "Yes, mess." He grinned sadly, showing uneven teeth.

Mag smiled and winked at Cat as Saba and Opin returned to the passenger cabin.

Cat leaned close to him. "Good idea, Dad, and that will give us something better to do than think about the end of the world."

After they left, Mag continued flying the shuttle toward Africa. Except for occasionally spotting stuff floating in the water, the ocean didn't appear much different than usual. The wind had died down, and the waves were choppy but not much more than usual. He gazed south at the ocean and couldn't see the forward edge of the tsunami any longer. The gray ash-laden sky prevented him from seeing far. Under the murky clouds, the ocean covered everything.

With nothing to distract him, Mag's mind turned to their desperate situation. As much as he tried to keep the children from worrying, he knew they realized how bad things were. With their home on Mateveco destroyed, they lost everything they had accumulated.

Mateveco had stood on a bluff overlooking a bay with turquoise blue water on a small island north of Solantis, where the continent stopped running east-west and went more north-south. No one else lived on the island, and the thick forest of tall trees protected the house he built from the fierce storms from the Western Middle Sea. Besides the wild goats and sheep that grazed on the island, they had a few pigs and a cow and had hoped to get a bull to start their own cattle ranch.

Always good with mechanical and electronic gadgets, Mag had pieced together an adequate solar energy grid and wind turbines, providing all the energy the family needed. Mateveco was too far from Atlantis to get power from the crystal towers, and since Atlantis never built them on Solantis, broadcasted electric power was unavailable from the south.

Mag stared at the ocean, realizing anew that everything was gone. Their little island was underwater. Their house was destroyed, and their animals were dead. Everything they owned was on this shuttle. He shook his head as deep, dark tiredness settled over him.

Cat entered the cockpit and slid onto her seat. "We put stuff back where it belongs. A few things got broken, but not too many. I got Opin and Saba sorting the food items and putting what is still edible into new containers."

"Good, that should keep them busy for a while."

"Are you okay?" Cat stared at him.

"I'm good. I was just thinking about beginning again, and that's a constant problem in my life. What is this, the tenth time I have had to start over since you were born?"

"I don't know. If you say so. I think starting over is a good thing." Cat stared out the window at the ocean.

"Why is that?"

"I think we need to settle down and focus on living for a while. Sooner or later, the revenge business will kill us. One slip-up, and we're dead."

Mag stared at her and smiled. "That sounds like your mother talking, but I think you're right. Revenge isn't solving anything and puts us at risk. What do you think we should do?"

"If the world is ending, the only smart thing is to try to get to the Atlantian Fleet and escape with them."

"That won't be easy. This poor old, beat-up shuttle would never get to the fleet. They aren't doing more rescue missions, so getting rescued is out. So, unless we can get aboard one of the last shuttles back to the fleet, I think we are stuck here."

"We know a rescue ship is headed for ISB2. Maybe we could get rescued."

"No time. They've already been to Nolantis. Besides that, we are a long way from there."

"I guess we blew that, huh?" Cat flounced on her seat.

"I don't think they would have let us onboard anyway. Rescue ships only hold ten people, and I'll bet more than ten were waiting for them when they arrived."

"What should we do?"

"Head south. Get as far away from the collision with Mars as possible. Find someplace safe and wait. Then rebuild and get into farming or ranching."

"On our own? Should we try to find a small community that we can join?"

"Yes, of course, but that has problems too. The people in Africa fall into two categories: one, the native population, and two, the rebels. The natives have no reason to trust us, not when Atlantians have enslaved many of them for eons. The rebels are probably not much better than the bandits we have fought for years. Brute power – the biggest brutes have the power." Magnus surveyed the instruments to make sure the shuttle was running at optimum.

"Not a good choice." Cat pondered the possibilities. "Maybe there's another possibility that we don't know about yet."

"Possible, I guess. We should expect to be on our own or join the rebels if they prove to be a real community, not just a dictatorship masquerading as a society. If we go our own way and prove to the natives that we're not a threat, we could wind up with a similar situation to what we had in Mateveco."

Cat glanced at her father. Since he was focusing on flying and lost in thought, she stared out the window at the ocean. She was ready for whatever the future would bring.

Hours later, they saw treetops sticking out of the water where the raised ocean had flooded the jungle inland for miles. Then, the trees and jungle seemed to rise out of the water as the land rose into hills and mountains. With the first mountain range holding back the water, they flew over the dense jungle and open grass-filled plains.

Below the ship, the land had been destroyed. Volcanoes erupted, adding smoke and ash to the already congested atmosphere while starting wide-ranging fires. Rivers, suddenly carrying ten times the amount of water, flooded large areas, taking out trees and the jungle in their rampage. Animals stampeded away from wildfires or floods. Elsewhere, Africans hurriedly climbed hillsides or mountains to escape disaster. Birds of every type flew south in numbers that blocked the clouds. As the evening grew darker, they flew south over a broad plain of tall grass.

"Hey, Dad, I see some vehicles. They are too far away to tell much. Hold on." Cat hurried into the back, got a pair of binoculars from her backpack, and then rushed back to her seat. She quickly located their headlights. "Yeah, I see six trucks and two trailers. They're following a trail through the tall grass."

"Yeah, I see them." Mag adjusted their course to keep them in sight.

"One trailer has a bunch of animals, and the other has household stuff. That's a good sign, right?" Cat rested the binoculars on her lap.

"Yes, but we should watch them for a while and not make assumptions. What we don't know could be bad for us."

"Okay, let's not scare them by flying too close. Let's circle in front of them and see where they go. Do you think they are also trying to find the rebels?"

"No idea." Mag flew farther east and increased their speed. "It's getting dark. See if you can find a place where we can land for the night and still see the vehicles."

A few minutes later, Cat pointed to a hillside. "There's a place. It's open, so we can see if anything comes close, and it's high enough that we can watch the grasslands."

"That sounds perfect." Mag brought the shuttle down and hovered over the hill. They saw no predators or people from above and landed in an open area at least a hundred feet from the trees.

As soon as the shuttle settled onto the ground, Cat jumped down and ran to the edge of the hill. The others joined her a few minutes later as she used the binoculars to search for the vehicles.

"Can you see them?" Mag asked.

"Almost too dark." Cat searched the grasslands carefully.

"Who?" Opin asked.

"We saw trucks that might be people moving south." Mag gathered Saba close and pointed to the area that Cat was searching.

"I see them. They drove out of the grass and stopped. Maybe they are going to set up camp for the night." Cat increased the magnification on the binoculars. "Wait, I see a faint light, and some people have walked farther into the open area."

"Probably too dark to go farther." Mag walked toward the shuttle. "Let's start dinner. I'm starving."

"Me too." Opin ran ahead.

"I'll follow you. I want to see if they stop for the night." Cat sat on a rock to stabilize the binoculars and watched the caravan until they turned around and headed back toward the tall grass. When they circled the trucks and built a fire, she walked back to the shuttle and found that dinner was ready. "They're camping, and we can wait until they are underway before we leave in the morning." She put her binoculars back into her pack and sat near the fire.

"All right, let's eat." Mag handed each person a plate and then served the food.

CHAPTER TWENTY-NINE

Acton's shuttle jerked to the right as a large chunk of DF shot past.

"Hey, I don't remember having to dodge debris during the whole trip to Earth before." Cass leaned forward to look through Acton's window at the millions of pieces of DF colliding with other pieces and being thrown into space.

Acton stared at the debris fall. While he watched, another large chunk of DF shot toward them. He quickly checked on the avoidance system as the ship jerked to the right. "It's definitely worse."

The shuttles were still above Earth's dark, cloudy atmosphere. Even this close, the ash and smoke were so thick that Acton couldn't see Earth. "Last week, we could see the ocean and sometimes even Poseidia and Atlantis from here." He keyed the comm unit. "Farl."

"Hey, Acton, what's up?" Her voice came over the ship's comm unit and their headsets.

"Just making sure you guys are using your avoidance system."

"Duh, for sure. What am I, a first-year rookie?"

"I guess I'm just a worrier these days." He unsuccessfully tried to smile.

"Hmm, that doesn't sound like the Acton I know."

"I'm not sure it's the Acton I know, either." He snorted.

"Don't get maudlin. You're the hero." Farl tried to cheer him up.

"Not feeling too heroic these days."

"Then buck up. It's get-dirty time. Smoke and ash dead ahead." Farl clicked off.

Acton checked all the gauges. "Here we go."

"Yep, I think it's only gotten worse." Cass studied the instruments and made sure his harness was tight.

As the shuttle entered the clouds, darkness instantly enveloped the ship. Turbulence made it shudder and shake, and the dashboard lighting came on.

"Man, that's thick as blood out there." Cass hung onto the safety bar.

"Yeah, even thicker than when we came through it this morning."

He wanted to speed up to see what was happening, but the shuttle was already going at the optimal speed for the avoidance system. Instead, he held his breath while they passed through the clouds. As long as the engines were getting oxygen, they were safe. In space, the ship used onboard oxygen to mix with the fuel for the jet engines. After entering Earth's atmosphere, the system changed to outside oxygen, but that couldn't happen at this altitude because there wasn't enough oxygen to trigger the switchover.

The ships descended, dodging DF every few seconds. The black clouds gradually dissipated and became dark gray, lighter gray, and finally lighter than gray as the ocean became visible. The shuttles swooped down through the haze and leveled out over the ocean, flying southeast toward Africa and Mt. Aswanga.

"This morning, we could see Atlantis from here." Acton stared out at the ocean.

"Doesn't look much different, just no Atlantis." Cass studied where the island used to be.

"It's different. Look closer." Acton pointed. "See? There and over there, things are floating in the water. That appears to be a small boat." He pointed at a mostly submerged, red and white shape.

Cass used the forward camera to magnify what was in the water. He could see furniture, boats, broken parts of ships, pieces of fences, cloth, and other items that were not as recognizable. Then he saw several bodies floating nearby, some face-up and some face-down.

"Shut it off! I feel like I'm looking into someone's grave." Acton turned away.

Cass turned off the camera. "Sorry, I didn't think. You don't really feel it until you see people, do you?"

They leveled off a thousand feet above the ocean and headed southeast on a course set by the pathfinder to Mt. Aswanga. The water extended to the horizon, and he had to focus to see if they were moving because everything appeared the same.

Nearly an hour later, he was starting to worry. "We should be over Africa. Look." Acton pointed in front of the ship. "The water must be hundreds of feet higher than before. Those are treetops sticking out of the ocean. The beach and shoreline must be underwater."

"Yes, I can see buildings under the water!" Cass leaned close to the side window and looked below the shuttle. "They must be a hundred feet below the surface! I can see all kinds of things floating in the water."

"Oh no, I wonder how much deeper it is."

"There are bodies down there. Animals and people... Oh my God, a lot of people."

"They must not have had enough warning." Acton studied the horizon and saw water covering all but the distant hilltops.

An hour later, most of the bodies and debris were behind them. The ocean still covered everything but treetops. "What if the mine is underwater?" Acton said.

"We'll know in a few minutes. As fast as we're going, we'll be there soon."

The shuttle jerked to the left to avoid DF that whistled past, leaving a smoke trail.

"The DF is much farther south than this morning." Acton watched as the DF hit the water below the shuttle, and Cass nodded his agreement.

As they flew southeast, they started seeing areas that were above water. On the horizon, hills and mountains became visible.

"Boy, I'm glad to see dry land." Acton suddenly realized how tense he was and leaned back to take a deep breath.

"Hey, that's Mt. Aswanga, right?" He pointed toward the mountain.

Acton leaned forward again and anxiously looked at where Cass pointed. "Yeah, I think you're right. That's it." His wrist comm chimed, and he punched it. "Hey, Farl."

"Mt. Aswanga is up ahead. I was worried," Farl said.

"Me too. See you there in a few minutes."

"Right." She ended the call.

Acton anxiously studied the mountain. The ancient volcano was shrouded in thick smoke, and at several locations, smoke or steam shot out of shaft openings. "Things are a lot worse."

The pathfinder showed they were over the mine, but the smoke was too thick to see the buildings or airfield. Watching anxiously, they dropped through the smoke.

"Something's wrong. I don't see anybody." Acton frantically searched.

"Yeah, there's nothing here. This is a different place than this morning." Cass used the rearview camera to also search behind the shuttle.

"There were two shuttles and four or five ore transporters here this morning. Now, they're gone." Acton brought the shuttle lower.

"Don't tell me we're going to jail for nothing. Did they go to New Hope on their own?" Cass demanded.

"I don't think so. Mya promised they would wait for us. And their shuttles couldn't fly well enough to get into space."

"But the transporters are gone too. Where else would they go?"

Acton brought the shuttle down and landed hard enough to bounce back up. He was out of his seat before the ship settled and left Cass to shut down while he bolted for the hatch. The stairs automatically extended when he opened the door, but he didn't wait and jumped to the ground. Shuttle 6756 landed fifty feet away, kicking up dust and making it harder to see.

Acton couldn't believe what he was seeing. The landing field was empty. Scattered across the area were pieces of paper, cloth, small tools, a comm receiver, office supplies, and lots of things so covered with dirt that he couldn't tell what they were. Cass, Farl, and Trice joined him a minute later.

"What's going on? You think they went to New Hope?" Farl asked.

"I don't think so. Mya promised to wait for us, and something isn't right. This wasn't an orderly departure," he said, pointing at the items scattered across the field.

"Yeah, I see what you mean. This stuff wouldn't be all over the place otherwise." Trice searched farther to the right than the others.

"Who's that?" Farl pointed to the mine entrance.

"Who?" Acton quickly looked at where she pointed.

"There are people over by the mine entrance," she said.

"I see them." Cass rushed forward.

"Wait, I think they're African miners. Don't scare them away." Acton walked calmly toward the cavernous opening as the others fell back to walk with him.

While most people in the mine entrance backed farther into the shadows, one sat on the ground, leaning against a beam near the front.

As they got closer, Acton thought he recognized him. "Shorty? Is that you?"

The man sitting on the ground looked at them. "Acton?" He tried to stand but collapsed.

"Yes, it's me. Where is everyone?" Acton got close enough to see eight people in the shadows, three Africans and five Gen-x AG people.

Shorty talked to the workers in a native dialect, and they stopped backing away. He returned to wrapping a dirty cloth around his bloody thigh.

Acton and his friends stopped near Shorty. As they listened to loud warning drums pounding a frantic pattern from several directions, Acton studied the area, expecting to see other people nearby, but there was only the small group in the mine entrance.

"All gone," Shorty said.

"Where did they go?" Acton tried to sound casual.

Shorty stared at them as though unsure of whether he should answer.

"Trice, Shorty is injured. Would you get a med kit?" Acton pointed to Shorty's leg.

"Oh, sure, no problem. I'll be right back." Trice ran toward her ship.

"Did they leave in the shuttle and transporters?" Acton sat on a crate near Shorty.

"No. Bad men come in shuttles. Shoot my friends. Take Mya, Monty, others. Take shuttles. Take transporters." Shorty stumbled over his poor Atlantian.

"When did that happen?" Acton tried to stay calm.

"Not long after you leave."

He nodded toward Shorty's injury. "Is that how you got injured?"

Shorty nodded. "Yes, I lucky. Two friends killed by men in shuttle. I shot when try to help Mya. They think I dead. Leave me."

"Did you see which way they went?" Acton said anxiously.

Shorty pointed south.

Trice returned with the med kit and patted a crate. "Sit here so I can look at your leg." She opened the kit.

Shorty struggled to get up until Acton and Cass helped him sit on the crate. Trice unwrapped the dirty cloth to find a nasty hole in

Shorty's thigh with scorch marks surrounding it. The wound was frayed, dirty, and still bleeding. As she gently cleaned the wound, using medical gauze and a bottle of disinfectant, Shorty cringed but bravely endured.

Acton joined Cass and Farl. "It has to be the rebels. They must have panicked and grabbed whatever they could before heading south." He checked his wrist comm. "And they have a six-hour head-start on us." The sun was setting, and the mine entrance was too dark to see each other clearly.

"Can we find them?" Farl sounded frantic as she stepped closer.

"I have to try. What choice do I have?"

"None. We came here to get them, and we will," Cass said.

Trice taped a bandage over Shorty's wound, then got a needle and a bottle of medicine from the kit. "I'm going to give you a shot to prevent infection. Understand?"

Shorty shook his head. "Shot?" he said anxiously.

"Show him the needle." Acton moved closer to Shorty as Trice showed him the needle. "Shorty, the medicine is in the needle. We need to inject it." He pantomimed, giving him the injection. "So no get sick. Understand?"

"Yes," Shorty said dubiously.

Trice filled the syringe, wiped Shorty's arm with disinfectant, and gave him the shot. He jumped when she inserted the needle. He stared at them nervously, rubbing his arm until they nodded approvingly and smiled.

"Shorty, can you survive here?" Acton leaned closer, but Shorty seemed confused. "Can you live here without the mine?"

"No. No food, no supplies. Mountain very bad. We leave or die." Shorty looked at the other miners and Gen-x people, who appeared to be exhausted. "Only here for can't walk."

"How many people are here?" Acton peered into the darkness, trying to count them.

"Many?" Shorty asked, confused.

"Number of people?" He pointed to the others.

"Oh." Shorty thought for a moment. "Ten, three like me, two wives, five Gen-x. Others dead or run away."

Acton looked to the others expectantly, and they nodded. "Shorty, you and your people are coming with us."

Shorty excitedly stood without assistance. "We go with you?"

"Yes, we can't leave you here to die. You better get the others."

Shorty hugged Acton. "Thank you, thank you!" He told the others while pointing at the shuttles. They excitedly jumped up, and several ran toward the cooking fires nearby.

As Acton and the pilots walked toward the shuttles, three Gen-x workers followed them, supporting Shorty as he hobbled along.

"So, how are we going to find the rebels?" Farl asked.

"I have no idea. I imagine the rebels went south to escape the coming catastrophe. But where exactly? We'll have to search until we them."

"Ah, it's pretty dark already. How are we going to find them in the dark?" Trice asked.

"Good question." Acton turned toward the mine entrance to see if the others were coming. Beyond the mine entrance, he could clearly see campfires burning brightly in the night. "Hey, it might actually be easier to spot them at night."

"Huh? Are you nuts?" Cass stared at him like he was crazy.

"No. Think about it. The rebel's camp must have hundreds of cookfires." He pointed to the campfires near the mine. "We should be able to see their fires for miles."

"Right, of course." Farl laughed. "Let's get going then."

Acton could see the other Gen-x, two native men, and two native women hurrying toward the ships, carrying their meager belongings. He stepped closer to Shorty. "Shorty, does everyone speak Atlantian?"

"Some yes. Some no."

"Make sure at least one person who can speak Atlantian is on each shuttle, four or five people per shuttle. We're going to find Mya."

"Good. Mya, good friend. Help us all time. I good spotter. Spot animals, food, and people too," Shorty proudly stated.

"Good. Then you come with me. We find Mya."

Shorty explained everything to the others, and the group broke into two parties. Shorty, his wife, another miner, and two Gen-x went to Acton's shuttle while the others went to Farl's.

"Cass, explain how the toilets work and show them where the food and water are located while I get ready to take off." Acton entered the ship. As he walked by Shorty, he stopped. "Shorty, you, and your people sit by the windows so you can spot the rebel camp. With hundreds of campfires, it should be easy to spot."

"Yes, I see more than most." Shorty tried to explain. "I tell others."

The Gen-x took several minutes to figure out how to sit on the seats. They finally sprawled lengthwise, and the Africans helped them fasten their harnesses.

When Cass joined him, the shuttle flew south into the murky ash and smoke-filled sky. Acton wondered what else could go wrong. In one day, he went from being the respected elder son of the royal family to a disgraced outlaw. What did his mother think of that? What problems did he create for his uncle, the emperor, Master Ono, and his father and his command of the fleet?

He glanced over at Cass, silently staring into the deepening darkness. Did he realize what this would mean to his future? And what about Farl and Trice? What had he done?

Acton shook his head and stiffened his neck. What had he done? He did the only thing he could to save Mya from a certain death.

Where was Mya? In the hands of the rebels, was she safe? Would they brutalize her? He tried to push the thrust forward, but the ship was going as fast as possible.

He grimly flew into the night.

The end of Book 1.

REFERENCES

CHARACTERS:

Acton Athu – is captain of Rescue 1 from SS New Hope, 22, male, 6′, black hair, blue eyes, athletic; son of Commander Cana Athu and Professor Nora Athu, and nephew of Emperor Maximus IV, ruler of Atlantis. He is a member of the Royal Family, and his girlfriend is Mya Moriset.

Alsa Gen-Aga – is a genetically altered receptionist in the Control Center of SS New Hope with four arms and two legs. She is a voluptuous woman with brown hair and blue eyes.

Asha Gen-Athu – is the wife of Cesa Gen-Athu, 50s, a Gen-x AG female (genetically altered human with four arms and four legs). She has dark hair and brown eyes.

Bola – is an African male miner, 20s, working at Mt. Aswanga Mines. He works for the mine manager, Monty Moriset.

Burger Vumguis – is the captain of SS New Venture, 50s, male.

Cana Athu – is the Commander of the Atlantian Fleet, SS New Hope, 52, male, 6′, athletic, graying black hair, blue eyes; brother of Emperor Maximus IV, ruler of Atlantis; husband of Professor Nora Athu; and father of Acton Athu and Pal Athu. He is a member of the Royal Family.

Captain Suga – is a shuttle captain bringing Nora Athu to New Hope from Atlantis.

Cass Keltu – is the co-pilot captain of Rescue 1, SS New Hope, 20s, male, 6′, black hair, blue eyes, athletic, and Acton's closest friend.

Cat Lipo – is an avenger who rescues women from bandits. She is 18, female, 5 foot 5 inches, with short blonde hair and green eyes. She is the daughter of Magnus Lipo and sister to adopted brother Opin, 13, and adopted sister Saba, 10.

Cesa Gen-Athu – is a Gen-x AG (genetically created human with four arms and four legs, like a centaur); 50s, male, farm manager for Athu Farms near Poseidia, the family home of the Athu family; married to Asha Gen-Athu and has three children, two male and one female.

Deez – A Gen-x Ag man who works at Aswanga Mine.

Denna Garric – a university student, 20s, male, swarthy, dark hair, brown eyes, 5′8″, and one of the students Genesi asks to lunch regarding Pal.

Dimitri Durias – is a farmer with Zeth Mercu's group, a white male, 30s, tall, fit, and muscular; husband to Vola Durias, father to daughter Ada (7) and son Ebe (5).

Duc Fenmenk – is a male university art student, SS New Hope, 20s, and Harcu Simoon's roommate.

Edo Tasari – is captain of Periphery Defense Gunner ship in Squad 51, 20s, a black male, black hair, brown eyes, long braided hair that hangs down his back, athletic; in Vin Neblu's squad, close friends with all the pilots.

Farl Falco – is captain of Rescue 2, SS New Hope, 20s, female, red hair, green eyes, thick eyebrows, close friends with Acton and Cass. Co-pilot is Trice Danti.

Genesi Forcu – is an Acolyte of the Church of the One God on SS New Hope, Master Ono's assistant; 20s, female, 5'8, brown eyes, long brown hair, and her boyfriend is Pal Athu.

Geta Cermius – is the wife of Perta Cermius, a farmer with Zeth Mercu; 30s, mother to son Nico (8) and daughter Thea (6).

Halo Hajac – Construction manager for the Fleet ships; 50s, male, gray hair, dark eyes, overweight but muscular. His wife's name is Baya Hajac, 50s, with dark hair, blue eyes, and stout.

Harcu Simoon –a university art student, 20s, male, red hair, green eyes, big ears, with a silly grin, 6', athletic, affluent in karate and judo; befriends Genesi and helps search for Pal.

Jonna Kerol –a university student, 20s, male, tall, fit, with blonde hair and blue eyes. He is a friend of Pal Athu and on his hoops team.

Kale Katalasou – captain of a striker in the Periphery Defense, Sector 52, SS New Hope, 20s, male, originally from Mu, and a close friend with the pilots.

Kayl Bezania – married to Volf Bezania, a farmer in Zeth Mercu's group, 30s, and mother to a son, Quina (7).

Kensa Storn – the Port Manager on SS New Hope, 40s, male.

Kona Torinus – farmer with Zeth Mercu's group, 30s, short, fit, with a short, neat beard, husband to Shea Torinus, and father to daughter Zala (5).

Lado Strifa – captain of Striker 113 in the Periphery Defense, Sector 51, SS New Hope, 20s, male, dark hair, brown eyes, tall, and fit. Friends with the pilots.

L.E.T. – Short for Law Enforcement Team, the police for Fleet ships

Linga Forst – a university student, 20s, male, tall, fit, with dark hair and brown eyes. He is a friend of Pal Athu and Genesi Forcu and is on Pal's hoops team.

Lola Laset – a tall female, 20s, with blonde hair and blue eyes. She was naked in a tree when Acton and Cass rescued her.

Magnus Lipo – an avenger who rescues women from bandits in Solantis. He is tall, 45, with dark hair, blue eyes, and a short beard. He is the father of Cat Lipo, 18, adopted son Opin, 13, and adopted daughter Saba, 10.

Mara – Master Ono's assistant in the Church of the One God, SS New Hope. She is in her 40s, female, with long dark hair and brown eyes,

Marlenel Nete – an Acolyte of the Church of the One God, SS New Hope, 20s, female, brown hair, and brown eyes, Genesi's coworker and roommate.

Marnin Clovus – the captain of SS New Hope, 40s, male, a little overweight, has short, sparse hair, and is a longtime assistant to Commander Cana Athu.

Maximus IV – the Emperor of Atlantis, SS New Hope, 56, male, tall, with black hair, blue eyes, in good shape; older brother of Commander Cana Athu and Acton's uncle.

Monty Moriset – the manager of Mt. Aswanga Mines and the father of Mya Moriset; 50s, male, and deathly ill.

Mya Moriset – the administrator at Mt. Aswanga Mines for her father, Monty. She is female, 20s, has long brown hair and brown eyes, is quiet and reserved, and is Acton Athu's girlfriend.

Nora Athu – a university professor on SS New Hope. She is 49, female, short, fit, with dark hair and brown eyes, the wife of Commander Cana Athu, the mother of Acton and Pal Athu, and in charge of the agricultural programs for the fleet ships.

Nolan Hasarius – the captain of a striker in the Periphery Defense, Sector 53, SS New Hope. He is male, in his 20s, with dark hair and brown eyes, tall and fit, and a close friend of all the pilots.

Nortin Ketsu – a captain with the L.E.T. on SS New Hope. He is male, in his 30s, has short, dark hair, mustache, and brown eyes. He is the policeman in charge of investigating Pal Athu's disappearance.

Norvis Scintillian – the Professor of Physics at the New Hope University, SS New Hope. He is a thin, frail male with thinning white hair in his 80s. He is the Chief Scientist for New Hope.

Ono – Master Ono is the Head of the Church of the One God and Master of the Way, SS New Hope. He is 64, male, a cousin to Emperor Maximus and Commander Athu, and Genesi's boss.

Ofre – the captain of SS Atlantis Pride.

Opin – Native Solantis boy, 13, 5', black hair, tattoos from waist to shoulders, designs carved on his upper body of fierce beasts, and adopted by Magnus Lipo.

Pad Nedin – the captain of Rescue 3, SS New Hope, 20s, male, 6', short dark hair, short beard, athletic, one of Acton's closest friends, and in Acton's squad.

Pal Athu – is a university student, SS New Hope, male, 20, tall, hoops player, youngest son of Cana and Nora Athu, and the younger brother of Acton Athu. After being missing for three days, his girlfriend, Genesi, starts the search for him.

Patel Derna – singer with the band in the Flight Club

Perta Cermius – a farmer with Zeth Mercu's group; white male, 30s, big, tall, muscular with a long, dark beard; husband to Geta Cermius; father to son Nico (8) and daughter Thea (6).

Saba Zylata – the wife of X'to Zylata, a Farmer in Zeth Mercu's group, 30s, black female; mother to daughters Ki (5) and Jea (3).

Saba – a native Solantis girl rescued from slave traders and adopted by Magnus and Cat Lipo; 10 years old, 4′, black hair, brown skin, brown eyes.

Salia Vericus – the Personal Assistant to Commander Cana Athu, SS New Hope. She is a female in her 20s with blonde hair and blue eyes.

Shea Torinus – the wife of Kona Torinus, a farmer in Zeth Mercu's group; 30s, female; mother to daughter Zala (5).

Shorty – an African miner at Mt. Aswanga Mines, 20s, male, over 6′, thin but strong, has exceptional eyesight and is a friend of Mya.

Steril Magneson – a captain and Assistant to Commander Cana Athu; male in his 40s.

Sula Kens – a university student, 20s, deeply tanned female with long dark hair and brown eyes. She is a lifelong friend of Pal Athu, as they grew up on farms next to each other.

Surg Sideral – the Base Commander at African Shuttle Base (ASB) and a male in his 40s.

Thegan – Captain in charge of communications on SS New Hope, male in his 40s.

Trice Danti – the co-pilot of Rescue 2 with Farl Falco, SS New Hope, a female in her 20s, tall, with brown hair and eyes, and close friends with the pilots.

Verl Madre – the captain of SS Grand Poseidia, a male in his 50s who is heavyset and has short dark hair and brown eyes.

Vin Neblu – the captain and Squad Leader of Periphery Defense Gunner ship 902 in Sector 51, a male in his 20s, blonde hair, green eyes, the dark complexion of a southern islander, athletic, and close friends with the pilots.

Vola Durias – the wife of Dimitri Durias, a farmer in Zeth Mercu's group; 30s, mother to daughter Ada (7) and son Ebe (5).

Volf Bezania – a farmer in Zeth Mercu's group and husband to Kayl Bezania. A male in his 30s, short, heavy set with short hair, father of a son, Quina (7).

X'to Zylata – a farmer in Zeth Mercu's group and husband to Saba Zylata. An African male in his 30s, he is short with short black hair and is the father of daughters Ki (5) and Jea (3).

Yassa Afari – the captain of a Periphery Defense Gunner ship in Squad 51, Vin Neblu's squad. He is in his 20s, a black Lamatian male with short black hair and brown eyes, and Vin's roommate.

Zeth Mercu – a farmer and leader of five air-corps friends moving south in Africa to escape DF. He is the husband of Zuzu Mercu and a white male in his 30s who is tall and muscular with dark hair and brown eyes. He is the father of son Feri (10), daughter Marta (8), and son Olly (4).

Zetu Ordia – the co-pilot captain of Rescue 3, SS New Hope, and a black Lamatian male in his 20s. He is 6′ 6″ and has long dark hair in braids down his back, bushy eyebrows, and dark eyes. He is one of Pad Nedin's closest friends.

Zuzu Mercu – the wife of Zeth Mercu, a farmer moving south in Africa. She is tall, has blonde hair and blue eyes, is in her 30s, and is the mother of son Feri (10), daughter Marta (8), and son Olly (4).

FLEET SHIPS:

Gunner 902 – a Periphery Defense Gunner ship in Sector 51. It is 30′ by 48′, is piloted by one person, Captain Pad Nedin, and has numerous blasters, cannons, and lasers mounted on his front and top and designed to shoot Mars debris before it can damage spaceships.

Gunner 903 – a Periphery Defense Gunner ship in Sector 51. It is 30′ by 48′, is piloted by one person, Captain Yassa Afari, and has numerous blasters, cannons, and lasers mounted on his front and top and designed to shoot Mars debris before it can damage spaceships.

Gunner 906 – a Periphery Defense Gunner ship in Sector 51. It is 30′ by 48′, is piloted by one person, Captain Edo Tasari, and has numerous blasters, cannons, and lasers mounted on its front and top and designed to shoot Mars debris before it can damage spaceships.

Rescue 1 – a sweep-wing rescue ship, red with the number 1 on its nose, underneath, and top. It is 39′ by 57′, has passenger space for ten people, has a flying scooter festooned with rescue equipment, and has a hover engine and two large jet engines. Two pilots pilot it; the principal pilot is seated on the left, and the co-pilot on the right. Rescue 1 is based on SS New Hope, and its captains are Captain Acton Athu and co-pilot Captain Cass Keltu.

Rescue 2 – the same as Rescue 1, except Captain Farl Falco and co-pilot Captain Trice Danti pilot it.

Rescue 3 – the same as Rescue 1, except Captain Pad Nedin and co-pilot Captain Zetu Ordia pilot it.

Shuttle 6122 – a passenger shuttle. It is blue, 51' by 57', carries 32 people in rows of two seats on each side of a center aisle and eight aisles, and has a storage or baggage area ship's length below the passenger area. It is piloted by Captain Acton Athu and co-pilot Captain Cass Keltu.

Shuttle 6756 – a passenger shuttle. It is blue, 51' by 57', carries 32 people in rows of two seats on each side of a center aisle and eight aisles, and has a storage or baggage area ship's length below the passenger area. It is piloted by two people, Captain Farl Falco and co-pilot Captain Trice Danti.

Space Construction Center (SCC) – a million-square-foot construction platform orbiting near the spaceships under construction. It is the warehouse for materials and parts for the construction of the spaceships and the office for construction managers.

Spaceship (SS) New Hope – is the white admin ship of the New Hope triad. The captain is Marnin Clovus. Home ship for the Athu family, Master Ono, and Emperor Maximus.

Spaceship (SS) Grand Poseidia – is the green agricultural ship of the New Hope triad. The captain is Verl Madre.

Spaceship (SS) New Venture – is the gray manufacturing ship of the New Hope triad. The captain is Emo Kodan.

Striker 113 – is a Periphery Defense Striker ship in Sector 51. It is 45' by 36', is piloted by one person, Captain Lado Strifa, and has numerous guns mounted on his front and top. All strikers stay above and slightly behind gunner ships and are the last resort to destroy debris headed for a spaceship. A striker is allowed to pursue debris, while a gunner has to stay in its position in the formation.

ADDITIONAL

RESEARCH SOURCES

Want to know more about the world of 12,600 years ago? The following videos and books will provide additional insight into the strange world that existed when Atlantis sank.

David N Talbott – The YouTube Channel *Symbols of an Alien Sky* has more than fifty videos detailing the ancient history of Earth based on human evidence – legends, myths, drawings, rock art, cave paintings, artifacts, and monuments erected commemorating what ancient man saw in the sky and the corresponding events on Earth. David's lifetime research documents the overwhelming evidence of tumultuous historical events in ancient times.

Edgar Cayce – "The Sleeping Psychic" detailed the psychic readings of past-track lives of over 2,500 people living on Atlantis as detailed in *On Atlantis* by Edgar Evans Cayce, published in 1968 by the Association for Research and Enlightenment Inc. through Warner Books. While most of the readings describe spiritual and religious events in people's lives, the society they lived in and the conditions of the world are vividly recorded. I used his references to advanced science and created an Atlantis with a hundred-thousand-year history and very advanced science – imagine our society ninety-eight thousand years from now.

Richard Firestone, Alan West, and Simon Warwick-Smith – *The Cycle of Cosmic Catastrophes: How a Stone-age Comet Changed the Course of World Culture,* Bear and Company, 2006. Exhaustively researched and well-presented, this book presents new scientific evidence about a series of prehistoric cosmic events that explain why the last Ice Age ended so abruptly. Their findings validate the ubiquitous legends and myths of floods, fires, and weather extremes passed down by our ancestors and show how these legendary events relate to each other. The findings also support the idea that we are entering a thousand-year cycle of increasing danger and possibly a new cycle of extinction. My story tries to show the same events, but instead of a cometary cause, I offer a closer and more remarkable reason – Mars and the breakup of the collinear system.

D. S. Allan and J. B. Delair – *Cataclysm! Compelling Evidence of a Cosmic Catastrophe in 9500 B.C.,* Bear & Company, 1997. Cataclysm presents a wealth of scientific information about a little-known but perhaps the most significant disaster affecting mankind. The evidence shows that it occurred in 9577 B.C., almost precisely when Atlantis sank in the Atlantic Ocean, as described by Plato. Coincidence? I think not. Though the authors show that a comet entered between Earth and its moon, worsening the Earth's tilt and distancing the moon, I have chosen to use Talbott's evidence to show that Earth was part of a collinear system of Jupiter, Saturn, Venus, Mars, and Earth, known as the "Eye of God," over the North Pole. The destruction caused by the comet intruder is accurate and well documented by *"Cataclysm."*

Graham Hancock, *Ancient Apocalypse Series* on Netflix. Graham Hancock has an excellent series of investigative reports on Netflix. The series shows ancient sites that defy conventional science and could only be built by advanced intelligence. Some areas date back 10,000 to 21,000 years ago. Graham's analysis shows an advanced civilization existed thousands of years before our current history and suggests it was Atlantis.

ATLANTEAN

HOOPS GAME

The Atlantean Hoops game is played on a hoops court. It uses a bright-orange, inflated rubber ball one foot in diameter. The object is to outscore your opponents in sixty minutes of playtime.

Playing Hoops

Using teams of five people, points are scored by throwing the ball through a single hoop or combined hoops. See diagram below:

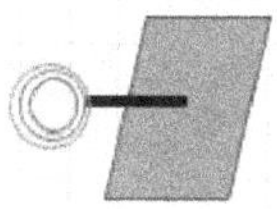

The red hoop is 18 inches in diameter, the blue hoop is 24 inches, and the green hoop is 30 inches. The hoops constantly travel around the court, a 100-foot by 50-foot wood floor with semi-circle ends 25 feet in diameter. Each hoop moves at a different speed. The green hoop moves fastest, the blue a little slower, and the smallest red hoop is slower still, allowing the hoops to line up occasionally.

The hoops fit within each other, and all three line up every five circuits around the track. Two hoops can also align as a double hoop, either green and blue, green and red, or blue and red. The backboard lights up to indicate a double hoop (a green light) or a triple hoop (a red light) is happening. Since the rings never stop moving, the double and triple score opportunities are brief.

The game begins with a buzzer, and the ball enters the court from one of the ten portals. Whoever takes possession of the opening ball has the ball first and the opportunity to score.

Players toss the ball to other team members, or they can bounce it to them. When players move with the ball, they must dribble it with every step.

When a team member has possession, other team members try to prevent their opponents from getting the ball or accessing the hoops, opening the way for the ball carrier to score. Opponents can intercept or knock the ball away from a player and take possession of it.

Since the hoops are constantly moving, multiple scoring options exist at any time, and numerous strategies exist to maximize the scoring opportunities.

See diagram:

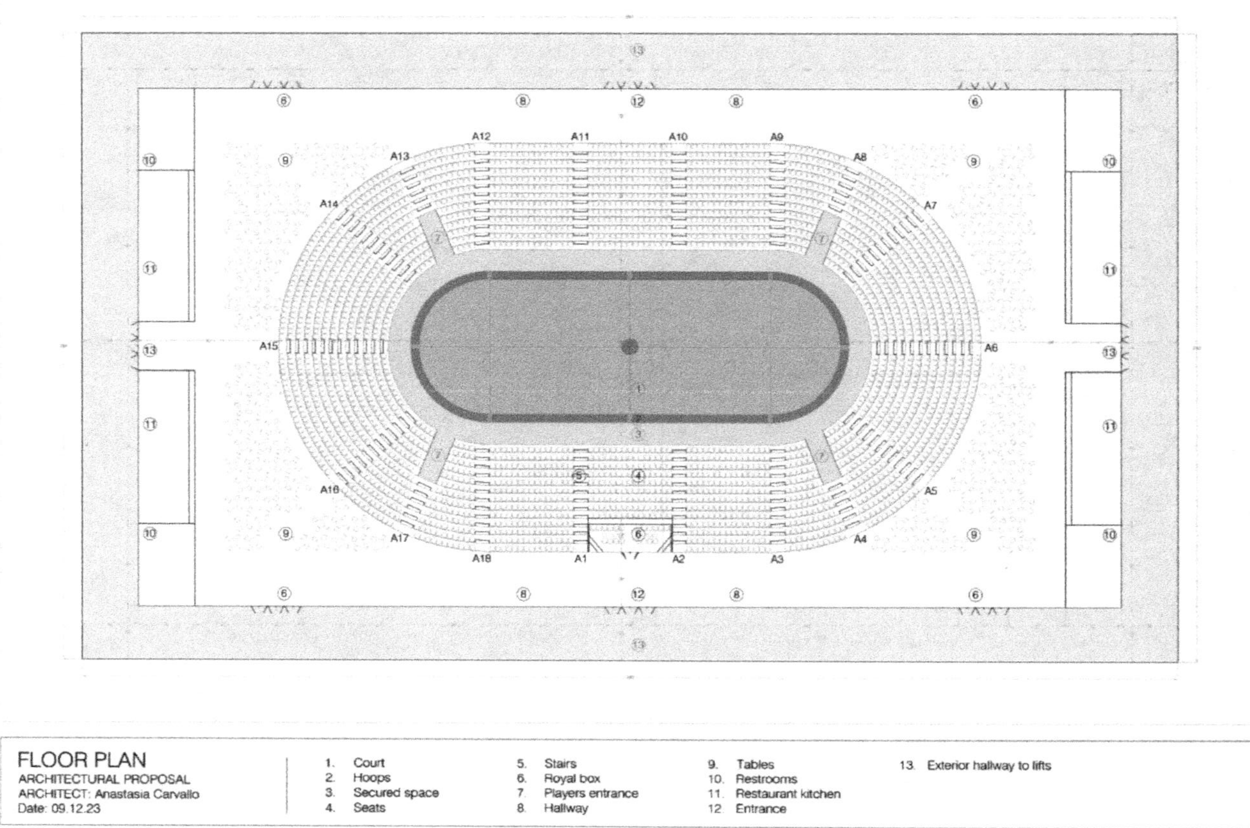

FLOOR PLAN
ARCHITECTURAL PROPOSAL
ARCHITECT: Anastasia Carvallo
Date: 09.12.23

1. Court
2. Hoops
3. Secured space
4. Seats
5. Stairs
6. Royal box
7. Players entrance
8. Hallway
9. Tables
10. Restrooms
11. Restaurant kitchen
12. Entrance
13. Exterior hallway to lifts